KAREN SLOAN-BROWN

Short Cut

This book is printed on acid-free paper.

ISBN: 978-1-944440-00-8

Library of Congress Cataloging-in-Publication Data on file.

Editor: Cornelius Brown

Short Cut

ShortCut

Prologue

It wasn't rage or passion that motivated the killing. It was merely something that had to be done, a necessary evil. Possibly even the lesser of several evils that could have resulted. It could even have been seen as merciful, like putting down a thoroughbred race horse after a catastrophic injury. There was no moment of terror. The victim never saw it coming. It was done in silence. No protests, no recriminations, with no witnesses. Nevertheless, it was a bloodbath, literally.

Chapter
One

Tires screeched, fireworks exploded from an automatic weapon, glass shatters. Instinctively they all froze waiting for the next signal to react. They've all heard it before. Each of them is poised to drop face down on the floor. Incoherent shouts strung together with cuss words are heard in the crossfire. Three single shots ring out and then, pop, pop, two more echo behind them. Engines gun, tires screech again, all to the background of heavy bass booming, swirling, and vibrating in the stifling summer heat even though it was early May. The sirens in the distance grow louder and louder.

It's nothing unusual; a drive-by shoot-out was par for the course on Friday afternoon or any other day or time outside the King Cut barber shop on Buchanan Street. Apart from the cheery bright spring sun in a nearly cloudless sky, it wasn't the kind of neighborhood where you see redbreast robins flying through a rose garden or hear blue birds chirping in tall trees. More likely you would see the sidewalk colored crimson with blood and hear a grieving mother singing the blues from an open window. It was hardcore, the hood, with young boys slinging, women hustling, older homeless men begging, music thumping, young girls booties bumping, and gangsta rap pumping from the four corners of the crosswalk.

Abandoned businesses and boarded up storefronts lined the street, half dead and dying from the growing spread of violence and rising poverty. Only the drive-in market/gas station, the liquor store, and the neighborhood Dollar Store seemed to be immune to the sickness. The fish, chicken, and pizza restaurant on the opposite corner was sucking for air. It was a four-way stop but it might as well have had a sign that said 'Dead End.'

Ernest was the owner and head barber at the King Cut Barber Shop. He exhaled as a crowd formed in the parking lot to view the aftermath. Luckily he had dodged another bullet in this latest melee. His store-front window had been busted out for the third time eight months ago and he didn't have another spare grand to pay another deductible for it to be fixed. After being there for ten years he accepted it as just another one of the hazards of living or working in the hood. He had been comfortable with it growing up around there, it was all he had ever known, but at thirty-five years old he wanted something different.

His mind drifted back into his past while he sharpened his straight razor for a shave. He remembered the excitement he'd felt back then when he was running the streets and the adrenaline rush of escaping a bullet. Back when he was thirteen years old it was like an amped up game of hide-and-go-seek. It made him feel significant and alive when his heart beat thumped hard and fast beneath his chest. Now looking back at his antics he saw he was a fool among fools. Instead of squabbling over territory that didn't belong to any of them he should have been hitting his school books. He should have run up his mama's electric bill with late night studying instead of lighting up a joint.

It bothered him that he would never know what other talents he had, what he could have been. Sure he could cut out the likeness of Barack Obama, Marcus Garvey, Martin Luther King, Jr., and Malcolm X with the words 'By Any Means Necessary' onto a client's scalp with his straight-razor that would rival a drawing by an accomplished artist, except he could have made his own mark in the world. Maybe have done something where another barber would be cutting his likeness on someone's head. Anyhow there was no way to go back. Aside from all that, he knew he was one of the blessed ones. He had never done more than a day or two in juvenile detention, never caught a bullet, and as his mama used to say, had enough sense to come in out of the rain.

"One of y'all could have called and told me they were shooting over here," Andrea protested as she burst through the door swinging her long ponytail, a gold-colored Michael Kors knock-off handbag in one hand, a carry-out container of food in the other, and late for her first client as usual. "These bullets out here don't have no name on them."

"That's why you need to be on time," Miss Morgan, her regular first client on Fridays fussed, still waiting for her press and curl with her arms folded.

Andrea, in her size 18 blue jean shorts, glittered flip-flops, and wearing a stretched-to-the-seams tank top that said 'Sassy since Birth' across her thick, smooth, peanut butter brown frame, ignored the comment. She set her things down at her station, walked past Miss Morgan to the soda machine, and bought an Orange Crush to wash down the fried hard livers and gizzards she had brought in for her breakfast/ lunch.

Andrea was the only beautician and female working in the barber shop. She and Ernest had gone way back, since high school, and she had run her own hair salon across the street for six years. When the landlord went up on her rent and the expenses got too high she asked Ernest about renting a booth at King Cut. It was supposed to be temporary until she found another spot but she got hooked on the drama, and being single, the steady influx of men in and out of the shop. She had real skills braiding hair and sewing in weaves and could have made long dollars and built a huge following but she was unambitious. She worked just enough to make her ends meet, play her share of tonk at $2 a hand, and hang out on Friday nights at Sensations.

"What's the deal out there?" Leon asked her, unruffled.

Leon was the oldest one in the shop even though he refused to allow gray hairs to set up camp on his head or face. Dark brown like apple butter, he kept his head shaved and his beard dyed natural black. He was old-school sharp, always wearing a shirt and tie under his smock. He had given Ernest his first job out of barber school and was the closest thing to a father that he had ever known. When he lost the lease on his own shop on Jefferson Street five years ago Ernest offered him a chair in King Cut.

"Two guys got shot," Andrea answered, opening up her carry-out container and popping a gizzard in her mouth. "I heard somebody say one of them was Junebug and the other was Pee Wee, so you know it's about to be on. You know how their family is."

Junebug and Pee Wee were twins. They were born premature so they were both slim and just over five feet tall but they raised more hell than ten men. Junebug was a small time drug dealer and Pee Wee was a thief, and neither of them bothered to leave the hood to do his dirty work. They came from a big family whose motto was, "whatever you do to one of us, you do to all of us." If it was true that they were the two guys being loaded into the ambulances, this was only the beginning.

Retribution would most certainly follow without hesitation.

It don't make no sense," Jeff said, looking out the window. "If that whole crew emptied their pockets right here right now it wouldn't add up to a hundred bucks.

Jeff was the youngest barber in the shop at twenty-six years old. He was tall and thin and looked a lot like a young Kareem Abdul Jabbar with braids. He had been at King Cut since Ernest opened it but he had dreams of running his own business one day. His booth was a one-stop-shop for his clientele. He kept it all organized on an iPad that was never more than two feet away from him. He made more money selling weed and bootleg CDs and DVDs in the shop than he did cutting hair.

Andrea laughed as she put on her hairdresser's smock. "I don't know why these young boys think they're extras in a New Jack City movie out here."

"In the movies, when your ass get shot you can get up for take 2," Jeff added. "They act like they don't know getting killed or going to jail is real."

Leon shook his head. "Folks act a fool when it gets hot outside. They don't even think."

Ernest removed the heated towel from Vince's face to do his shave. Vince had been his first client on Fridays since he opened the shop. The two of them had been closer than brothers since they were eight years old. They could even pass for brothers, deep brown like chestnuts and built like redwood trees, strong and tall. When they were kids Vince and his mama, Eileen, lived on the other side of the duplex where Ernest and his mama lived. Ernest was more of a hustler while Vince was more of a jock but together they ran both sides of the streets in the hood when their mamas weren't looking. Both of them played high school football at Pearl and had dreams of going pro together after college.

The other difference between them was that Vince's mama planted a seed in him that made him believe that he could do something better, the same seed that was passed down to her from her mama. Ernest's mama never got that seed, she never knew her mama. So she couldn't give Ernest what she didn't have, he didn't know he could do better. The divide in their lives came when Vince got an athletic scholarship to go to Tennessee State. Ernest had lost his chance with a misdemeanor conviction that cost him the football scholarship and his financial aid eligibility.

They remained close with Ernest enrolling in Barber College and Vince excelling as a tight end for the TSU Tigers. After a notable college career Vince graduated with a business degree and was chosen by the Tennessee Titans in the seventh round of the draft. He'd retired a year ago after playing twelve years and now had a cushy position in their front office.

"I can't afford to get caught up in this ghetto nonsense, E," Vince said through his teeth while Ernest applied the fresh mixed Magic Shave to his face. "I worked my ass off to get where I am and half the crackers in the office still look at me cross-eyed. Plus, I've got to set a positive example for the young brothers on the team. We're going to have to work out something else for me to get my cut and shave. It's not worth me coming over here."

"Come on, man, it's not that serious," Ernest said, meticulously cutting the line just under his ear with his straight razor. "I know most of these dudes. I cut their hair. They got respect for my shop. Ain't nothing going down here."

"Man, you crazy. They out there trying to kill each other and you think they care about you," Vince said, holding his head still. "I got too much to lose, man."

Jeff chimed in, "You not going soft on us, Vince, are you?

These are the same niggas you was running with before you got saved."

"What you talking about, fool?" Andrea laughed with her fingers scratching Mrs. Morgan's head through the suds, "You mean before he got drafted."

"Hell no, he knows what I'm talking about," Jeff smirked.

"Are you talking about that Sunday when his mama drug him up to the front of the church?" Leon chuckled, remembering the day.

"Naw," Jeff said, "I'm talking about when Ernest took the fall for him when the cops caught them with that crack back in the day."

"That's so old, man," Ernest said, trying to diffuse the situation and hating that Jeff had brought it up. "I don't even remember that."

Vince chewed the inside of his jaw. He did remember. His mama was kicking it with this drug dealer who let him and Ernest borrow his car. They got pulled over and the cops found some crack in the glove compartment. Ernest had taken full blame for the few vials they found in the car. The incident got him six months on probation and Vince still felt like he owed him. Even though they were still juveniles it would have cost Vince his eligibility too. He didn't even like to think about how his life might have been if Ernest hadn't stepped up.

"You know you're my brother, man, but this is my last time coming back over here," Vince told E, putting those memories in the back of his mind, "I can't risk it."

Ernest walked around to face him. "Come on, man, we grew up around here."

"You're right, E, and we're grown now. I got responsibilities," Vince said, avoiding his gaze.

"We all got business," Ernest said, taking offense.

Vince took off the blue striped drape and checked himself in the mirror. "What you need to do is move your business elsewhere."

"It's not that simple for me," Ernest responded, feeling put down and insulted.

"It's on you, man, if you want to deal with the low-life," Vince said, handing him a fifty dollar bill. "From now on, come by the crib or the office to hook me up."

It was as quiet as a library in the shop as Vince walked out in his designer suit. Four sets of eyes followed him as he moved towards his black Escalade, one set in envy, one in disgust, one in approval, and one in lust. He pushed his key fob, got in, revved his engine, and drove off.

Jeff spoke first. "Your boy thinks he's too good for us now, E. He's just like the rest of them niggas who make a little money and forget where they came from."

"You're wrong about that, Jeff," Leon objected. "Why should he keep coming back around here in this damn war zone, dodging stray bullets? He worked hard to get where he is."

"Cause niggas need to be loyal, that's why," Jeff said indignantly.

"To who?" Leon asked, "He's got to protect himself first. If I could I'd get out of here too."

Jeff shook his head as he locked and unlocked the joint in his right knee. "I'ma tell you like my Black Panther brother Eldridge Cleaver said, "If you're not a part of the solution, you are a part of the problem.""

"Shut up, Jeff," Andrea said, wrapping Mrs. Morgan's head in a towel, "Ain't nobody in the mood for arguing today."

Ernest didn't comment. This definitely wasn't the time to tell them that he had already been thinking long and hard about how to make his next move. He wanted something else, something more, something better to fill the void that was growing inside of him. Vince had turned him onto a few top shelf clients with money that he serviced on their locations. They smelled good, looked good, wore designer threads, sported expensive watches, and drove nice rides. They were running things on higher levels. There wasn't any reason why he couldn't live that lifestyle. He was as much a businessman as they were. He just needed to up his game.

Ernest's cell phone rang bringing him back to his reality. He saw his mama's name across the top and answered the call.

"What's going on down there, baby?" she asked with concern, "I heard they was shooting around there again."

"Yeah, they say two guys got shot out here."

"How are you doing?" she asked as her fears eased, finding comfort in the sound of his voice. "Is everything okay?"

"I'm cool, Mama," he said with a chuckle, not wanting her to worry.

"I want to make sure for myself. Stop by here on your way home," she insisted.

"All right, but it'll probably be late though. You know its Friday."

"I don't care what time it is, you hear me."

"Okay, Mama, I'll see you later," he said, appeasing her.

Ernest wasn't what you would call a mama's boy but he loved his mama more than anyone else in his world. He wasn't ignorant to the sacrifices she had made for him, and because of that he never said no to whatever she asked him. Besides, she never asked for much and he didn't want to disappoint her.

The bell of the door jingled as two more customers walked in. One sat in Ernest's chair. With his phone still in his hand, Ernest dialed his wife, Rochelle, before he started on his next cut. He knew she would be the next one calling. They had been contently married, if not happily, for fourteen years and had three kids, two girls and a boy. Rhonda, the oldest at seventeen, Rhiana at fourteen, and the baby, Ernest Junior was eighteen months.

"Hey, what's up," she answered after the second ring, preoccupied with an episode of Maury.

"I wanted to call before you hear about it and get hyped up. There was some more shooting on the corner down here, but it's done. The shop wasn't hit."

"Did anybody get shot?" she asked, sitting straight up and getting excited.

"I think two, nobody died as far as I know."

"You still want me to bring E.J. down there?" she asked, unsure. She got off on the drama but she didn't want her baby in harm's way.

"No, I'll get him cut before the weekend is out. I gotta go."

"I'll check with you later," she said, looking over at their 18 month old son playing with his toy truck. He was the only thing slowing her down or she would have already been at the shop.

Rochelle had loved Ernest from the first moment she saw him and that love had grown so much that she had forgotten her own life. He was her life. Back when they first got together she was jealous and insecure, but then again she had reason to be. Over the years Ernest had played around on her more times than she cared to count and she was sure there had been other incidents that she didn't know about. It was a subject of contention between them. They fussed and fought especially whenever he hung out with Vince. She knew that thirsty gold-diggers were all over them and his crew hoping that their next baby-daddy might have some ducats they could latch onto. Even Andrea's female clients coming into the shop had been the source of many arguments between them but he had sworn to her that he was on the straight and narrow. His player days were over and she didn't have anything to worry about.

Ernest left the barbershop late that night. It was around 8:00 when he finished with his last client. It had been a long day and that's the way he liked it. The longer the day, the longer the pay. Andrea still had a few hours left before she would be done. There was one client in her chair, one under the dryer, and another one she hadn't touched. Ernest never had to worry about her being safe, he could count on Leon to stay at the shop until her last clients were styled and club ready, and clean the place a bit before he locked up.

Tired, more mentally than physically, he was too restless to go home. More than anything he wanted to drink an ice cold beer and drive around for a while to wind down but he didn't want to keep his mama waiting or show up with beer on his breath. A couple of minutes later he pulled his black Ford Expedition over to the curb in front of the duplex.

He sat there for a moment before he got out of the car looking at the front window and door of the place that held so many of his memories. He couldn't help wondering when and if he would ever be able to say goodbye to this duplex. It seemed so small and vulnerable to him now. He had begged his mama to let him move her someplace where there was peace and quiet but she refused, telling him that she was happy and comfortable around the people she had known for more than thirty years. She would always say that they might raise hell and act crazy but they were family, the only family she had ever known anyway.

***

This was where Ernest had grown up, raised in the third Section 8 duplex from the corner of Sherwood Lane, the only child of Sheila Shaw. His father, Tyrell Gibbs, was a fast talking car dealer who owned a car lot full of used lemons. He met Sheila when he was visiting his twin brother, Tyrone, who lived next door to Sheila's foster mother, Miss Gerri, in Edgehill.

The first time Tyrell saw Sheila she was sweeping the sidewalk in front of the house wearing shorts and a t-shirt that exposed her long slim brown arms and legs. He thought she looked like an Ethiopian queen. He winked at her and flashed his front teeth that were framed in gold as he strolled to his brother's screen door. To Sheila, the attention from him was like rain in a desert for a parched nomad. The next week when he came by to visit his brother she was watching and waiting from the living room window and smiled back at him.

It was on the following week that he came over across the fresh cut lawn and struck up a conversation with her while she sat on the porch singing to the radio.

"Hello, young lady," he said, propping his right leg up on the steps and leaning on his knee. "I had to come and tell you that it sounded like Aretha Franklin was over here singing."

"Thank you," Sheila said, blushing, "She's my favorite singer."

Tyrell grinned and leaned in closer to her. "Well, she better watch out. With that voice you got you might take her place."

Sheila smiled big with all her teeth showing as she relished the thought. "I could never be as good as her."

"You could be better," he said, showering her with compliments, "You're pretty enough to be a model, you might even be a movie star."

Nobody had ever made Sheila feel so special. She was ready to buy anything he was selling or at least put it in the layaway. For the first time in her life she didn't have to compete with somebody else to be noticed. He made her feel like it was like her birthday. The fact that he was strong, handsome, and mature was simply icing on the cake.

After a while Tyrell started coming by to see Sheila instead of his brother. That's when Miss Gerri started making a fuss. She said he was too old to be talking to a girl Sheila's age. Yet Sheila wasn't about to give up the person that made her feel like sunshine on a cloudy day. That just meant she had to sneak around to see him. Every other day she would wait for him down the block and around the corner. He would take her to the Dairy Queen, buy her a burger, fries, a strawberry milkshake, and drive her over to Shelby Park where they could talk and have their alone time. That was where she lost her virginity.

Sheila was thrilled to be loved by a grown man, it made her feel protected. Three months later when she told him they were going to have a baby he told her about his wife and their family of four children across town in East Nashville. Sheila got out of the car at the park, walked all the way back to Edgehill, and never saw him again.

Pregnant at seventeen years old, Sheila refused to consider abortion or adoption. When Ernest was born she got a job working at Mary's Bar B Que Pit, saved her money for a year to get her own place, and moved out of Miss Gerri's house. It was 1978 and she was nineteen years old. She didn't need anybody's permission, she was grown now. And even though she'd never gotten the chance to be a child in her young life, she vowed Ernest would always be her baby.

As pretty as she was, after Tyrell mislead her, Sheila never gave the guys who tried to talk to her a second look. She didn't know who she could trust and she wasn't about to make the same mistake twice. In her eyes, Ernest was her angel, someone for her to love and someone who would always love her. Sheila wanted to raise him right so she took him to church every Sunday. When Ernest started school she changed her hours to the second shift so that she could be there when he left in the morning and be there when he got home. Despite the fact she cooked most of the food at Mary's Bar B Que, she never brought him food home from work, she cooked him a fresh meal to put on the table everyday whether he ate it or not.

Ernest made her proud with the better than average grades he made in elementary school and then being on the honor roll when he got to middle school. Sheila was determined that the As and Bs would continue throughout high school. Every afternoon before she locked the door behind her on her way to work she made sure he was busy doing his homework.

Ernest's brilliance in school wasn't so much intelligence or due diligence, it was dumb luck. He was born with a photographic memory. He indulged his mama and never hit the door until he was sure she was busy cleaning, slicing, and seasoning the chicken and ribs in the kitchen at Mary's Barbecue Pit. So for the many hours she figured he spent pouring over his books he was actually out dabbling in petty street hustles with Vince trying to be a gangsta.

During the summer when he turned fourteen, Ernest's voice changed from El Debarge to Barry White, and the shadows above his lip and around his face turned to fuzz. Sheila, having always been raised in a household of girls, had no idea what to do for a boy going through puberty. She bought him a deluxe grooming kit for shaving and a pair of clippers and trimmers as his birthday gift. He learned how to use them in more ways than she imagined. With the straight razor he learned how to give himself a perfectly smooth shave and cut a flawless hair line, and when he hung out with Vince and their crew he kept it in his pocket at all times ready to slice anybody who stepped to him.

***

Sheila heard his car pull up on the street and watched her son from behind the sheer curtains as he sat out in his car. She worried about him more now that he was a man than she did when he was a boy. Back when he was younger his problems weren't so big and she could make most things all right again. She could tell he had a lot on his mind lately and she didn't want to add any more things for him to worry about but there was some news she needed to give him.

She walked to the front door, opened it, and waved. Buttons, the poodle he bought to keep her company eleven years ago was yapping beside her in the doorway.

Ernest turned off the ignition when he saw her standing in the doorway wearing her flowered housecoat. "Hey, Mama," he said, getting out of the car.

"Come on in here, child. What you doing out there wasting gas?"

"Taking a minute to think," he said, walking up the short concrete path.

"What you thinking about?" she asked, looking up at him as he came through the door.

"A friend of mine is thinking about opening up a full service barber shop downtown. Something like a spa for men."

She nodded her head. "Uh- huh. You hungry? I got some whiting fried up in the kitchen," she said, closing the door behind him.

"Yeah, that sounds good," he said, following her through the narrow hallway with Buttons trotting in front of him.

He took his usual seat at the small round table while she made him a plate. She poured him a glass of sweet tea, a glass of cola for herself, and pulled the chair out across from him. As soon as she sat down Buttons jumped in her lap for the family meeting.

"So tell me what your friend has on his mind," Sheila said, comfortable and ready to listen.

This was the way they had communicated ever since Ernest went to kindergarten. They talked about everything, but always in third person. "Mama, a friend of mine wet his pants, a friend had to go to the principal's office, a friend cut class, a friend of mine got suspended, a friend of mine likes this girl, a friend tried smoking, a friend was drinking, and a friend got this girl pregnant. Sheila knew who he was referring to from the time he was five years old, even though she never let on that he was the "friend."

With his eyes on the fried crisp fish, some greens, and a sliced tomato he started talking.

"He's thinking that there's not a lot of cash floating around in the hood right now and if he wants to get ahead and make some real bread he has to go where the money is."

"So where does he think that is?" she asked intently, wanting to get the full gist of what he was saying.

"Downtown, midtown, or in the Gulch somewhere," he said before he took a bite of fish.

"I can't argue with that," she said, pondering over it. "Even so, it sounds like something he needs to give a lot more thought to before he steps out there. He don't need to run out half-cocked and lose everything he's worked for. Ain't no short cuts in this world. I would tell him to take his time, save his money, and when the time is right he'll be ready."

"It's time now, Mama," Ernest said anxiously. "It's pastime. I know how he feels. My business has been slacking too. Brothers are growing their hair long, wearing corn rows, nappy twists, and dreads again. I need to expand my clientele and get some of that white money."

Sheila nodded, understanding his dilemma. "All I know is that it's not a decision your friend needs to rush into. If I could, son, I would help you do something like that but right through here I can barely make my own ends meet."

"What are you talking about, Mama?" Ernest asked, taken aback. He wasn't about to see her struggling again. "You know to call me."

"I didn't want to bother you with it," she said, staring into the glass of brown soda. "I've been off sick from work a lot lately and my check has been short. The doctors say my kidneys are weakening. They probably gonna go out on me."

Ernest shook his head and pushed the plate away. He was caught off guard but he couldn't say he was surprised. His mama didn't like water and she never drank it. She preferred Pepsi or Coca-Cola, whichever one was on sale. He looked down and frowned at the plate of food with his appetite lost. Sheila looked down too searching for a hidden message among the lines inside her hands. She hated to trouble him. She wanted to make it all right for her child as she always did when he was a boy but he was a man now with adult sized problems. In Ernest's mind those problems had just gotten bigger.

"So what else did the doctors say?" he asked, breaking the silence.

"They say I might have to go on the dialysis machine soon," she said downheartedly.

"Don't focus on that, Mama. It doesn't have to go like that. All you got to do is take better care of yourself. Try to leave those cokes alone and drink more water."

"I can't stand the taste of water. Besides, it's too late for me to change anyway. The damage is done."

Ernest got up from his chair, mad and sad. He couldn't stand to hear her giving up so easy.

"Try for me, Mama, and the kids," he urged, scraping his plate in the trash before he rinsed it in the sink. "It might help and do you some good."

"I'll be all right, baby," she said, standing up and walking behind him to the door. "Anyway, I was thinking about that thing you said your friend wanted to do. Even if he doesn't decide it's the right time for him to step out there, I think it might be a good idea for you to do something like that. You got a lot going for you."

"I was thinking that too," he said, turning around to give her a hug before he left.

She called out to him before he got to his car. "Be patient, son, keep doing what you're doing and I know it will come together for you."

He turned around. "Thanks, Mama. I love you. Make sure you lock the door."

"You're my heart, Ernest. Be careful," she said as she shut the door.

***

His cellphone rang as soon as he turned the key in the ignition. He pulled it out of his hip pocket and saw it was Rochelle. Ernest let it ring. He didn't feel like talking. He wanted to listen to his own thoughts until he got to the house. He sent her a text message that he was on his way home so she wouldn't start tripping.

He and Rochelle had been together off and on since their

sophomore year in high school. Short and petite, she was more cute and sassy than beautiful. Whenever she wasn't sporting a almost-to the-waist weave she wore her hair permed and cut short. She was golden brown like baked chicken with big dark brown eyes that she framed with press-on lashes. She was the kind of girl who would prop her hand on her hip and tell you about yourself without question. He liked kicking it with her back in the day but he was just having fun. Whenever they got together he used a condom if he had one, pulled out when he didn't. She got pregnant in their senior year. His mama was pissed when he told her. She was just starting to think that maybe he could go to college, that he might be smart enough to become a doctor.

The baby and his run-in with the cops forced him to review his options. He did go to college even if it wasn't the one his mama had planned on, Barber College. When he finished he rented a booth in a shop on Jefferson Street with Leon for a few years while he saved to get his own spot.

Rochelle wasn't the only female he was dealing with at the time but after she got pregnant again he decided to marry her. He wasn't crazy in love with her but he didn't want her to be his baby-mama and his kids to grow up like him, without a father. He never denied cheating on her a few times before their marriage, maybe a couple of times after, and her family never let him forget it. They were always giving him side eyes whenever they came around. He didn't consider himself a player or a dog. He just had a weakness for sweet lips and heavy hips.

The main reason his attention wandered is that he and Rochelle didn't have anything in common aside from their kids. Over their sixteen years together he developed a broadened horizon and she sustained chronic tunnel vision. He's a dreamer, she's a realist. He's ambitious, she's indifferent.

He wants it all, prestige, money, status, everything that Vince has. She doesn't care about any of that; they're only additional things to come between them.

By the time Ernest got home he had made up his mind. He parked on the driveway outside of the garage of their three-bedroom home, pushed the lock on his car fob and went inside. He wasn't sure how he was going to bring up the subject of opening a spa with Rochelle but it didn't matter. She was going to raise hell no matter what he said.

"What took you so long?" Rochelle fussed as soon as he came through the door.

She didn't like coming across angry all the time but he always gave her a reason. He was the one who made her feel insecure about their relationship. She'd only had the third baby to tie him tighter around her.

"You know I went by to check on my mama," Ernest said defensively, "She cooked so I ate."

"I wish you thought about me half as much as you think about your mama," she said, blocking his way.

"Now you're being ridiculous, Chelle. You need to stop. It doesn't make no sense for you to be jealous of my mama."

"That's if the only place you stopped was at your mama's," she remarked.

Ernest walked past her. "I'm not going through this with you tonight. You just want to argue."

"That's not what I want," she said with her tone softening. "I don't have much choice when you want to hang out all the time."

Ernest immediately canceled any plans he had for talking about his idea, waved her off, and went down the hallway towards their bedroom to take a shower. He heard the TV on in Rhonda and Rhianna's room. He stuck his head in the door.

The girls, lovely mixtures of him and Rochelle, were laughing and watching some horror movie.

"Hey, ladybugs, what y'all watching?" he asked, smiling.

Rhianna who kept her headphones on all the time waved.

Rhonda answered, "Hey, Daddy, its *Scary Move IV*. You want to watch it with us?"

"Not tonight, sweetheart, I'm beat."

"Okay," she said with her attention turning back to the show.

Ernest turned on the shower in the master bath, undressed, and sat on the edge of the tub while he waited for the water to get hot. The whole day replayed in his head, then last month, then last year, and then five years ago. By the time the bathroom had filled with steam it was clear to him that it was now or never.

Chapter
Three

On Saturdays, Ernest always opened up the shop early. When Leon, always the second person to come in, got there to ruminate over his morning coffee it gave him a chance to go and meet Vince at the gym for a workout. The two of them had been doing that since high school to stay connected as the directions of their individual paths began to deviate.

Vince was working with some medium weight barbells when Ernest walked in.

"Is that all you got?" Ernest teased as he pulled his t-shirt over his head.

Vince laughed. "Man, you know this is my cool-down, I did a world class workout before you got out of the bed."

"Yeah right," Ernest said, slapping his hand. Then he grabbed a pair of 15-lb dumbbells to warm up. "All I need is a minute to catch up with you."

Vince put down the weights and picked up a towel to wipe the sweat from his face. He and Ernest were running dogs from way back and they were always honest with each other but after he left the shop he thought about what he said and regretted the way he had come off.

"I wasn't trying to crash on you yesterday, man, but I'm serious about what I said," Vince told him. "You need to up your game and bring it out of the hood. There's nothing going on there. You don't owe anybody there anything. You can make some real dough downtown with high end clientele that would never set foot in King Cut."

Ernest knew it was true. He thought about Theo Brooks, the CEO of Black and Blue Entertainment. He was one of the clients that he serviced at his location. It was a pent-office suite with a view over Riverfront. He paid Ernest $100 for his cut and shave and tipped him an extra $100 every two weeks.

"I hear you, man. I was up all night thinking about it," Ernest said, putting his knee on the weight bench and picking up a 30-lb dumbbell.

"With your skills there's large money to be made out there for you. I'm talking about professional brothers who like to keep their look tight at all times."

"I've been wanting to go that route for a long time, man, but whenever I think I'm ready something always comes up. Now my mama is sick and missing days from work. I know her check has been short and I have to cover her expenses with the shoestring I call my budget. My money is not even funny, it's fucking hilarious."

Vince chuckled. "That's deep, man, but you can still make that move. I got you, whatever you need. Just say the word. You're my brother."

"Thanks, man, I appreciate that but I can't borrow from you. Money can take out a friendship quicker than anything else. It made Judas turn on Jesus."

Vince laughed again. "I hear you, but don't let it go. Take some time, put a proposal or business plan together, and go to your bank and apply for a business loan. There are other private investors out here too. We can go in together."

"That's a bet," Ernest said, taking the heavy barbells from his friend. "To do this right I need to get in there with the big Benjamins."

***

Ernest was restless all day Sunday. He was itching to get through their weekly family ritual of his mama coming over, her cooking dinner with Rochelle, and them all sitting around the dining table with the kids for an hour. He had a ton of work to do to get ready for his appointment at the bank tomorrow. He hadn't mentioned it to Rochelle or his mama. If he didn't get the loan he wouldn't have to worry about telling them that either.

The dinner of pork chops and gravy, macaroni and cheese, cabbage, and corn bread tasted as good as it looked. Ernest practically inhaled his plateful. For the rest of the time he bounced his foot impatiently under the table while Sheila and Rochelle went over every song, chapter, and verse of the morning church service including the sermon between their bites. E.J., sitting next to him in his highchair was just as fidgety as his Dad, playing more with his food than eating it. Rhonda was focused on reading her Facebook page in her phone, and Rhianna, wearing her usual headphones was singing under her breath.

"Finally," he thought when the chatter died down and they were all full to the brim.

Rochelle wiped her hands and took E.J. out of his high chair to let him roam around on the floor. "All right, girl-friends," she said to Rhonda and Rhianna, "Y'all don't need to wait until late to clean the kitchen."

"I've got to study for my final exams," Rhonda, the oldest said, getting up from the table. "My chemistry teacher don't play."

"I got homework too, Mommy," Rhianna said, hoping she wouldn't have to clean the kitchen all by herself.

"You girls go on and hit those books," Sheila said, rescuing her granddaughters, "I'll help your mama do the dishes."

"You don't have to do that," Rochelle said with a sigh, "It's no big deal. Ernest can go on and drive you home so you can relax. I know you're probably tired."

"I'm all right," Sheila said, pushing back from the table. "As long as he gets me home in time to watch the "Real Housewives of Atlanta.'"

Ernest checked his watch. "We might need to ride now, Mama, I have to stop for gas," he said, anxious to get back and put his proposal together.

"Don't let Ernest rush you, Miss Sheila," Rochelle said, going into the kitchen. "There's probably some game coming on he wants to watch."

"That's fine, I'm ready to get out of these clothes anyway," Sheila said, lifting her purse from the back of the chair. "Come over here, E.J., say goodbye to your grandma."

"Go on and take him with you," Rochelle said in an afterthought. That way she would be sure Ernest didn't make any other stops on his way home.

It didn't matter to Ernest. He couldn't wait to get back. He picked his son up and headed out the front door with his mama behind him.

"What's got you on edge?" Sheila asked after he got E.J. in his car seat.

"Nothing," Ernest said, dodging her question. "I was thinking that we might need to move to a bigger place so you can stay with us if you need to."

"Well you can stop thinking about that. I like my privacy."

"If you don't want to live with us, it would make me feel better if you lived closer to us."

"Child, I'm only across town, not in another state."

"All right, I'll leave it alone for now."

Ernest let it go and mentally began organizing his business plan. Sheila looked out the side of her eye at him while he drove. She had raised him, so she knew there was something more on his mind that he was keeping to himself.

When they were almost there, she casually turned to her window. "What did that friend of yours decide about opening up his shop?"

"He's going to see if he can get a loan from the bank to finance it?"

"I wish him the best on that," she commented, still gazing through the window. "He should do fine as long as he's careful not to step too high too fast and get carried away."

"He won't, he's got his head on straight," Ernest said confidently, pulling in front of the duplex. "Plus you can't get anywhere if you're afraid to move to the next level."

Sheila opened her car door. "I'll be praying for him," she said, getting out of the car.

"Slow down, Mama," Ernest said, opening his door to get out of the car. "I have to get E.J. out of his car seat."

"Leave him be, he's sleeping," she said, looking in the back seat. "I don't have no problem going in the house by myself."

Ernest closed his door and rolled down the passenger side window.

"Okay then, I'll stay here and watch until you get inside. I love you, Mama."

"You're my heart, son."

Ernest watched her from the street wishing she would let him do more for her. When she got the door unlocked and opened he saw Buttons jumping up and down on her hind legs happy to see her. Sheila waved back at him to let him know everything was all right before she closed and locked the door.

Usually Ernest drove down 4th Avenue to Broadway and then down 8th Avenue to get home, but tonight he jumped on the interstate to save time. When he got back home E.J. was still asleep. He carried him from the car into the house, laid him down in his bed, and slipped off his shoes. Rochelle was in their bedroom on the phone with somebody discussing what was happening on her TV show. Quietly he went downstairs in the finished part of the basement that he had transformed into his man-cave. He kept a desk and a file cabinet there to handle the business for King Cut.

He started with his last three tax returns, a list of his assets, checked his inventory, and got his bank balances in order. Then he leaned back in his office chair and did a full contemplation on opening a male spa. He weighed the pros and the cons before he opened a blank word document on his laptop and began his proposal.

***

On Monday afternoon while Rochelle picked the kids up from school, Ernest strolled into the Third National Bank downtown on Commerce Street. He was dressed in a dark blue pinstriped suit, a lavender shirt with white stripes, a lavender pocket square, and navy Italian wingtips. He was cleaner than the board of health, as his mama's boss at Mary's Bar B Q Pit used to say. With his leather-bound portfolio under his arm, he was the picture of a successful businessman, photo ready for the cover of Black Enterprise.

Inside the heavy brass-trimmed glass doors you could almost smell the money. Without a doubt you could see it in the grain of the cherry wood furnishings, the gleam of crystal from the lighting, the immense Oriental rug centered on the floor, and the impressionist art that lined the walls.

He approached the information desk in the center of the lobby.

"Hello," he said with a smile, speaking to the young white woman sitting there. "I have an appointment to see Glenn Charles."

She smiled back at him. "He's on the fifth floor in suite 524. When you get off the elevator make a right."

"Thank you," Ernest said.

His heels clicked against the marble floor as he moved towards the three elevators in the lobby. He pressed the brass button with the arrow pointing up and waited in front of the middle elevator. From there it didn't matter which door opened first. The door on the left parted first and Ernest walked on by himself. He pushed the number five and looked at his reflection on the brass wall of the elevator until the muted bell sounded that he had arrived on the fifth floor.

Down the hall on his left he saw the half-opened door of suite 524. He peeped inside and saw a man about fifty-five years old, thin salt-and-pepper hair, silver-wire framed glasses, wearing a gray plaid suit sitting behind a huge walnut desk. Ernest knocked softly on the door to get his attention. The man looked up straining through his glasses.

"Mr. Shaw," he said with it sounding like a question.

"Yes," Ernest said, extending his hand to shake.

Mr. Charles stood up and shook his hand. "Hello, Mr. Shaw, good to meet you. Come on in and have a seat. Let's talk about your business venture."

Ernest sat down in one of the two dark wood chairs with blue tufted seats in front of his desk. He slid it a little toward the center where he could look between the Chinese Bonsai tree and the orange orchid plant on the front corners of the desk.

"Thank you, Mr. Charles, for meeting with me today," Ernest said graciously. "I didn't expect to be able to get an appointment with you on such short notice."

"Please call me Glenn. You know what they say, time waits for no man and time is money. Here at Third National we understand the urgency of the business world. We want to be able to assist you in all your financial needs."

"I appreciate that very much. I called here first because I've been doing business with Third National Bank for years."

"Can I get you something to drink?" Glenn asked, raising his hands as if he had forgotten something important.

"Water would be fine," Ernest answered.

Glenn reached up and handed Ernest one of the bottles of water from a nearby shelf. Then he leaned both hands on his desk and said, "So tell me what you have in mind for the expansion of your business."

"I'm not interested in expanding, Glenn. I want to begin something totally new. It would be a full service spa for men. I have a proposal with me for you to take a look at," Ernest said, opening up his portfolio to show his budget and plans.

"Wow," Glenn said, going down his line-item column. "This is much more than I expected. The initial investment is over 250 thousand, that's right at our cap for small business loans."

Ernest ran his hands back and forth over the creases in his pants legs as his confidence in the outcome of this meeting wafted like a birthday balloon quickly losing air.

"I built my other shop from nothing and it has been profitable for seven years," Ernest said to assure Glenn he was worth the risk.

Glenn shook his head slowly from side to side. "For this sum we would have to try for a Small Business Administration-Guaranteed loan. We'll need financial statements from King

Cut and cash flow projections for the new venture to complete the application."

Unable to gauge his reaction, Ernest shifted back in his chair while Glenn read the rest of the proposal and turned the pages. The exotic colors of the orchid bloom on the right corner of the desk kept drawing his eye. It seemed out of place among the cool dark colors that decorated the office. With every passing minute Ernest felt more like that bright flower. He wanted to show his talents to the world and flourish but he was destined to be held down in an isolated place where he couldn't be valued.

When Glenn finished reading the proposal he handed the papers back to Ernest. "Like I said we'll need a little more to evaluate the loan."

"Whatever you need, let me know and I'll put it together," Ernest replied with only a fraction of the enthusiasm he had when he walked in.

Glenn stood up and walked around to the front of his desk signaling that the meeting was over. Ernest zipped up his portfolio and rose to his feet in front of him. Taller by at least four inches he gazed down at Glenn's face as he walked him to the door.

"Put together a list of your business assets that we can use for collateral and get it to me as soon as you can," Glenn said, stopping in the doorway, "I'll take your application to our review committee and we can make the loan request to the SBA if need be."

"I'll get that back to you in a few days," Ernest said, knowing that wouldn't help boost his application very much. Most of the equipment and furnishings he was working with were old and probably needed to be replaced.

While they were standing there an attractive black woman walked towards them in the hallway and Glenn's face lit up.

"By the way, what area are you looking at for your new location?" he asked Ernest.

"Downtown or in the Gulch would be prime spots for me," Ernest answered, turning to leave.

"Hold on for a second," Glenn said, smiling as the woman got closer. "Hello, Eva, nice to see you. How have you been?"

"No complaints, Glenn. How about yourself?" she said, returning his greeting while giving Ernest a lingering once-over.

"I'm great. I might have a client for you," he said, glancing at Ernest. "This is Eva Hamilton. Eva, this is Ernest Shaw. He's in the market for some commercial real estate for a new business venture he's planning."

Eva nodded and smiled at him in approval. "It's a pleasure to meet you, Mr. Shaw."

"Likewise," he said, eager to get to the elevator.

"Here's my card, call me," she said, handing it to Ernest and making eye contact. "I'm sure I can help you find the perfect spot."

"Sure, I'll do that," Ernest said, sliding the card in his breast pocket and stepping backwards a few steps before he walked away.

"What's his story?" Eva asked Glenn as she watched Ernest walk away.

"He runs a barbershop in North Nashville, King Cut. He wants to open an upscale men's barbershop/spa downtown somewhere."

"How's it looking?"

"He's done all right for himself, however, at first look he might be trying to bite off more than he can chew but we'll see what collateral he can bring to the table."

"Interesting," Eva murmured as Glenn walked back into his office. Actually she was more than interested, she was intrigued. The fact that he hadn't given her a second look struck a chord with her. That didn't happen often. Staring down the hallway at him she thought, "I don't know what that man is asking for but if he can deliver what I need, he's going to get it."

When Ernest got off the elevator he passed the information desk in the lobby on the way out. The young white woman sitting there called after him, "Have a nice evening."

"Same to you," Ernest replied with a fake smile, knowing the odds were against it.

He had planned to pick up Rochelle and the kids after the meeting to go out to eat but there was nothing to celebrate. When he got to his car, he tossed his portfolio in the trunk, took off his jacket and tie, laid them in the back seat, and drove straight to the shop. The steering wheel suffered intermittent jabs all along the way even though he was pissed at himself. His financial statements from the barber shop were a sham and wouldn't match up with his IRS filings. Nearly all the proceeds from his business were paid in cash and half of them weren't even reported. He shook his head in exasperation; every time he tried to give himself an edge he stabbed himself in the back.

Chapter Four

Eva Hamilton was born Eva Watkins and raised in Chocolate City, Washington, DC, the only daughter among three older brothers. Both of her parents were teachers. Although they spoiled their only girl, they also made sure she hit her books. She had a good head on her shoulders, looking like a young Diahann Carroll with brains to match. In her senior year of high school she was voted prom queen and the most-likely to succeed. She got her bachelor's degree from Howard University and her master's from Georgetown University. For ten years she was a workaholic employed at the Maryland Financial Bank, advancing until she reached the glass ceiling as Chief Lending Officer. She made the move to Nashville after she was headhunted by the Pinnacle Financial Group. That's where she met her future husband, Mitchell Hamilton III, vice president/chairman of the board.

Even though her main interest was her career, Eva was social and dated regularly. At thirty-seven years old and still single, her mother had given up on grandchildren from her daughter, telling her she was too self-absorbed to be in a relationship or raise a child. Her cavalier attitude didn't deter

Mitchell. He was attracted to her model good looks, five-foot-ten, a perfect size six, and flawless skin the color of nutmeg. Wasting no time with a long courtship, he wined and dined her every weekend in a different city, Miami, New York, Los Angeles, Las Vegas, and then he proposed in St. Thomas. Eva said yes without hesitation, she wasn't so much in love with Mitchell as she was with his spontaneity. She also loved the fact that with him, unlike all the other men she had dated, money was no object.

Born in 1941, Mitchell was a self-made man, having come up during a time when black men were considered to be boys from the day they were born to the day they died. He had fought for every quantity of education, every employment position, and every dollar he ever earned. He had no qualms about enjoying the fruits of his labor and indulged himself with the finest houses, cars, food, wine, and women.

Mitchell had always preferred younger women. It was a trait handed down to him from his father, Mitchell Hamilton Jr. His dad had always told him, and repeated it on his death bed at ninety-two years old, that a young wife will preserve a man's youth. Mitchell following his example had been married twice before. His previous wives had become unhappy with his disinterest and disregard for them as they matured. He liked that Eva was independent, and at sixty-eight years old he didn't require the constant attention of a wife.

The only objection to their union was from Natalie, Mitchell's daughter by his second wife. She was only ten years younger than Eva. Despite being a plastic surgeon with a successful practice she hated fake people. People who she thought pretended to be something they weren't. Natalie thought Eva was as fake as they come, an opportunist looking for a way or a man to promote herself to a higher status. She disapproved of the marriage from the start believing that Eva was incapable of real feelings or connecting to another human being on an emotional level.

At Mitchell's request, Eva left the company after they were married. With no desire to be a trophy wife she started her own real estate firm. Hamilton Realty was remarkably successful as a black enterprise from the beginning given her access to super wealthy white commercial and residential clients funneled her way from Pinnacle Financial. Mitchell and Eva were both satisfied personally and professionally for the next six years until he began to have health concerns that changed the whole nature of their relationship. He was diagnosed with a degenerative muscle disease.

You don't have to be Einstein to know that energy is neither created nor destroyed. Power is not lost, it simply changes hands. Inevitably the dynamics of the marriage between Mitchell and Eva began to change. As Mitchell's condition slowly deteriorated she gradually became more vibrant. Every ounce of strength he lost she gained and became stronger and more assertive. Mitchell accepted his fate as he had with all the fortunes and misfortunes that life had bestowed upon him with the wisdom that most of what you get in this world you don't deserve, good or bad. He never gave her permission to cheat but suspected that she wouldn't remain faithful to him. Discretion was his unspoken requirement.

Eva had a few dalliances but none of them meant anything to her or threatened her marriage in any way. They were all purely physical. She was more fixated on building a conglomerate of companies over which she would rule. To her, Ernest Shaw could possibly fulfill two purposes. Aside from his physical appearance, his business plan had piqued her interests. She tapped his name and King Cut into her iPad.

***

Ernest was doing everything he could to keep the way he was feeling from showing on his face. It was Friday, his busiest day at the shop, and he was disheartened. He had done the best he could to prop up his books from King Cut, had put together his home, SUV, and car as collateral for the loan, and had faxed all the additional information over to Glenn Charles at Third National. It had all been a waste of time. He could tell as soon as he saw Glenn's expression when they met yesterday afternoon in his office.

"I have to tell you, Mr. Shaw, a new business is a difficult proposition. We don't want you to lose your investment and the bank doesn't want to lose its investment."

"Are you saying my loan wasn't approved?" Ernest asked feeling discouraged.

"The news is not all bad, Mr. Shaw. We can't get you the approval on the amount you requested but if you could find a more modest location we might be able to work something out."

"I'm not sure what you mean, Glenn. Are we negotiating the amount here or is this a denial?"

"Please understand, Mr. Shaw, we want to see you be successful in your endeavor. Growing your business too fast can set you up for failure. We feel it would be wiser to gradually scale up. Allow your clientele to grow with you, possibly at a less expensive location."

Ernest held his tongue. No reason to argue, get angry, or play the race card. There wasn't anything more to say. In no uncertain terms they had denied his loan. He took one more glance at the exotic out-of-place orchid and stood up.

"Thanks, Glenn, for your consideration," Ernest said without looking at him.

"As I said, we're here to help you," Glenn said, standing up behind his desk. "Don't hesitate to let us know how we can do that."

Ernest nodded once and walked out. "What the fuck is he talking about?" he thought as he strode to the elevator.

"That's what I was here for. How in the hell are they going to help me if they won't give me the money. That's the only reason I went through all this bullshit."

He'd left the bank and gone by Donks' to have a drink before he went home, to mellow out, but it hadn't helped much. Even after four shots of Hennessey and two beers he couldn't sleep. It was hard to let his dream go. Hard to pretend to be satisfied when he had the desire for much more. The next morning he'd gotten up at dawn, showered and left while everyone was still asleep. He stopped at the McDonald's drive-thru on Trinity Lane for a cup of coffee and drank it in the parking lot while he watched the cars merging onto the interstate. He felt like they were all moving forward while he was stuck in one place.

When he'd gotten to the shop that morning Leon had already opened up, and his first client, Noah, who did landscaping was already there waiting and watching the news. Ernest put his smock on and motioned for him to come sit in his chair.

"Morning, man" he said, "Sorry you had to wait, my bad."

"It's all good," Noah said, shifting in the chair while Ernest organized the tools of his trade.

Leon sat in his own chair next to Ernest's station drinking a cup of coffee. He had worked with Ernest for more than ten years. He wasn't sure what the deal was but he could sense that something was out of sorts.

"You're moving kinda slow this morning, Doc," Leon commented, "I got a shot of Five-Hour Energy if your need it."

"No, I'm cool," Ernest said casually as he put the neck strip and then a fresh drape around Noah's shoulders. He combed through Noah's hair absentmindedly for a couple of minutes before he picked up his clippers and began to cut.

Seeing Ernest who liked to joke with Noah being unusually quiet, Leon pushed a little more to see what was wrong. "I'm not trying to get in your business, E, but it seems like you got a lot going on. Everything okay at the house?"

"Definitely, I just got some things on my mind," Ernest said, wishing Leon would let it go.

Leon kept pressing. "How's your mama?"

The question made Ernest stop brooding and think about his mama for a moment. "Not too good, her kidneys are acting up. Her doctor says she might need to go on dialysis soon."

"That's rough, man," Noah said, joining in the conversation. "All I can tell you is make sure she gets a second opinion. Half these doctors don't know what they're doing. If they make a mistake, you're the one who has to pay for it."

"I heard that," Ernest said moodily.

Figuring that was what was bothering him, Leon turned his attention to the news on the TV while Ernest finished up the cut.

Ernest sharpened up Noah's hairline with his straight-razor, brushed away the stray hairs on his neck, and dabbed it with alcohol before he removed the drape.

"Thanks, man," Noah said, slapping a twenty dollar bill in his hand. "I hope your mama feels better. Tell her to start drinking cranberry juice."

Ernest gave him a brother handshake and said, "Thanks, man."

Jeff pulled the door to the shop open just as Noah was walking out.

"What's up, fellas?" he asked, dropping his duffel bag full of CDs, DVDs, and who knew what else on the counter beside his station. He grabbed the remote for the TV from the wooden end table between the waiting chairs and pressed the 'off' button. Then he changed the radio station to 101.1 FM and pressed the volume button higher. "It's the freaking weekend, my niggas, time to turn up."

Leon shook his head in disgust. "I don't know why you starting with all that noise in here, it's barely 10:00 in the morning."

"Old as your ass is, Leon, it's going to take all day to get your blood flowing," Jeff said on his way back out to smoke a cigarette.

Ernest laughed, forgetting about his troubles for a minute.

A minute later Andrea pulled into the parking lot with her music blasting. She got out of her car wearing a hot pink maxi sundress and a glittered baseball cap, carrying an over-sized fake Gucci satchel in one hand and her usual take-out plate in the other. She stopped outside the door where Jeff was smoking and they stood out there laughing and talking like it was the end of the work day instead of the beginning. Then Jeff dropped the cigarette on the ground and lit up a joint. He took two tokes on it and then put it out.

"That's why we can't get nowhere as a people," Leon complained, looking at them. "Black folks don't understand that you don't play around on your job, you handle your business. I can't tell if they come here to work or come to party."

"Hey there," Andrea hollered at them when she finally came in. "Ima tell you right now I'm hungry. I didn't have any breakfast this morning. What are we eating today?"

"You call it," Leon said, shaking his head again. "It don't make no difference to me."

"What you want to eat, Ernest?" Andrea asked, noticing he was unusually quiet.

"Rochelle is probably going to bring me something later," he said, sounding subdued.

"Y'all know I want me some Prince's hot chicken," Andrea said, putting down her stuff and clapping her hands, "That's how I roll on Fridays."

"Get me an order of gizzards," Leon added.

"Call it in and I'll pick it up," Jeff said, coming in the door.

Pee Wee and two of his crew with pants sagging waddled in behind Jeff. Pee Wee got in Jeff's chair, another got in Ernest's, and the third went over to Andrea's corner to get his hair braided.

"You feeling all right, Pee Wee?" Andrea hollered across the room. "I was worried about you when they said you got shot."

"Ain't no thang," he hollered back. "You know I'm not going out like that. It's gonna take more than one bullet to lay me out."

"You ain't Superman," Leon said, cutting in. "Keep up what you doing and you gon' get another chance to look death in the eye."

"You joking, man," Pee Wee snickered, "I'm the one out here taking names. Those niggas that shot me, they lucky they in the pen. If they was out here on the streets they wouldn't make it through the night."

"Hell yeah, that's truth right there," the guy in Ernest's chair added.

"You bad to bone, Pee Wee," Jeff laughed, "I ain't mad at you."

The bell on the door rang again. It was Bishop Rayburn coming in. He was the pastor at Mount Pisgah Baptist Church two blocks away. It was more than 85 degrees outside and he was more than 285 pounds but he was wearing a suitcoat with his white shirt buttoned up to his neck. A hush went through the shop as he ambled his way over to Leon's chair.

"Good morning, Bishop," Leon said respectfully as he shook out a fresh drape. "How are you doing today?"

"I'm blessed and highly favored," Bishop Rayburn answered with his voice booming like he was in the pulpit. He took a handkerchief from the inside pocket of his jacket and wiped the sweat from his forehead. Then he reared back in the chair, looked around, and asked, "How are my brothers and sister in Christ doing?"

"We're all blessed too, Bishop," Andrea said with her fingers pulling through the corn row on the guy's head that came in with Pee Wee.

"How's your mama, Ernest?" Bishop asked while Leon stirred up his hair dye.

"She's hanging in, sir," Ernest answered.

"Praise, Jesus," Bishop said, leaning back so Leon could put the dye on his beard.

Jeff was finished with Pee Wee in no time. Wearing short dreads, he only wanted a line. Ernest had quickly hooked up his homey with a faded Mohawk. They waited out front for their other friend, more than ready to get out of there before Bishop's greetings turned into a sermon.

***

An hour later there was a totally different set of folks in the barber shop. Andrea had one under the dryer, one in the shampoo bowl, and all the seats in the shop were filled. Chattering on cellphones and conversations in the room drowned out the jams on the radio. The steady flow of customers increased and by noon they were getting backed up and some waited on the sidewalk outside shooting the breeze.

After 2:00 the shop turned into a hub of activity. School was out and the rush of moms bringing their boys in for cuts had begun. Ernest and Leon worked steadily with the sound of clippers and shavers blending in with the rest of the noise.

Andrea was in her area working her fingers to the bone with weaves, perms, and still feeding her face. Jeff was busy burning custom CDs while he cut.

LeShay, one of the neighborhood boosters who did most of her work in Wal-Mart, came by with a fresh haul of products to sell. She had everything from laundry detergent, bath soap, powders, deodorants, toothpaste, and air fresheners. She even had some tube socks and crew socks. She sold it all, took some orders, and left promising to be back tomorrow. Next Terrance wheeled in his trunk full of knock-off hand bags and put on a show for the ladies, rhyming as he displayed his collection.

It was around 6:00 when there was a lull in the flow in and out of the door. That's when a white-on-white Mercedes drove up and parked in front of the shop. Ernest recognized her through the window. He remembered her name, Eva. She stepped out of the car and all the eyes in the shop were fixed on her. She was ready for it, wearing a tan pencil skirt, a safari style jacket, and light brown pumps. Her eyes were shielded from all the stares by a pair of white frame sunglasses. Leon, the only one of them who didn't have someone in his chair, hurried to the door and opened it for her.

"Welcome to King Cut, pretty lady," he said, sounding proper. "How can I help you?"

Eva took off her glasses. "I'm here to see Mr. Shaw," she said with a smile, knowing she was the center of attention.

"Please have a seat," Leon said, pointing to the waiting area, "He'll be right with you."

Eva sat down in a chair where she could watch Ernest work. She folded her sunglasses and put them in her purse as she enjoyed the view. She thought there was something sexy about watching a man at work, particularly if he used his hands. Casually dressed and wearing a smock he seemed more rugged than when she saw him at the bank. Even still, she recognized his taste for the finer things in his True religion jeans, Ralph Lauren polo shirt, and Cole Hann boat shoes. She noticed that he was very meticulous in his craft. He didn't rush; making sure every hair was in place.

Across the room Andrea's eyes widened with a questioning look to Ernest, then they shifted to Jeff and then to Leon. Jeff and Leon shrugged their shoulders. They didn't know who this woman was or what she wanted but it was obvious she wasn't from around there.

Ernest took longer than necessary as he worked on the teenager's high top fade. He hadn't told anybody in the shop about his desire to make a move much less his loan application. He didn't care to discuss any of that in front of them. He wasn't even sure what this lady was doing there. The kid in his chair was getting restless so he sprayed his hair with oil sheen and took off the drape. The young man gave him a folded up ten dollar bill and headed out.

Without speaking Ernest motioned for Eva to sit in his chair. The whole room got quiet as she sauntered over to his station. You would have thought he was about to perform major surgery. When she sat down her perfume engulfed him like thick fog.

"What can I do for you?" he asked in a low voice after she was seated.

"Can you arch my eyebrows for me?" she asked, relaxed.

"Certainly," he said, putting a fresh drape over her.

Her brows were flawless but he was sure that wasn't her reason for coming. He put some cream around her brows and sterilized his straight razor. Eva closed her eyes and took a deep breath. She could smell his cologne; she guessed it was Calvin Klein's Obsession. She felt his firm hand against her skin but could barely feel the sharp blade as it brushed above her eyelid. It felt more like a feather. She liked the feeling but it was over too quick.

"You're done," he said after a couple of minutes.

He held a mirror up for her to judge his handiwork.

"It looks good, thank you," she said, getting a glimpse of his chest in the mirror.

He removed the drape and told her, "Ten dollars."

She gave him a twenty. "I'm a little nervous," she whispered, "Would you mind walking me out to my car?"

"Sure, no problem," he said.

He held the door for her and they walked out. Eva got in her car and rolled down the window before she said anything.

"I hadn't heard from you, Mr. Shaw, so I thought I would drop by and see how things are going on your project. I've got some spots that I believe would be ideal for you."

"I didn't get the loan," Ernest said brusquely.

That was something Eva already knew, she had called Glenn Charles earlier in the week to check on the status of his application.

"That's unfortunate but it's not the end of the world. You still have options."

"Opening another corner barbershop is not an option for me," he said, losing patience and wanting her to go.

Eva smiled. "That's not what I was referring to. I like your idea but I like you even more. Let's talk about it some more over lunch or dinner. I'm sure we can make your spa happen."

Ernest was thrown off, first by her coming to the shop and now her interest in his project. Yet, if there was any spark of hope of reviving his plans he definitely wanted to pursue it.

"Why not," he said.

"Good, met me at Ruth Chris tomorrow at 6:00," she said, handing him another business card and rolling up her window.

Before Ernest could figure out an explanation to give to Rochelle tomorrow he needed one to tell his crew as soon as he stepped foot back in the shop. He knew they were all itching to hear what the mysterious woman's visit was all about.

Jeff was the first one to jump on him when he went back in. "What's up with your side piece, man?"

"Show some respect," Leon fussed in spite of his own curiosity.

Ernest decided to tell half of the truth. "It's not like that. She's a real estate agent. She's checking with the businesses around here to see if they are looking to lease somewhere else."

"She was pushing up on you, E," Jeff said.

Ernest shook his head no. "I don't need that kind of drama, man. Been there done that."

"I know that's right," Andrea chimed in, "Don't start none, won't be none."

"Well if you're not going to hit it," Jeff laughed, "Give her my number."

The rest of the shop joined in on the conversation and Jeff kept them laughing and talking with his antics until they closed up for the evening. Ernest looked towards the window and saw his own reflection. What had changed about him? When had it happened? He wasn't sure. He only knew that he didn't fit in his small world anymore. It was time to move on.

For their Saturday morning workout Ernest drove over to the TSU campus. Vince wanted to meet there so they could shoot some hoops in the Gentry Center. When he got there Vince was already running and dribbling up and down the court. Ernest watched him take a shot from the three-point line. The ball banged against the rim like a brick.

"You're looking raggedy, man," Ernest yelled at him, setting his gym bag down on the first row of the bleachers.

"I know, man. You gonna have to hook me up after this."

"I'm not talking about your line, bro', I'm talking about your game."

"Not hardly, hit the floor. I'm about to embarrass you," Vince said, tossing him the ball.

Ernest shot it from the perimeter and it went in smooth. "Not in this lifetime," he bragged.

"Uh-oh, what's got you cronked?" Vince asked, giving him a high-five before he went out for the ball. "You must have got the bank loan?"

"No, man, they shut me down," Ernest said, going out for a pass. "The thing is I met this chick on my way out of the bank who deals with real estate. She came by the shop yesterday and wants me to meet her for dinner today."

"Hold up," Vince said, stopping in mid-stride of blocking his shot. "Is this about business or pleasure?"

"It's all business, man, she wants to talk about some ways I can make my plan work," Ernest said, going around him and landing a bank shot.

"Is that right?" Vince said suspiciously after he caught the ball.

"Yeah, that's right, and I need you to cover for me," Ernest replied, holding his hands out for the ball. "I don't want Rochelle tripping for no reason."

"How old is this chick and how does she look?" Vince asked, going for a layup.

"She's a little older but she looks damn good," Ernest said, knocking the ball out of Vince's hand and going to the hoop. "What difference does that make?"

Vince looked down at the floor and shook his head. "Come on man, I know you. Plus, Rochelle's folks will kick your ass if you mess up again."

"I'm not messing up. I'm trying to do something big for our family. Didn't you say it was time for me to make that move?"

"Okay, you're right. I'll call the house later."

"Thanks, man," Ernest said, giving him a high-five.

"I got your back, E, you know that."

"Hell yeah," Ernest said, going in for a dunk.

They played one-on-one for another hour before Ernest had to go to work.

"I'll come by in a few," Vince said with a nod.

"Cool," Ernest said, grabbing his towel.

***

Eva felt excited, almost thrilled as she sat at her dressing table applying her make-up. She didn't know why this man had this effect on her but she was eager to find out. He hadn't made any efforts or attempts to impress her. Truth be told, he acted as if he wasn't interested in her at all. His indifference only made him more attractive to her. It had taken her nearly a half hour to decide what dress to wear. Gazing at her reflection in the mirror, she hadn't felt this much anticipation since she'd gone on her senior prom. It was on that night that she'd chosen to lose her virginity. She hoped and prayed that this night would be as eye-opening.

"Is there something I've forgotten about?" Mitchell asked, somewhat surprised when he saw her come down the stairs in one of her black cocktail dresses. "Do we have plans this evening?"

She had hoped to dodge him on her way out and call him on the phone later but he was passing through the foyer on the way to his study just as she was leaving.

"I forgot to mention that I was having dinner with some clients," she answered sweetly. "I'm close to finalizing a deal I've been working on."

"You look beautiful. Would you mind if I joined you?" he asked. "We could celebrate the contract being signed."

"That would have been nice except I'm already running late, sweetheart," she said, giving him a quick kiss on the lips. "If everything goes well we can celebrate when I get back."

"All right, my love," he said, squeezing her in a tight hug. "I'll miss you."

Eva cringed when his cold fingers touched the bare skin on her back.

"I'll try not to be too late," she said as she rushed out the door.

***

The smell of his cologne set off an alarm in Rochelle's head. It was telling her that something wasn't right. For the last couple of weeks, ever since the last drive-by outside of the barber shop, Ernest had been in a funk. Now he was humming while he got dressed. She always could tell when he was up to no good because he couldn't look her in the face. "I'm not having it," she said to herself, "I've been through too much."

"Where are you going?" she demanded angrily when he walked into the living room.

"You heard me on the phone with Vince. I'm going over to his place. I'm going to give him a cut and a shave and then some friends of his are coming by to play some cards."

Rochelle propped her hand on her hip and cocked her head to the side. "You must either think I'm a fool or crazy. What kind of friends, Ernest, female friends?"

"Come on now, Chelly, just some guys drinking a couple of beers and hanging out."

"That's bullshit. You don't need to wear cologne to hang out with a bunch of guys."

"First of all, I put on cologne like I do deodorant, it doesn't have anything to do with where I'm going. Second, I'm not a child and you're not my mama. I don't know why you're acting crazy all of sudden."

"You do know why, because I can't trust you," she said loudly. "I don't know why you keep trying to play me. I'm not stupid."

"Here we go again," he said wearily, "Why do you keep doing this to the kids? They don't need to hear this all the time."

"You're the one who puts me in this position. This is not how I want to be."

Ernest had willingly accepted the responsibility for his actions in the past. He knew he was wrong for cheating on Rochelle but most of that was before they had gotten married. Aside from a slip here and there he had been faithful to her but she couldn't let the past be the past. Every time he stepped out the door she was accusing him of going to see another woman. He was trying to be patient with her tantrums, trying to be a good husband, but he couldn't turn back time and erase what happened.

"Look, baby, I'm going to catch some air and chill with my boys. Why don't you let Rhonda or Rhianna watch E.J. and you go out with one of your girls."

"Why can't we just spend some time together? Isn't that more important?" she asked, crossing her arms and legs.

"I'm out," he said with a sigh, and walked out the front door.

Ernest looked back at the house as he drove away, truly sorry that they couldn't make each other happy. If he would have told her the truth she still would have been mad. They had known each other for eighteen years and still didn't know the other's needs or how to satisfy them. He wondered if anyone in the world was truly satisfied.

***

Ernest parked in the Loews Hotel parking garage and walked through the hotel entrance to Ruth Chris Steakhouse. He came in and scanned the room and saw Eva having a cocktail at the bar. As he walked in her direction he unconsciously checked his watch to make sure he hadn't kept her waiting.

"No worries, you're right on time, Mr. Shaw," Eva smiled when he reached the bar. "Our table is ready."

Eva eased out of the bar stool leaving her drink on the counter and led the way. Her hips drew Ernest's eyes as they swayed beneath her tight black dress to a table near the rear of the restaurant. Always a gentleman, he pulled out her chair before he sat down.

"I hope you don't mind, I ordered for us," Eva said, "I had a busy day, missed lunch, and I'm starving."

"Not at all. If it's not good, then I can blame it on you," Ernest said lightheartedly.

"So you're not intimidated by a woman who takes charge?" Eva asked as he sat down.

"I'm used to it," he said casually, "I was raised by a single mother."

Just then the waiter approached the table with crab cakes and a bottle of wine. He popped the cork and filled their glasses.

"Your meal will be out shortly," he said, nodding towards Eva.

"Thank you," Eva said, putting a fork full of the crab cake in her mouth.

Ernest didn't care much about the food or the wine. That wasn't what he was hungry for. He wanted to hear all about how he could move forward with his plan. He gave Eva a chance to take a sip of wine before he folded his hands on top of the table and broached the subject.

"Mrs. Hamilton, I really appreciate your interest in working with me. I'm anxious to hear what suggestions you might have for me to finance my project."

Seeing he wanted to get down to business, Eva put down the wine glass and her fork.

"Glenn let me take a look at your business plan and I'm positive that I can get you the investment that you need to get your project off the ground and running."

"That's excellent," Ernest said, rubbing his hands together. "That's what I wanted to hear. Is this an investment group or a finance company that you work with?"

"As a matter of fact it is," she said, dangling the loan in front of him like a carrot in front of a hungry rabbit. "Whenever you're ready we can get started looking at possible locations."

"That sounds great," he said guardedly, "I hope you won't mind me holding off on that until there's a contract or loan approval. I don't want to find the perfect place and then get let down again."

"That's nothing you have to worry about, I can guarantee you that. However, if you want the deal in writing to look over I can have that done within a few days."

"That would be fantastic," Ernest said, feeling optimistic again.

The waiter returned with their meal, steaks, rice pilaf, and asparagus.

"Now can we relax and enjoy this dinner?" Eva said happily.

Ernest thought she acted like it would be easy, except nothing in his life had ever been easy. Before he met her his spa dream was practically dead in the water. She had thrown him a lifeline. Now she predicted it would be smooth sailing. Yet something about the deal made him feel uneasy, like there was an undertow swirling below him.

"I don't want to look a gift horse in the mouth but I just have one more question," he said after poking at his food for a minute. "Is there any flexibility on the loan amount? The cost of the space, fixtures, supplies, utilities, and personnel can vary with quality."

"I can assure you that once we begin working on this you won't have to cut any corners. Why do it if you're not going to do it right."

"My philosophy exactly," Ernest said, smiling widely and lifting up his glass for a toast.

"Put you mind at ease, Mr. Shaw, and start thinking of a name for your business," Eva said, touching his hand softly.

With those words Ernest's hunger came back. He cut a

big slice of steak and put it in his mouth. "I have a name," he said, chewing on the tender beef, "I'm calling it the In Earnest Gentlemen Spa."

Eva repeated it over in her mind. Then she said, "I like it, it has a classy ring to it."

Eva watched him eat while she took tiny nibbles from her plate. It wasn't that she didn't have an appetite; it just wasn't for anything on her plate. Ernest's eyes were fixed on his food as visions of his new enterprise became more focused in his head.

"So what is your timetable, how soon would you like to be up and running?" Eva asked to get his attention.

"I'm ready now. I've been wanting to do this for a long time."

"The process will move quickly once you decide on your location. As a matter of fact I have some prime spots I'd like to show you next week."

Ernest swallowed the last bite on his plate. "All I can say is that I'm glad I bumped into you at the bank."

"This is only the beginning," she said with a seductive look. "Let's drink to a mutually satisfying endeavor."

"Absolutely," Ernest said, clicking his glass against hers and then draining it. He could feel a subtle change in the vibe between them but he knew better than to read anything into it.

The waiter returned to clear the table. "Would you care for dessert?" he asked politely.

"No thank you," Eva said, still looking at Ernest. "I couldn't ask for more of a treat."

"Enjoy the rest of your evening," the waiter told them with a smile, "The check has been taken care of."

Eva had taken care of all the arrangements when she arrived. It was one of the reasons she came early. She didn't care to go through another one of those awkward verbal tussles at the end of meal over who would pay the check. She had been through enough of those, particularly with men. She learned from Mitchell how to avoid them. She reached for her purse, stood up, and smoothed her dress. Ernest followed suit as he got up, pushed his chair back under the table, and paused. The fragrance of her perfume swirled around him.

"I enjoyed this," she said, "Now, would you mind walking me to my car?"

"Not at all, where are you parked?"

"I'm in the hotel garage," she said, making eye contact.

"That's where I'm parked too."

Eva slipped her arm through his and moved closer as they walked out. She was dropping hints left and right but he kept stepping over them like a soldier in a mine field. He had to admit she was sexy as hell but he didn't need the drama. He was glad when another couple got on the garage elevator, which made it easier not to make conversation. When they got to her car she turned and gave him a hug, or more accurately, a caress. Ernest didn't respond and opened the car door for her.

"I'll be in touch," Eva said.

Ernest nodded and walked away. He came to this meeting to get answers about financing but now he had more questions about the terms of the deal. He looked at his watch and it was still early. When he got to his car he called Vince.

"What's up, man?" Vince said.

"Hey, what you got up for tonight? I need to holler at you for a minute."

"I'm at the crib, come on by."

"I'm going to check on my moms first."

"Aw right, man. I'll be here."

***

Buttons started barking when Ernest first knocked but Sheila didn't open the door until after the second knock. He had a key and could have gone in, but number one, he respected her privacy, number two, he didn't want to scare her and get hit over the head with a frying pan.

"I didn't expect to see you tonight," she said, sliding her slippers back across the floor to the living room where she was watching TV.

"I wanted to find out how your doctor's appointment went today?" he said, trailing her and Buttons to the sofa.

"It wasn't good news," she said, sitting down. "They said these little bumps on my arm and the itching mean I'm in stage four of kidney failure. I have another appointment next week for them to go ahead and put a shunt in my arm to get me ready for dialysis."

"That's messed up, Mama," he said, sitting next to her. "I think we need to see some other doctors. We need another opinion before you do all of that."

"Look here, child, I've been to enough doctors," Sheila said firmly, "My kidneys have run out, that's all there is to it. I knew this day was coming for a while now."

"You don't know that for sure. I can take you to a specialist," he urged.

"I'm already seeing a specialist and they have put my name on the list for a transplant."

"You don't have to wait on that. You know if you need a kidney, I'll give you one of mine."

"Hell no," Sheila argued, "There's no way I would let you do that. You have a family to take care of. One of them might need a kidney from you one day."

Ernest knew his mama. She had always been stubborn and set in her ways. Her last word on something seldom changed. He looked at the half-empty cola bottle sitting on the end table.

"We might be able to put the dialysis off for a while if you would stop drinking those sodas."

"I don't have no regrets, son, and I'm not stressing it either," Sheila said, looking towards the TV. "It's too late for me to worry about that now, so don't worry me. I like my colas and I'm going to keep drinking them."

"Even if it kills you?" he asked sarcastically.

"Something is going to kill all of us. If it's a cold drink for me, so be it."

Ernest was beyond frustrated. He hated to hear her talk like that.

"I know you don't want to hear this again but I really think it might be time for you to come and stay with us."

"Ain't no way, child. I've been on my own all my life and that's the way I like it. You and Rochelle already got your hands full with E.J."

Ernest raised his hands up in surrender. "I'll leave it alone for now."

"Forget about me, I'm fine. What's going on with you?" Sheila asked, changing the subject.

"I might have some good news about opening up the new place I was telling you about. I think I have the financing worked out. I'll know in a couple of days."

"Now that's what we needed, some good news. What about that friend of yours, how is his plan working out?"

"He's working on a deal with this woman he met at the bank. He wants to keep it purely professional but he thinks she wants to get more personal."

"He needs to be careful," Sheila warned, "That sounds tricky to me. The only business I know that involves money and sex is prostitution and that's still illegal last I heard."

"It's nothing like that. She's just real flirtatious."

"Uh-huh, I got your flirtatious. All that means is that she

sees something she wants and she's gonna say and do whatever she has to do to get it."

"I doubt that, Mama. He says she's fine. She can pull guys all day long."

"Uh-huh, well tell him I said not to get involved with her. She sounds like trouble to me."

"I'll do that," he said, kissing her on the cheek and standing up to leave. "I love you, Mama. Make sure you lock the door."

"You're my heart, Ernest," she said to him as he walked to his car.

Traffic was light for a summer Saturday night. Ernest pressed his foot down on the gas as he merged onto the interstate. For some reason he couldn't get past the warnings of his mama. After talking with her, he was having some second thoughts.

***

"Come on in, player," Vince said, grinning at the door.

"Don't try it, man. It's not even like that." Ernest said defensively.

Vince laughed. "Chill out, man, I'm just messing with you. You want a beer."

"I'll take one," Ernest said, following Vince out back to his patio.

Vince tossed him a beer. "So how did it go?"

"It went perfect. She's hooking me up with an investment company that will finance my whole project."

"That's what's up, man," Vince said, giving him a 'low five' handshake. "Congratulations, you lucked out."

"I hope so," Ernest said, suddenly realizing he didn't even know the name of the company.

"What do you mean? I thought you said it was a done deal."

"Basically it is, but I can't stop wondering why she's interested in getting in this deep with my business."

"You said she's in real estate, she's probably going to make a killer commission when you find a location."

"Yeah, that's probably why she was all up on me."

Vince laughed again. "She's letting you know that there are some fringe benefits along with the deal."

Ernest shook his head no. "I don't have time for that, man."

"You mean you don't want to hit it?" Vince asked, half-teasing.

"She's fly for real but I'm past all that. I'm coming correct."

Vince took a big gulp from his bottle. "I never thought I would see you give up your seat at the players table."

"I'm all about my family and my business now."

"Nothing wrong with that, family is a beautiful thing," Vince said seriously, "I'm proud of you, man."

"You'll find out if you ever decide to settle down."

"Naw, man, marriage is not for me."

"Keep doing what you're doing and you're going to get caught one day."

"I'm too fast for them," Vince joked, "They look for me and I'm gone."

"I hear you. Anyway, I've got to go if I want to keep peace at the crib," Ernest said, finishing the rest of his beer.

***

Rochelle was calm when Ernest got home, unusual for any other Saturday when he went out. The difference was that instead of sitting around the house brooding and worrying about who he was with for the whole night she had gone out to see if he had lied to her. She was appeased and set at ease when she saw his car outside in Vince's driveway. She had even gone so far as to sneak around the back just to be sure. The two friends were just talking and drinking beer. So when Ernest walked through the door she greeted him with open arms and a wet kiss.

Ernest had planned to tell her about his plans for opening up a new business when she started cussing and fussing but she caught him off guard with her good mood. He wasn't about to spoil the atmosphere talking about something he figured she didn't want to hear about anyway. For a change, they made love without the anger or frustration that was normally there. Ernest lay on his back smiling at the ceiling fan spinning above him. Finally, all the pieces of his life were coming together.

***

Eva turned over back and forth in the bed of the guest suite. She'd told Mitchell the truth this time when she explained that she was restless and didn't want to disturb him. Lying next to his weakening body was more than she could stand. It had been several months, more months than she wanted to count, since she'd had a man satisfy her passion. She hadn't been on the hunt but like a lioness that spots an unsuspecting prey she was motivated by her hunger. The hotel room she'd reserved at Vanderbilt Loews had disappointedly gone wasted. She had thrown out enough bait over dinner but Ernest hadn't taken any of it. Now her desire had turned into a troublesome itch that moved from one spot to another making her uncomfortable.

Mitchell was in their bedroom wondering what new imprudence he would have to contend with from Eva. He abided with her sleeping outside of their bedroom occasionally despite his objections to her requiring some personal space. In his mind it was rude. He may not be able to satisfy all of her sexual needs any longer but she was still his wife and her place was by his side.

Chapter Six

The Tuesday morning after Memorial Day seemed like the best time to begin to tell Rochelle about his business expansion plans. The kids were out of school for the summer and things had been mellow around the house between them lately. She might be in a more receptive frame of mind. If by chance she wasn't and flipped out or started an argument over it, he could easily cut it short by telling her that he had to go to work.

He figured he could make some extra brownie points by whipping her up a ham and cheese omelet while she finished bathing and dressing E.J.

"What's up with you?" Rochelle asked with amazement when she walked into the kitchen with E.J on her hip and saw the food on the table. "I can't believe you cooked breakfast for me."

Ernest smirked at the look on her face. "Don't go there, baby, I do things for you every day, you just don't notice."

Rochelle put their son in his high chair. "Never mind, don't spoil the moment by telling me how you keep the roof over my head."

Ernest laughed. "As long as you know."

He poured her a glass of grapefruit juice and filled E.J.'s sippy cup with milk and handed them to her. She sat down in her chair next to E.J.

"Don't get full of yourself, boss man," she said, taking a sip of the juice. "You couldn't even afford to pay for the work I do around here."

"Probably not," he said, sitting at the table across from her.

Rochelle grinned with contentment as she ate, taking a bite and then feeding a small morsel to E.J. Ernest, pretending to read the morning newspaper, was going over his spiel in his head. When she was almost finished it was time to throw out his pitch.

"I've been thinking about a new location for the barber shop," he said offhandedly. "All the gansta bullshit around King Cut is bad for business. I'm losing clients."

"Why should you have to move?" she said indignantly. "You don't have to chase after nobody. If they think they are too good to come to your place of business, then forget them."

"It's not about them, Chelley. It's time for me to move on to something bigger and better."

"Ernest, we grew up around there. It's home."

"It's not what it used to be around there when we were coming up, things have changed, and the area is going down."

"That's because all the businesses keep leaving," she said, exasperated. "They make a little money and then they bounce."

"You know why. What choice did they have? You can't make a living if the young thugs rob and vandalize your place of business every other week."

She shook her head no. "They know you, Ernest, they ain't bothering you."

"It's not just that. I want something special for myself, for you, and for the kids."

"That's just you. I'm happy and the kids are happy. We don't need anything else."

"I'm the sole provider for this family and my mom's health is shaky. She won't be able to work much longer and living off disability won't cut it. I need to set myself up somewhere I can make better money."

"You don't need to do all of that. If we need more money, I can get a job. I'm tired of being stuck in the house with E.J. all the time anyway."

"All those years that I told you I could use your help, you ignored me. You didn't want a job. You're the one who said you wanted to be a fulltime wife and mother. Besides, where are you going to work? You don't have any experience."

"If we need money so bad right now how can you afford to think about moving someplace else anyway?"

"I can get a business loan to get me started."

"That doesn't make any sense," she said with her voice getting louder. "You don't even know if your regulars will come to another location."

E.J. started to whine and fidget in his chair, getting upset with the tension growing between them. Ernest took it as a signal to end the conversation.

"That's a chance I'm willing to take," he said, getting up from the table.

"To find yourself deep in debt," she snapped.

Ernest stopped at the door. "Look, Rochelle, I would like you to support me on this."

"Why are you asking me? You're gonna do what you want anyway."

Ernest turned and went out the back door. Before he got to his car his cell phone rang. He thought it was Rochelle to argue some more but it was Eva.

"Hello," he said hesitantly, half expecting to hear her say she couldn't work it out.

"Good morning, Mr. Shaw," she said cheerfully. "I was trying to reach you early to see if you could put me into your busy schedule sometime today."

"Do you have some good news for me?" he asked, bracing himself.

"Something I think you'll be happy with."

"Where's the office, I can be there in thirty minutes," he said, totally relieved.

"The paper work isn't completed yet but there are some prime hot spots that we don't want to miss out on."

Ernest checked the time on his phone. "I've got some regulars this morning. I can get away after 2:00."

"All right, that sounds great. Meet me at the Starbucks on Metrocenter at 2:30."

"I'll be there," Ernest assured her, bolstered by the call.

He got in his car and drove to the shop bopping all the way, even with the radio being off. Based on Rochelle's reaction he decided not to say anything to the folks at King Cut until the deal was finalized and he had found his new location.

***

Ernest could see Eva waiting in her white Mercedes at Starbucks when he pulled up to the light on Metrocenter. He made a right on the red light and turned into the parking lot. For just a second he hesitated before he pulled up beside her and rolled down his window.

"Where's the first stop?" he asked, throwing his initial caution to the wind.

"Park your car and we can ride together," she answered with a smile.

Ernest parked his car in the empty space next to hers, opened the front passenger side door and got in. Sitting deep in the bucket seat he felt like he had dropped down into the lap of luxury. "This is how you should be led to the promise land," he thought to himself and chuckled with a grunt.

"I bought you an iced coffee if you like," she said, motioning towards the two drinks in the cup holder.

He reached for the one closest to him and took a sip.

"Thank you," he said feeling the cool brown liquid roll down his throat.

"I want to take you downtown first," Eva said, sounding upbeat.

Ernest put his elbow on the armrest, leaned back, and exhaled. "Whatever you want, ma'am, I'm riding with you."

Eva zipped out of the parking lot and down 8th Avenue. When they got downtown she turned down 4th Avenue and paused near the Arcade.

"There is some space available inside there," she said, trying to get a feel for what he was interested in. "But I don't think it has the atmosphere you're looking for."

Ernest looked up the dark corridor and frowned. "Definitely not for me."

Next they drove through 2nd Avenue dodging pedestrians that jumped in and out of traffic. Eva stopped for a minute in a no-parking zone for Ernest to take in the view. To him, very few of the prospective male clients looked like they would spend more than $15 for a haircut, and with all the cowboy boots, sneakers, and flip flops strolling by it was evident that getting a pedicure might not be high on their list of priorities.

"I don't think this gives you the upscale feel you're after," Eva said, gauging his reaction.

"Not at all," Ernest said, "Too many tourists and it feels honky-tonk."

Eva drove a few blocks up to an office complex near the Music City Center and parked in a reserved space.

"Let's go inside," she said, opening her door and getting out before he could respond.

Ernest got out and followed her through the automatic doors. The entrance was immaculate with tented glass walls, slate flooring, and pewter light fixtures that hung from the high ceiling.

Eva made a left down the hallway, stopped, and opened her arms like a model presenting the showroom prize on the *Price is Right*. A sign on the door said, 'Available Space.'

"What do you think?" she asked, looking pleased with herself.

Ernest weighed it for a few seconds. It was a high profile location on the first floor.

"It has some potential. What is the square footage?" he asked, looking inside the windows.

Eva pulled a set of keys out of her handbag and unlocked the door.

"It's around 2000 but it's pricey," she said, leading him in.

"How much are they asking?"

"No less than $27 per square foot a year."

"The price isn't the problem with it," Ernest said with some disappointment, "It doesn't have enough space. I want to have a large area for the booths, a massage area, a steam room, and maybe even a room for some exercise equipment."

Eva nodded and walked to the door. "In that case let's keep it moving."

They made a quick stop near Cummins Station on 10th Avenue. The price was unbeatable at $10 per square per year and the space was a bit larger. Eva pointed out the office building across the street could possibly bring him a ton of business. Ernest thought it was nice, more of what he was looking for, but he wasn't feeling it. It seemed secluded from everything.

"I appreciate your patience," he told her apologetically. "I don't mean to take up all of your time."

"Not at all, I have all day," she said unworried on the way back to the car, "I want you to get your ideal location. The Gulch is a few blocks up."

They parked in the lot where 12th and 11th Avenue merge and walked up the half block to the new construction on 12th Avenue. Ernest could feel his heart begin to beat faster as they approached the building. From the outside it was perfect. The windows on the first floor were large enough to be welcoming but not over exposed. He like the ample parking in the area and the easy access from the street. He paused at the door for a moment to take it all in because somehow he knew that his destination was just on the other side.

Eva led him through the entrance. "This location has 5000 square feet, more than enough space for all the things you want to provide."

The interior was decorated with sky blue paint, glass and chrome, with rustic teak floors. It was more than he had dared to imagine even in his wildest dreams. Ernest walked through the entire space visualizing where everything would be situated.

"How much are we talking about?" Ernest asked, holding his breath.

"The space in this building runs between $12 and $15 per square for the year."

"That's pushing my limit," Ernest said with a sigh.

"Not necessarily," Eva said. "This location will more than pay for its self. Don't under estimate the potential here. You're moving to a totally new clientele with deeper pockets."

"I get that but I don't want to start out operating under financial pressures."

"Don't worry about that," Eva said nonchalantly, "I have one more place to show you."

Ernest followed her out to the car but he didn't want to see another place; his mind was already settled there. The only thing left to do was work out the financing details. He was going to make it work even if he had to borrow money from Vince.

Eva sped along the 65 South interstate humming to a CD while Ernest stared out the passenger side window of the car without seeing anything. His focus was on a mental math session of how to make one plus one equal eleven. He was confused when she stopped the car in front of a large home for sale in a Brentwood subdivision.

"What is this place?" Ernest asked curiously as she got out of the car.

"Come on in," she said with a smile.

She unlocked the door with another set of keys and he trailed her through the foyer. Inside, the house was fully furnished and staged for potential buyers. It was impeccably clean with a sterile feel to it, almost like a hospital. Eva put her handbag down on the sofa. "Make yourself comfortable," she said, leaving him in the living room.

Ernest sat down on the sofa wondering why in the hell they were there. He wasn't looking to buy a house. All he wanted to do was finalize his loan and get busy bringing his dream to reality.

"I was thinking we should have a pre-celebration toast to In Earnest," Eva said, coming back in the room with two glasses of wine.

She handed him a glass, sat down close beside him, and looked him square in the eyes. That's when he could clearly see where this was going. Ernest knew the game, he had played it himself more than once.

"I'm very pleased that you found your location today," she said, placing her hand on his leg.

"I am too," he said, looking away. "You have been a real blessing to me and I don't know anything about you."

"There's not much to tell," she said, scooting back on the sofa. "You and I have a lot in common. We are both ambitious people whose families don't always understand that about us."

"What makes you say that?"

"You seem to be alone in this venture; I've never seen anybody accompany you."

"Not completely, I want to get the pieces in place before I get anyone else involved. It keeps everyone else from being frustrated when obstacles get in the way."

"I see your point," she said, patting him on the leg before she stood up. "Come on, let me give you a tour of the house."

Ernest downed the rest of the wine and got up. He followed her past the kitchen, through the den area, and down a hallway to what looked like the master bedroom. It was dim with all of the blinds closed but it was decorated in brass and cherry wood.

"What do you think of it?" she asked, looking at the bed.

"It's very nice," he said, gazing around the room.

Eva was tired of being coy. She moved in close to him and rubbed her hands across his chest.

"I really like you, Ernest. I was attracted to you the first time I saw you."

He grabbed her hands. "I think you look good, real nice, but I'm married, Eva."

"So what," she said, pulling her hands away. "I have a

husband and I'm not looking for another one."

"I've made some mistakes in the past. I don't want to do that anymore."

Eva wanted him and rarely accepted no as an answer. She took off one of her shoes and started to run her foot up and down his leg. Ernest stood there frozen, still reluctant to cross the bridge in front of him.

"Aren't you ready to take that next step and have everything you want?" Eva asked, undoing the buckle on his pants.

Here she was holding the loan and the keys to his future in front of his face like a casino dealer offering him loaded dice at the craps table. How could he lose? It was tempting. He was too close to back up and walk away. Without a word he reached behind her, zipped down her dress, and pulled it off her shoulders.

Eva stepped out of it, stood before him proudly and asked, "Do you like what you see?"

"You're very sexy," he said, surprised at out how fit and firm she was.

"I never had any babies to tear my body down," she said, lying down on the bed.

Ernest took off his clothes and joined her. If this would push his loan through faster he could live with it. It wasn't personal, he hadn't even kissed her on the mouth.

Eager to have him inside her, Eva nixed his efforts of foreplay. The sex between them was hot and intense. Ernest couldn't believe what he was doing and he couldn't deny that he enjoyed every minute of it. She was so different than Rochelle in bed. Eva wanted him so badly, needed him so much, and she wasn't shy about telling him. Rochelle made it seem like she was doing him a favor most of the time.

"Can I get you anything, a drink, or something to eat?"

Eva asked, running her fingers through the curly hairs on his chest after they both climaxed.

"I can't stay," he said, having gone farther than he had promised himself. "I've got to get back and close my shop."

Without saying another word he got up, went into the bathroom, and took a shower. Eva wanted him to take another chance at bat but she wasn't disappointed. More than she needed a man to satisfy her, she needed to have a man who would respond to her touch. She needed to know she still had that power. Ernest had given her everything she desired.

***

The silence in the ride back to Starbucks was extremely awkward for Ernest. He didn't know what to say. They were way past small talk about the traffic or the weather. He didn't have to bother though; Eva was satisfied in every way. She smiled as the most passionate moments of the afternoon filled her head. Her right hand rested on his left thigh as she drove and she gave him a squeeze every time she felt an aftershock or tremor from her orgasm.

Ernest got out of the car back at Starbucks without a word. When he closed the car door she rolled the window down. "I should have everything ready for your signature by the end of the week."

Ernest nodded, "Thanks a lot."

"No, thank you," she said with a smile, "It's a pleasure doing business with you."

It was only when he got in his car that he could think clearly. The whole day was a blur, like a white-knuckle ride on an exhilarating rollercoaster. He had lost control of the situation. That rarely happened to him. It was thrilling in a way yet he knew it was extremely dangerous. He headed towards King Cut. It was around 6:30, Leon would probably still be there and he needed some time to get his nerves settled before he went home.

"That was a mighty long lunch," Leon joked when he walked in, "Where was the restaurant, in Memphis?"

"No, man, I had some other things to do," Ernest said, sounding low key. Guilt was beginning to pour over him like a rain storm.

"Everything okay? Your mama all right?" Leon asked, observing his mood.

"Yeah, she's got an appointment to get the shunt put in tomorrow."

"That's tough, man."

Ernest went back in his office to get away from any more questions. He was having serious doubts about what had gone down. He didn't have any paperwork, a contract, or a loan approval letter. What if the whole thing was a scam, a twisted game, and there was no money. Maybe all his dreams about the spa were just fantasies. It was too good to be true. He had gotten caught up and had gone too far.

Seven

"Are you sure you don't want me to come to the hospital with you?" Rochelle asked him. "It's no problem. I can drop E.J. at my cousin's house."

"No, you don't need to do all that," Ernest assured her, "The doctors told her it should be over in less than two hours and she can come right home afterwards. I'll probably stay over there with her for a while."

"Why don't you just bring her over here?" Rochelle suggested, feeling excluded.

"She'll be more comfortable at home," Ernest said, going out of the door.

Although Ernest felt like he could handle everything with his mama at the hospital without any help, the real reason he didn't want Rochelle to come with him was because he was afraid she might be able to sense something was amiss. He was feeling paranoid after last night's indiscretion. To him, her eyes were like ultraviolet lights that could visualize Eva's handprints on his body or that her nose was like a bloodhound's and could detect faint residues of perfume on his skin. Being in the same room with her made him very uncomfortable.

When Ernest got to the duplex Sheila was sitting in a chair on her stoop waiting for him. He got out to open the door for her as she walked to the car.

"How are you today?" she asked, sliding down into the seat.

"I'm good, how about you? Are you having any second thoughts?"

"No way, child. I'm ready to get this over with," she said, turning the radio over to 92.1 where they played gospel on Wednesday mornings.

Donnie McClurkin's *We Fall Down* was playing and it touched a nerve inside of Ernest. He pressed his foot down hard on the gas pedal after he merged onto the interstate. He wanted to get his mama to the hospital as quick as he could. It seemed like everybody knew his business.

"Slow down, son," Sheila said, noticing the speed. "We're not late."

Ernest eased off a little. "Sorry, Mama."

Thankfully the hospital wasn't too far from the house. In less than ten minutes he was exiting the parkway. They pulled into the parking area right after the first verse of *Sinner's Prayer*.

"Do you want me to let you off at the front entrance?" he asked.

"No, Ernest. I can walk," she answered slightly agitated, wondering why he was acting so strange.

After he found the closest parking spot to the entrance he got out and hurried around to the passenger side to help his mama get out. The double doors parted as they approached and they veered to the right where the patient registration office was located. After all the questions and paperwork were completed, a short Latino nurse wearing dark blue scrubs came to escort them to an examining room. Inside the room there was a hospital gown lying on the bed.

"Change into the gown, Mrs. Shaw, and I'll be back in a few minutes," the nurse said kindly.

"You can go on out to the waiting room," Sheila told Ernest. "I'll be fine."

"We'll come and get you when she's done," the nurse said, smiling at him.

Ernest walked past the waiting room and straight out of the hospital. He needed to get some air and moreover he was too wired up to sit still in a room full of people sneaking looks at each other between watching 'Flip this House' on the TV and scanning their Facebook pages. He paced across the front of the building for a few minutes before he decided to wait in the car. He moved it to a spot in the shade where there was a slight breeze, rolled down his windows, leaned his seat all the way back, and closed his eyes.

The sound of his cell phone woke him up about forty-five minutes later. It was the doctor saying that the procedure was over, everything went fine, and he could pick his mother up in the recuperating room. When he got there the nurse directed him to bring his car around to the exit doors at the end of the building. When he got there she was waiting beside his mama who was sitting in a wheelchair with a bandage on her left arm.

"How do you feel?" he asked, helping her into the car. "Are you in pain?"

"I'm still drugged up so I don't feel too bad," she said in a low voice.

Ernest looked at the clock on the dash. Less than three hours had passed and they were on their way home.

"Are you hungry, Mama?" he asked once they were closer to the house.

"My stomach is kind of queasy right now," she answered

with her eyes closed. "Stop at Mary's and get us some chicken plates, we can eat it later."

He shook his head. "I don't see how you can still eat their food after all these years."

She chuckled. "I want to see how it tastes without me in the kitchen."

Ernest got the food while his mama waited in the car.

"At least it smells good," Ernest said when he returned with the plates.

"Smell don't mean nothing, it's got to taste right," Sheila fussed.

Buttons met them at the door of the duplex yapping and jumping up and down when they came in.

"Did you miss me, sweetie?" Sheila said, rubbing the dog's head with her free hand. "You can stop worrying. I'm back home, safe and sound."

"Why don't you eat a little and then take a nap," Ernest suggested.

"I'm not tired," Sheila protested. "I haven't done any work today."

"Sit down, Mama," he said, ignoring her stubbornness. "I'll make you a plate."

Sheila sat in her chair with Buttons in her lap and watched Ernest dish out the food. He had been with her all morning but he seemed like his mind was miles and miles away. It got her thinking about the last conversation they'd had.

"Whatever did that friend of yours decide to do about that woman at the bank?" she asked, wondering if he had listened to her advice.

Ernest took a deep breath before he spoke. "He agreed with what you said but she took him out to look at some properties, then they went by this house she had on the market, and things went farther than he wanted them to."

"How far?" she asked bluntly.

"All the way to the end zone."

"Lord have mercy," Sheila said, slapping the table and scaring Buttons, "Get me a cola out of the fridge."

"Mama, what is wrong with you?" Ernest said, totally outdone. "You know drinking those cold drinks is not good for you. We just got back from the hospital to put a shunt in your arm for the kidney machine."

"What harm can it do to me now?" she asked, agitated.

"It doesn't matter," he said, getting her a glass of water.

"Never mind," she said, gathering her composure. "Your friend had my nerves going there for a minute. Anyway, what's done is done, but he shouldn't let it go any further. He needs to lose that woman's number."

"What if she comes through with the loan? Things can still work out all right."

"He should know that money has strings attached. If that romp down the field was good to her she's going to want to have a replay."

"So if she comes through you don't think he should accept the loan?"

"No I don't," Sheila said firmly. "Your friend has stepped in some shit. Best he take his shoes off and walk away before he tracks it all through his home and his job."

Ernest looked at Buttons who was staring back at him and knew his mama was right.

***

The last seventy-two hours had given Ernest some perspective on his situation. After talking to his mama and considering everything she said, he was convinced that Eva was trouble. Definitely the kind he didn't need. It was back to square one as far as he was concerned. He would start all over again with a new application at another bank. The complication was that

Eva had been blowing up his cell phone for almost a week. He had been ignoring all of her calls and trying his best not to think about the ideal space she had shown him in the Gulch.

On Tuesday morning he drove to the Titans Headquarters in Metrocenter where he had started coming to give Vince his weekly cut and a shave. He parked and got out the duffel bag he carried in his trunk. It was packed with a clipper set, drape, combs and brushes, a mixing kit for his shaving cream, and a hand vacuum for clean-up. His straight razor was always on him.

Coming to this complex always left him disconcerted. Everything about it was first-class. If it weren't for that one mistake he might have been there under completely different circumstances. He was happy for Vince and his success but he was damn tired of looking in on how the other half lives, being invited in for a few hours, and then having to leave. It was even harder today with his dream back on the shelf.

"What's up, dude?" Vince said, getting up and greeting his friend with a handshake and a shoulder bump when he walked in his office.

"Man, more than you would believe," Ernest said, still not quite believing it all himself.

"What you got going on?" Vince said, slipping out of his suitcoat.

Ernest unzipped his duffel bag and put on his barber's smock.

"It's that chick I told you about, the one who was getting me the hook-up," he said while he placed the paper strip and drape around Vince's neck.

"Aww, man. Don't tell me you hit it."

Ernest lined up all his tools on a towel on the desk and began working on Vince's cut.

"She was showing me some spots for the spa, then she

took me to this house out in Brentwood. It was like I had to do it to close the deal."

Vince started laughing. "You're right, man, I don't believe it."

"I'm serious, man, it's not like you're thinking. She showed me this place in the Gulch that would be perfect for my shop before we went to the house. She said the loan was guaranteed but I hadn't seen the money yet. I felt like if I shut her down, she might not come through. Now she's been blowing up my phone."

"Oh, shit. You got your hands full on that."

"My moms said I should forget about all of it and go to another bank."

"It might not be that deep," Vince said lightly, "She's a grown woman. She probably just wanted to get her freak on. She's trying to get paid too. Business is business."

"That makes sense but the whole thing has me on edge. She's bold as hell."

"What's the name of her company?"

"Her card says Hamilton Realty."

"Hold up a minute and I'll have my lawyer check it out."

Vince reached for his cell phone and made a call to his lawyer.

"That'll work, man," Ernest said, finishing his cut.

"No problem, he'll get back with me in a few. So anyway, how was ol' girl?"

"Close your mouth so I can do your shave."

While he worked Ernest told Vince about his mom preparing for dialysis and how she seemed to be taking it in stride. He was done and packing up his things when Vince's phone rang. It was his lawyer. He chewed the inside of his jaw nervously while they talked.

Vince listened, nodded, and then hung up. "She's

completely legit, man. Her company is worth several million dollars and her husband is at the top of the food chain at Pinnacle Financial. I wouldn't worry about the deal," he said, putting his suitcoat back on. "The money is in the bank."

"It's a lot to think about," Ernest said, not completely convinced. "We'll talk later."

***

When Ernest got to the parking lot at King Cut he could see a police cruiser in front of the door and Leon standing outside with an officer. He cursed under his breath knowing that whatever had gone down it wasn't good. He scanned the outside of the shop and didn't find any sign of crackled glass. Then parked perpendicular to the shop he saw the windshield on Leon's car. In the sunlight the pattern of the shattered lines through the glass gleamed like the facets of a diamond. Ernest hung back until the cop finished his report before he went to the door.

"Man, what happened to your car?" he asked Leon as if he didn't already know.

"My battery quit last night. Andrea had some late clients and when we left it wouldn't start. Neither of us had jumper cables so she gave me a ride home. I rode the bus in this morning and this is what I found. The cop told me they were shooting out here late last night."

"Damn," Ernest said, shaking his head at the car.

Something clicked in his head. Maybe it was the last straw. The sight of the bullet hole reminded him of all the reasons he wanted to cut his ties in the hood. He had to make that move. These new millennial thugs were too hard to be around. It was time for him to go somewhere more peaceful and prosperous where he could start something bigger and better.

"Sorry that happened, man," he told Leon.

"Me too," Leon groaned, "I don't have nothing but liability on my car."

"Don't sweat it, man, I'll get you a new windowshield," Ernest said, going into the shop.

He went straight back to his office and called Eva. She answered with a hello that sounded like it had ice all over it.

"I want to apologize for not getting back with you sooner," he said sincerely, trying to smooth things over.

"Did you get my messages?" she asked with the edge still in her voice.

"I saw that you called but I haven't had a chance to listen to my voicemails."

Eva wasn't about to let him get off that easy. "Is this how you handle your business?" she snapped, "It's a little unprofessional for my taste."

"Not under normal circumstances," Ernest said without calling her out on her own version of professionalism. "My mother has been having some serious health issues. Please accept my apology for not returning your calls sooner."

"I'm sorry to hear that," Eva said, warming up some. "I was beginning to think you weren't interested or had changed your mind."

"Absolutely not, I'm very interested and want to get my project moving at full speed."

"Can you come by my office this evening?" she asked with an alluring tone.

"No doubt, I'll be there."

"I'll text you the address, be here at 7:00," she said before hanging up.

"No more second-guessing," he thought, "Why was I tripping so hard? She didn't mention anything about what had happened in Brentwood."

After all, he wasn't getting anything free and she wasn't buying him. It was a loan, a business transaction with a legitimate firm. Once the papers were signed he wouldn't have to deal with Eva at all.

***

Eva smiled as she watched Ernest sign the loan agreement. Now she had him exactly where she wanted him. Whether he realized it or not, she was the one who held the purse strings to his project. His ignoring of her phone calls let her know that he hadn't learned the rules to the game yet but he seemed relatively intelligent, he would learn very fast.

Ernest wasn't stupid. Every page of every document that he signed was stored in his head like a picture. Even details he wasn't conscious of at the moment could be pulled out later and studied. At first glance the terms of the loan were cutthroat but he expected that. It was straightforward with no fine print necessary. He noted that the funds were to be drawn from a subsidiary of Pinnacle Financial and not the bank itself. Repayment was to begin six weeks from today and the consequences of a default of the loan would be the seizing of his property and real estate which were deemed as collateral.

None of those things bothered him. It was the home stretch and Ernest was feeling like the winning jockey at the finish line of the Kentucky Derby. He had pulled off the long shot of his life. Still he knew there was no time to bask in his victory. He would have to expedite the whole process of out-fitting his shop without breaking his bank. His usual mantra would not change, "Don't stress it. Make it work." He signed the last page, closed up the folder, and slid it across the desk in front of her.

"I'm glad that part is over," he said with a sigh, "This is a great opportunity for me."

"For the both of us," she said, smiling as she placed the

papers in the top drawer of the desk.

Ernest stood up to leave and offered his hand to shake on the deal. Instead of taking it, Eva walked around to the front of her desk and in one quick motion hopped on top of it and pulled her dress up to her waist.

Ernest took a step back, a little shocked, but not totally surprised. She definitely couldn't be described as shy or inhibited.

"I'd prefer to keep the arrangement on a professional basis," he said, holding his hands up.

"I can be your best friend on this project, or not," she said with a no holds barred tone.

"I'm not here to make friends," Ernest said, taking offense, "I'm here to make money."

Eva didn't blink. "All I'm saying is, if I'm happy you'll be happy. I wouldn't want you to lose your option on the lease in the Gulch."

With that said, Ernest got the message loud and clear. The neurons in his brain were firing like rockets searching for a soft target. He didn't see an out-clause on the contract he'd just signed but that didn't necessarily mean much. If the deal was solid, he could take his chances on another agent and keep looking for a comparable location, except he had his mind settled on the one in the Gulch. He dropped his head in capitulation refusing to look at her. Then he took off his sport coat, undid his belt buckle and the fly of his pants, and snatched off her panties.

Eight

The next morning, Ernest had a notification and a text waiting in his phone. The notification was for a deposit of $450 thousand into his new business account. The text had a photograph of a lease agreement for the Gulch property on 12th Avenue to Earnest Shaw and Hamilton Realty. The joint lease was the bad spot on an otherwise perfect contract.

He wanted to call his mama, Vince, and Rochelle to share his news but something told him to wait. He wasn't prepared to answer all the questions that were sure to follow. Plus, in his own mind it was all too new to trust. He decided to keep it all under wraps until he had something more tangible to show them.

When he arrived at the barbershop he barely said hello, heading straight into his office to get down to business. His first call was to the management company of the property to arrange for the keys to be delivered to him at King Cut. The next thing on his list was the barber chairs. He got online and ordered three top-of-the-line Constantine antique barber chairs and barber stations. He was partial to red but he didn't have the money to redecorate the interior of his space so he settled for black. He ordered an assortment of mirrors, storage closets, and tons of fresh towels. He ordered two manicure/pedicure stations and one massage table and two massage chairs. He decided to hold off on the exercise equipment until he organized the space.

He made an appointment with a plumbing company that could install the sinks where he needed them and build the steam room. Preferably, he would have wanted to save the money of hiring an interior decorator but he didn't have the time to creatively bring it all together himself while he worked. He thought about the duo decorators who had done Vince's house. He liked their contemporary style. He looked up their number and scheduled an appointment with them, explaining that time was of the essence. Fortunately the plumbing company and the decorators agreed to meet him at his location on Thursday morning.

He was about to order cards and stationery when he heard his name.

"Hey Ernest," Leon called again, "Noah is out here."

"I'm coming," Ernest shouted back.

"What you got going on back in there?" Jeff asked when he finally came out of his office. "You've been back there all morning and now you coming out with a smile on your face."

"I need to check and see if he's got somebody tucked back in there," Andrea added jokingly but half-serious.

"What's up, my man," Ernest said to Noah, ignoring their remarks.

"It's all good," Noah said, getting in his chair.

"Watch out, Noah," Jeff said, "Make sure he washed his hands."

"What is y' alls problem?" Ernest said, playing it off. "Why can't a man have a smile on his face without you getting all suspicious?"

"It's all right with me," Noah said, enjoying the humor, "Do what you got to do man. I want him relaxed when he shaves me. That way I don't have to worry about getting cut."

"Talk to them, man," Ernest said with a grin.

"Whatever you got back there I need to get some of it," Leon said, joining in with their teasing. "I can't hardly stand up, my gout is acting up again."

"Y'all need to stop. There ain't nothing in my office, no woman, nothing to drink, and nothing to smoke," Ernest said, snapping the drape in the air before he put it around Noah's neck.

"Then Rochelle must have put it on you last night," Jeff said, chuckling.

Ernest didn't comment and the smile dropped off his face as he thought about what went down with Eva after he signed the papers. He'd thought that once the deal was closed he could distance himself from her but after last night he wasn't so sure.

Leon noticed how his mood changed and quickly came to his defense.

"Get out the man's business and get some of your own," Leon said, scolding Jeff.

"If you don't have anything better to do why don't you go out and get us some lunch," Andrea said to Jeff, hearing the bell ring and seeing her next client come in. "I'm hungry."

***

For more than a month Earnest had been working his fingers, feet, and ass to the bone between holding down his clients at King Cut, meeting with his contractors, meeting with delivery people, and paying bills. Every evening when he got home he fell into bed, sometimes too exhausted to eat. He barely had enough energy to read a book to E.J. before he went to sleep.

Rochelle's overactive imagination was starting to work overtime. She saw Ernest was going out of the house early and coming home late and tired. She noticed that on some days he was dressed a little too nice just for work. She knew something was up and she wasn't about to be nobody's fool again. On the morning of his mama's first treatment on the dialysis machine she put a sippy cup with milk and a small bowl of dry cheerios in E.J.'s crib to keep him occupied while she went to confront Ernest. He was eating some toast with his coffee in the kitchen.

"Who are you messing with, Ernest?" she demanded, standing in front of him with her hand perched on her hip.

"I don't feel like going there with you today," he said, dreading each word he knew would fly out of her mouth. He had heard them all before, too many times in fact.

"I'm not crazy, I know when something's up with you."

"Look, I've got to go to the clinic with my mama in a few. We can talk about this when I get back," he said, pushing his plate away and getting up from the table.

"Believe that, Ernest. We are going to talk about it," she hollered at his back as he hurried out the door. Frustrated as hell she stomped into the living room and called one of her girls to vent.

***

Sheila had arranged transportation with the Metro Transit Authority for an Access Ride Van to take her back and forth to her treatment so Ernest drove directly to the dialysis clinic. He didn't know what to expect when he got there. He didn't think he could handle it if his mama was broken down. She was the strongest person he had ever known.

"I'm looking for Sheila Shaw," he told the receptionist right inside the entrance.

"Hold on for a sec," she said, picking up the phone.

A minute later, a chubby white woman with dark curly

hair dressed in flowered scrubs came through a door to the right of the information desk.

"Good morning," she said without making eye contact. "Come on back."

Ernest followed her down a hallway to the area where the renal patients were being treated.

"Grab a chair over there," the woman in scrubs told him, waving a finger at the wall.

The dialysis patients were all spaced evenly in a row like the stations he trained on back in Barber College. He saw his mama at the end of the line with a blanket over her legs reading a magazine. He made his way across the room without glancing at any of the other patients who were connected to the machines.

"Hey, baby," she said, smiling when she saw him.

"How're you doing, Mama?" he asked, placing the folding chair on the other side of her.

"It's not a walk in the park but I'm not complaining," she said with a sigh.

"Are you cold?" he asked, nodding towards the cover on her legs.

"The air conditioner is on too high for my taste," she said, "How've you been? I haven't seen you in a few days."

"I'm great, Mama. I applied for the loan I needed to open up a new spot and I got it."

"That's beautiful, son," she said, letting go of her reservations and hoping for the best. "Where is it going to be? I've got to come see it."

"It's 317 12th Avenue South, in the Gulch. It's going to be called "In Earnest.""

Sheila wanted to clap her hands except she couldn't with the left one connected to the pump. Instead she slapped her thigh in excitement.

"I'm so proud of you, Ernest, I can't even say."

"Once things are up and running like I want them to it's going to change things for us. I'm going to move you out of the duplex whether you like it or not."

"All right, child, we'll see," she said happily. "I hope we get to have that argument."

"Count on it, Mama," he said, wishing they were both somewhere else.

They sat in silence for a minute but the sound of the dialysis machine churning his mama's life blood and the noise of its motor humming were unnerving for Ernest. He couldn't stand the thought or the sight of his mama being hooked up to this contraption.

"You feeling okay while all this is going on?" he asked, pointing towards the machine.

"Not too bad. The worst thing is they want me to cut out my cold drinks. They say the brown color has phosphorous in it which isn't good for me. They say I can drink ginger ale or Sprite."

"You got to listen to them, Mama. You need to take care of yourself until you get a transplant. If you don't they'll take your name off the list."

"I don't know about all of that," she said, dismissing the idea. What she really wanted to talk about was if he had taken her advice. "By the way, what happened to that friend of yours who wanted to start him a business too and the woman who was plaguing him?"

"Things worked out for him. She came through with the money and the loan was all legit."

"Did he have to pay her some more dues?" she asked, eyeing him closely.

Ernest looked down at his hands. "She got him for one more but that's the end of it. He's not going to get tricked up with her. He's got his business to pull together."

"I sure hope he doesn't," she said, looking back down at her magazine.

Sheila knew how these hussies were when they get a taste of a younger man. They can't get enough. She said a silent prayer for her boy. She was too sick and too tired to have to go and kick some old woman's ass over her child.

***

It was an hour before lunch when Ernest got to the shop. Jeff was outside smoking a cigarette and talking on his Bluetooth. He gave Ernest some dap on his way in. Leon was doing some clean up at his station and Andrea was working on two of her older regulars from her church. One was under the dryer while she was setting the other's hair on small rollers.

"How'd your mama do?" she asked, pausing with the roller only halfway on.

"I think she did okay, but you know how she is," Ernest said with a touch of sadness. "She wouldn't have let me know if she was in pain or uncomfortable."

"I know that's right but I don't think she could hide it if the treatment was really bothering her," Leon said, trying to ease his mind.

"I hope you're right, Leon," Ernest sighed as he put on his smock. "Anyway I need to holler at you in the back for a minute."

"Sure thing, man, what's up?" Leon asked, trailing him to his office in the back.

Ernest sat down in his chair and took a deep breath while Leon sat down in front of him.

"I'm ready to switch things up in my life," Ernest said sincerely, "I've got some plans in motion that I need to tell you about."

"It's about time, E. I knew something was going on. You've been out of pocket here for a couple of months now."

"Leon, we go back a long way. You know how it was. Back in the day I cut hair for weed, pussy, and a hot plate of chicken for lunch. You were the one who gave me a spot to do my thing and I'm grateful for that. From there I was able to open this place. It's been all good but I'm ready to take my game to another level and make some serious money."

Leon leaned forward in the chair. "So what's on your mind?"

"I'm opening up another shop. It's completely upscale, over in the Gulch."

"That's what I'm talking about," Leon said, holding out his hand for a low five. "How soon are you talking about?" he asked, getting energized.

"A month or two at the most."

"Damn that's quick."

"Leon, I've been waiting for this chance for a long time."

"I'm ready to make that move with you, man."

Ernest inhaled before he spoke. "I wish you could, man, I really do. I could surely use your help but I need you here to run this place. You're the only one I can trust to do that. If you don't, I'll have to shut it down."

"Wow, that's deep," Leon said, sobering up, "I don't know what to say, E. This is a lot to digest."

"I know it seems like this was all of a sudden but it's been on my mind for a while. I need to come up, man. I couldn't wait any longer. Now that my mama is on dialysis she won't be able to work. I've got to hold her down and take care of my family."

"I feel you," Leon said, nodding up and down. "I'm happy for you, man, and I've got your back here. You don't have to worry about the shop."

"Thanks, man," Ernest said, "Now I've got to tell the rest of the crew."

Leon patted him on the back as they walked back out to their work stations. He knew Jeff and Andrea would have a lot more to say about the news than Leon did. Just as he was about to speak the door was snatched open and the bell jangled fast and loud. Eva was standing there in a fiery red dress and leopard pumps, infuriated, with her chest heaving like the top on a boiling pot getting ready to spill over.

Ernest had been dodging her calls and canceling after she'd set up several times for them to meet. He was trying to run one business and get another up and running and he didn't need the hassle of catering to her. Even still, he didn't think she would have the nerve to come to his place of work and call him out.

"I thought we had an understanding," she said indignantly.

"We have a legal agreement," Ernest responded.

The whole shop went quiet. They were all watching and listening to the interaction between Eva and Ernest like it was the final episode of *Empire*.

"I don't take kindly to being treated like this," Eva said with her temper flaring.

"This is my place of business, where I make my living," Ernest said, staying composed. "You need to respect that?"

"I don't have a problem with any of that as long as you respect me," Eva snapped. "Don't forget who made all your plans possible. When I call you answer."

Ernest lost his patience with her tirade. "How do you figure that?" he asked irately.

"You're not stupid," Eva fired back.

After a few more grunts and whistles among the folks in the shop intrigued by the show, Ernest took her by the arm and pulled her out of the door.

"I don't know what's going on inside that head of yours but you're asking for trouble," he hissed in her ear.

"Meet me at the house tonight," she said in a sweet voice. "I didn't mean to cause a scene."

Her whole demeanor had changed. Ernest looked at her like she was psycho.

"I'm done with this," he said, waving his hand. "I got work to do."

"I just need to see you again," she said, pulling on his smock. "I don't know why I'm so crazy about you. Meet me tonight whenever you get finished."

"I'm married, Eva. I can't see you whenever you feel like it. It's not that kind of party. Plus, I told you before that my mother is sick. I have to check on her when I get done here."

Eva knew she had gone too far. She had never acted like this before. Her intention wasn't to embarrass him or herself. She was acting like a drug addict who needed a fix. She was definitely out of control.

"Forgive me. I'm sorry about you mother," Eva said, pulling herself back together, "I hope she feels better."

Ernest turned around, went back in the shop, and walked through the hushed room into his office and shut the door. Leon took his clients for the rest of the afternoon while he placed some ads for the new shop and checked Craigslist for recruits to work at the spa.

When the last client of the day was cut and the shop door was locked, Leon knocked on the door and came in.

"You might as well drop the bomb while you got them dazed," Leon said.

Ernest would have preferred to talk to Rochelle first but after Eva's performance he didn't have much choice. He walked out to the front where Jeff and Andrea were sitting in their chairs waiting to hear what led up to the episode.

"So it's like that," Andrea said, shaking her head.

"I'm going to skip to the bottom line and be straight up

with y'all," Ernest said, "I'm opening up another shop in Midtown. I don't know if you all remembered the woman who came in earlier. She's the real estate agent who helped me find the location."

"That's a bet," Jeff said, "When do we pack it up and make that move?"

"I'm going alone. It's going to be more than a barbershop, it's a gentlemen's spa."

"So what are you saying?" Jeff said, "We not good enough to work there."

"It's a whole different clientele," Ernest explained.

"So you chasing the white dollar now?" Andrea asked, still mad.

Ernest sat down in his chair. "Dollars aren't white or black, they're green."

Jeff shook his head. "Sounds like you're being a sellout, man."

"I don't have nothing to prove to anybody out here. I've been on this street for more than ten years. It's just time for me to move on. My leaving doesn't have to affect y'all. Come to work and do your thing like you usually do. Leon is going to manage this place for me."

"Why him, he's past his prime," Jeff argued. "I could do that better for you."

"Come on, Jeff, you're not serious," Ernest said, "You haven't even decided if you want to hustle or cut hair."

That hit a nerve and Jeff jumped out of his chair. "Who said I have to choose. I can do both. All of it is a hustle."

"I can't argue with that," Ernest said, "Everybody in this room is grown and responsible for themselves. We all have to eat. I'm not standing in nobody's way. I started at the same place where you and Andrea are now."

"Whatever happened to reaching down and pulling a

brother or a sister up?" Andrea asked, feeling let down.

"You're not ready, Andrea," Ernest said to her. "You treat your livelihood like a hobby. You only want to work three or four days out of the week and you treat your clients like shit. None of them should have to spend the whole day with you just to get their hair done. I'm not going to run my new place like that. It'll be purely professional."

His comments made Andrea's hurt turn to anger.

"I thought we were all family in here but you're only caring about yourself, E," Andrea said snidely.

Ernest shook his head in disagreement. "Truth be told, if I didn't care about you two, I would take Leon with me and shut this place down in a heartbeat."

"That's coldblooded, E," Jeff said.

"That's the problem with our people," Ernest said in his defense. "We're always thinking somebody owes us something. I follow the James Brown philosophy, "I don't want nobody to give me nothing, open up the door, I'll get it myself.""

Jeff chuckled. "Are you sure you got it for yourself or did that bitch who was in here earlier get it for you."

"Speak some more truth," Andrea said, egging him on.

"I don't get into anybody's business in here," Ernest said plainly. "I expect the same in return."

Chapter Nine

Ernest wanted to stop for a beer on his way home to smooth down his edge before his overdue conversation with Rochelle but he knew crazy news travels fast and the story about Eva in the shop was probably already on the wires. He went straight home but he still wasn't fast enough. Andrea had put in a direct call.

Rochelle was pacing around the house with a temper so hot she couldn't sit down. It was all she could to keep from calling her sister and two brothers and have them waiting there with her when Ernest came home. She was tired of him playing with her emotions. She needed to remind him that if he didn't love her she had family who did and they wouldn't hesitate to give his ass a beat down. When she saw his car pull in the driveway she rushed out to meet him.

"You got all kinds of secrets," she said, pushing him in the chest as soon as he got out of the car. "Who's the bold bitch who came up in the shop and called you out?"

Ernest walked past her to the front door. "I'm not about to put my business in the street. We'll talk about it in the house."

Rochelle stomped in behind him. "From what I hear, your business is already in the street."

"Where are the kids?" he asked. He knew it was about to get wild and he didn't want them to hear all the arguing.

"They're in the den watching TV," Rochelle snapped.

"Rhonda," he called out loudly and waited in the entryway.

"Hey Daddy," she said unperturbed when he came into the living room. She had heard, seen, and been in between their arguments all her life and now they didn't faze her.

He reached in his pocket and pulled out three twenty dollar bills. "Take your sister and brother to the mall for a couple of hours."

"Okay," she said with a big smile on her face.

Rochelle stood in the middle of the floor with her arms folded. She was still there fuming when Rhonda came back through with Rhianna and E.J. on her hip.

"Make sure your brother is fastened in his car seat," Ernest said as they were leaving. He went into the kitchen, got a cold beer out of the refrigerator, and came back into the living room where Rochelle was still standing. "Why don't you sit down, we have a lot to talk about."

"I don't feel like sitting down," she said angrily.

"I know you want to hear about the female who came in the shop today but that's not the only thing we need to talk about. I've mentioned to you several times that I wanted to open another shop in a different area of town. I applied for a loan and got financing to move forward on that. The real estate agent who helped me find my location was the woman who came by today. The new place is really coming together. Most of the equipment and supplies have already come in. The only thing I have to concentrate on is getting the right personnel and we'll be on point."

"Are you cheating with this ho', are you in love with her?" Rochelle asked in a huff.

Everything about the new shop had gone in one ear and out the other.

"Baby, you're tripping. I'm not in love with anybody else. I don't need anybody else."

"Then why was she down there pushing up on you?"

"She wanted to take things further than business but I'm not interested."

"Is that right," she said full of sarcasm, "You come in all hours of the night, eat, and then you fall asleep. Why are you so tired all of a sudden?"

"I told you. I've been busting my ass trying to keep money coming in while I try to set up the other place. Plus, you know I have to keep a closer eye on my mama. I'm doing all I can do."

"Not quite. You haven't been spending any quality time with your wife."

"You're the mother of my children and I love you for that but most of the time I can't get close to you. You've got a wall up so high there's nothing I can do to climb over it."

"That's the only way I can protect myself from getting hurt by you. The way things have been around here it doesn't seem like your family is important to you."

"You know better than that, Chelle. My mama didn't have anybody. I didn't have anybody but my mama. My family means the world to me. I can't erase the things that happened in the past and you won't let me live it down. I've done everything I know to do, given you everything you wanted, and you're still not happy."

In the middle of their conversation, Ernest felt his phone vibrate in his pants pocket. He kept talking and five minutes later it vibrated again. He reached down and turned it off without taking it out of his pocket.

Rochelle cooled down a little as the sincerity of his words rained over her.

"One thing that would make me happy is if you would get your head out of the clouds and concentrate on your family for a change," she said without yelling.

"Everything I do is because I want to make things better for you and the kids."

"No, don't even fool yourself, Ernest. You're doing that for yourself, for your ego, and because you're trying to keep up with Vince."

"That's not true, Chelle."

"You're lying to me and yourself. It's time for you to make your choice. Do you want me and the kids or your big dreams?"

Ernest frowned in confusion. "That doesn't make any sense."

"It does to me. I don't want you in our bedroom until you figure it out," she said, storming out of the room.

Ernest sat there on the couch dumbfounded for almost a half hour. He couldn't believe that Rochelle didn't care one ounce about the new shop. She didn't ask any questions about it or ask to go and see it. He pulled his phone out of his pocket. There were three missed calls from Eva.

He stepped out on the front porch and called her back.

***

Eva was feeling things she'd never felt before, emotional, vulnerable, and desperate. It had to be some kind of pre-menopausal symptom triggering changes in her hormones that had caused her to become sentimental and have fits of jealousy all within a minute. She was bewildered by the unfamiliar feelings and wanted to turn off the reactions like a light switch but it wasn't within her power. She wasn't herself. The only thing that she previously had strong feelings about and wanted to possess completely was money. Profits and making record sales had fallen off the top of her to-do list. Ernest had taken the highest spot. Being with him or thoughts of being with him consumed her, morning, noon, and night.

It was August 20th, Natalie's birthday. Eva was fulfilling her mandatory duty as hostess for Mitchell's annual dinner birthday party for her with her latest boyfriend and a few of her sorority sisters and friends. Eva was struggling through the festivities because she was mentally and sexually frustrated. She had taken a Xanax earlier but it hadn't kicked in yet. She needed her drug of choice, Ernest in bed. It had been 48 hours since her last dose and she was getting edgy. She had already excused herself three times to go to the restroom to call Ernest and the main course hadn't even been served.

Natalie noticed her distraction and was glaring at her every time she came back to the table.

"You might need to see a doctor and get that checked out, Eva," Natalie sneered, "I know the bladder weakens as women get older but I'm sure they have some pill that can alleviate that."

"Thanks for your concern," Eva said scornfully, "But you don't need to worry about me, it's not good for you. And since you're celebrating another birthday, have you considered a consult with a colleague about some work? Your frown lines are getting deeper."

"No I haven't, but whenever you're ready to go under the knife for those overgrown crow's feet around your eyes I'm ready for you, stepmother," Natalie snapped back. "I'll even give you a family discount."

Eva narrowed her eyes with contempt. "Thank you, my dear step-child; I'll keep that in mind."

"Now, now, my favorite ladies, stop the needling or you'll ruin the mood of our celebration," Mitchell said with a strained smile.

The dessert was about to be served when Eva felt her cell phone, which she'd tucked into her spanx, vibrate against her inner thigh. She smiled and quickly excused herself again.

"Hello," she said frantically inside the half-bath, praying he hadn't hung up.

"Hey, you want to meet me at the house tonight?" Ernest asked seductively.

"I'll be there in an hour," she answered in a hushed voice.

Eva could barely contain her pleasure with the call. A wave of heat rolled over her. She looked at her reflection in the mirror and her face was flushed. She reached for a tissue and dabbed her cheeks.

"Are you feeling all right, sweetheart?" Mitchell asked when she returned to the table.

"Actually I'm not," she said, needing a reason to exit the dinner party, "I might be coming down with some kind of virus."

"You have to be careful where you go and the company you keep," Natalie chimed in, "You could catch all kinds of germs."

"That's a hazard of working with the public," Eva said, ignoring her snide remark.

"Some ginger tea would help," Mitchell said. "Have Loretta make you a cup."

Her name was Loretta, Loretta Lopez. She was the cook/housekeeper and had worked there for fourteen years ever since she came from the Dominican Republic by way of New Jersey with her daughter. When the head of Human Resources at Pinnacle found out she didn't have a green card they fired her. Mitchell, feeling bad for her, hired her to come and work for him.

"I think you're right," Eva said, getting up from the table. "I don't want to spoil the rest of the evening. You all enjoy yourselves. I think I'll go to bed early."

"I'll come up with you," Mitchell said, reaching for his walker.

"No, no, honey," she said, patting his shoulder and kissing him on the cheek. "This is Natalie's day. You all have a good time. I'll be fine."

Eva left the dining room and went straight out the front door where her car was parked along with the other guests. She drove away without looking back. The pile of lies she had been concocting for the past few weeks was surely above her head by now but she didn't care. She was addicted to this thing that was starting to feel like love.

***

Eva wouldn't have received any awards for her acting performance at the table from Mitchell or Natalie, primarily because it lacked originality. Mitchell had played the role much better himself and Natalie had seen it so many times that she found it boring. Mitchell was always aware whenever Eva stepped out of the bounds of their marriage, not only because he knew all the signs, but because he had a private investigator keep close tabs on her. Far from naïve, he believed that when you took someone's hand in yours, whether it is in friendship, fellowship, marriage, or any kind of contract, you best know what the other hand is doing. It was the key to him rising to the pinnacle of success, pun intended.

Not many years ago, Mitchell was the one giving flimsy excuses for making quick exits to meet a lady on the side. Nevertheless, nature has a way of leveling the playing field. He had gotten older and his body, more obstinate every day, refused to obey his commands. On an irreversible course, he was slowly losing his independence and freedom. As a man who once ran wild and free, it was a bitter drink to swallow.

Still, it wasn't in his nature to put Eva on a short leash. His concern was that in this instance she seemed to be getting tangled up. He felt that it was time to stop chasing her rabbit and come back home. After all she wasn't just some stray dog running around like she was in heat. He had given her his pedigree.

Natalie, on the other hand, never liked Eva or her "I'm God's gift to the world" attitude. She knew her Dad was nobody's fool and always insisted on prenuptial agreements but Natalie felt he shouldn't have married Eva. She didn't believe a man his age with his money could ever find someone to truly love him; they would always love the money more. She preferred the wives who were young, dumb, and knew their position.

The birthday party wrapped up around midnight with all the guests going home tipsy or totally drunk. It was a few minutes before 1:00 when Eva's car pulled into the front entrance. Natalie went to the bar and poured herself a Scotch, her first drink of the night. She wanted to be clear-headed when Eva got home from her rendezvous.

"Ooh, you startled me," Eva said nervously when she saw Natalie standing on the other side of the door. "I'm surprised to see you're still here."

"I wanted to wait for you to get back home," Natalie said dryly, "You left in such a hurry after saying you were sick. I thought you were probably headed to the Emergency Room. It must have been more than a stomach virus since they kept you so long."

Eva knew Natalie was being sarcastic but she played along. "I thought it would be helpful if I went to Walgreens and picked up some medications."

Natalie nodded. "You were probably just dehydrated. Did you get something to put fluids in your system?"

"As a matter of fact I did," Eva said, "You shouldn't have worried. I'm feeling much better."

"My father was the one who was worried, Eva. He doesn't need to be bothered with your fake fevers while he's facing real health issues."

"Why don't you take care of your own life or better yet find yourself a husband to care about," Eva said through narrowed eyes.

"You're not deceiving anybody," Natalie said, staring her down.

"Why are you still here?" Eva asked, irritated.

"For your information I belong here. This was my mother's house and she willed it to me. I'm the only one who will be here after my father's death."

"Don't be so sure," Eva snapped, flashing her a devious smile.

"You're not going to break my father down you scandalous bitch. If you do anything to hurt him in any way I will kill you with my bare hands."

Eva laughed and walked up the stairs to the guestroom. She wasn't about to allow Natalie's miserable ass to cast a shadow on her afterglow. She undressed in the dark and got into bed, running her hands over the spots where Ernest had touched her.

***

Eva could hear Mitchell's slippers scuffling against the floor before he turned the corner into the room. She wasn't ready to face him after being with Ernest last night. It had been different from the other times. Last night she could feel his desire. It was like he wanted to lose himself inside her body. Her head was still spinning from the passions that had been stirred up. The parts of her life that she thought were settled, like her marriage and her future, seemed to be back up in the air again. The only thing she was sure of was that she wanted Ernest.

"Good morning, love," Mitchell said, ambling into the kitchen still wearing his pajamas and bathrobe.

"Good morning, my dear," Eva responded, putting on a fake smile while on the inside she was wishing she had left ten minutes ago. She wanted to blame Loretta for brewing the pot of fresh coffee and its aroma for drawing her in but it was her fault.

"Are you feeling better this morning?" he asked, easing down onto one of the barstools in front of her. "You look lovely."

"As a matter of fact I am," she answered without any further explanations. "I was just leaving to get an early start at the office."

Eva poured the remaining half cup of coffee in the sink and proceeded to walk past him. Mitchell grabbed her hand tightly and pulled her next to him.

"I'm sure as my wife you can spare your husband a few minutes of your time," he said, putting his arm around her waist. "You seem to be in such a hurry lately. Come sit by me. All my senses have missed you, hearing you, seeing you, touching you, smelling you, and tasting you."

"I don't mean to neglect you, honey," she said, rubbing his shoulders. "I've been preoccupied with some problems at work."

"Oh, what's going on? Maybe it's something I can help you with."

"One of my new agents has a problem with the broker's fee and shared commission on a sale from one of my clients. It's nothing I can't handle."

"You know, we both have been so stressed with work and doctor's appointments it would be a good time for us to take a couple of weeks off and get away for a while."

"That sounds wonderful, honey, but I've got a lot of irons in the fire myself and traveling might be difficult for you right now."

Mitchell feeling her reluctance, insisted, "Between the two of us, we'll be fine. I'm not a total invalid, at least not yet."

"No, darling, that's not what I meant," Eva said to appease his growing anger.

"Try to wrap up your business this week," he said firmly. "I'll make the arrangements. In the meantime don't forget we're attending the Tennessee Performing Arts Gala on Friday."

Eva swallowed the words of protest that rose in her throat. "I'll do my best," she said before kissing him on the cheek and rushing out.

Chapter Ten

It had been the fourth hottest August on record in Nashville but the air in the Shaw household was frigid at best. Ernest was doing everything he could to get Rochelle to warm up to him after their disagreement but she wasn't having it. Two weeks later she was still giving him the silent treatment and sleeping in the room with E.J. Under these circumstances, Eva's chasing him down had become a turn-on.

The new shop had created a wedge between him and Rochelle, and Eva had inserted herself into the divide. At the outset when he slipped he wanted to put it behind him. He wanted to be honorable but then again and again he was tempted. He started rationalizing the situation, telling himself it didn't make a difference if he does it or not. Rochelle had been accusing him for years. He was still going to catch hell. He had already suffered her punishment enough times when he was totally legit. Wasn't he owed a few infractions?

Earnest looked at the clock on the wall of his office. If he left now he would have time to go home, spend some time with the kids, and get over to Vince's place before kickoff. The NFL's last preseason game was coming on tonight and Vince had invited him to come by to watch it. With Vince tied up with training camp and exhibitions and him busy preparing for the new shop opening, they hadn't had a chance to hang out in a while and he was looking forward to it. Vince was the only person he could talk to about all the things that were going on.

"Oh hell naw, man," Ernest exclaimed when Vince opened the door with the beginnings of an afro and a patchy beard. "I don't believe you're walking around in public like that. You're going to ruin my reputation."

"Cut it out," Vince said, feigning insult as he shut the door. "I know I'm a little scraggly but it's not that bad."

"Not bad if you've been stranded in the woods for a month."

Vince laughed as he led his friend back to the great room where the TV was already blaring.

"Hey, it's that time of the season but trust, I'll be the first one in line for your opening."

"I got you reserved, man," Ernest said, getting a cold beer out of the bucket of ice sitting on the floor beside the couch. "You got the set-up in here."

"You know how I do it, hot wings, Italian foot longs, and my barbecue skins," Vince said, uncovering the trays he had ordered from Publix.

"Who are you pulling for tonight?" Ernest asked, making himself a plate. "No changing halfway through the game."

Vince popped the top on a fresh beer. "I hate Pittsburgh so I'm going for the Eagles."

"Okay, that'll work," Ernest said, plopping down on the big leather sectional. "We're on the same team for this one."
"So what's the official opening date for you place? How long I got to wait?" Vince asked, leaning back in his recliner.

"It's September 13, two weeks away. It's a lot to pull together but I'll be ready."

"I'm proud of you, man, you made it happen," Vince said, leaning forward to slap his hand in congratulation.

"The rest of my life is out of order," Ernest sighed, "But hey, it's all good."

"Trouble in paradise again?"

"It never ends. Rochelle heard about Eva coming in the shop and now she's tripping. She thinks I'm messing around on her again."

"Are you?" Vince asked nonchalantly, watching the TV screen.

"I wasn't at first, but if I'm going to take the heat, I might as well make it worth the trouble."

"I don't believe you went there, man," Vince said, turning to look at him, "That wasn't a good move. That has danger written all over it."

"It wasn't my bad; she made the move on me. Believe it or not, I was the one dodging a piece of ass. Then it seemed like I didn't have many options at the time. It was a part of the loan process."

"You mean she played you like a bitch."

"We've both done worse things to get paid and we've told a lot of lies to get the panties," Ernest said, being defensive.

"I thought those days were behind us," Vince said seriously.

"So did I," Ernest said, looking at the floor. He knew getting involved with Eva was not one of his better decisions and he was sure the day would come when he regretted it, but for now she had him mellowed out and was really there for him when it came to his new shop.

"Shut her down, man, immediately," Vince told him, "You got too much to lose. That's how you eat and feed your family. You know the rules, 'don't shit where you eat.'"

"You're right, man. It's got to be done but it's not that

easy. She's sexy as hell and Rochelle's not giving me anything but a hard time."

Just then Ernest's cell phone light flashed indicating that he got a text message. It was Eva wanting to see him. He sent a message back that he was watching the game.

She texted back, "All I need is halftime."

He answered, "Not tonight."

"You're playing with dynamite," Vince said, shaking his head.

"I'm trying to be like you, man."

"I'm by myself, E. If some shit blows up in my face I'm the only one going down."

"Get off my case," Ernest said, putting his phone in his back pocket. "The Eagles are getting ready to score."

***

Listening to a Sade playlist, Eva dressed alone for the gala in the guest bedroom that had become more than occasional refuge. Mitchell had been throwing innuendos at her all week and she was weary of ducking and fending them off. In the past they had always given each other space and independence. Now whenever she was in the same room with him she could practically feel him breathing down her neck. She knew it was partly, if not mostly, her fault for the change in their dynamic. She had never let a dalliance of hers interfere with her obligations as his wife before. Why she was so obsessed with this barber she couldn't explain. Possibly it was because he was unpredictable, and his resistance only made him more desirable.

She sprayed her neck with Joy, her favorite cologne, but it didn't do much to change her frame of mind. She was edgy, disgruntled, two small steps from being outraged. All because Ernest chose a meaningless football game over her last night. Feeling like a junky in need of a fix again, the last place she wanted to be was stuck by Mitchell's side all evening with Natalie watching her every move.

"We're waiting for you, love," Mitchell called from downstairs.

Eva took another glance at her reflection in the full length mirror. The violet gown fit her perfectly. She looked beautiful, she always did, but something in her face was off. She moved closer to find the imperfection. Her eyes were shadowed flawlessly. Her cheekbones were perfectly contoured. The line of her lipstick was precise. It was probably just her imagination.

Loretta tapped softly on the outside of the guestroom door. "The car is here, ma'am."

Eva grabbed her beaded evening bag and strutted out the door and down the stairs. She was determined not only to get through this evening but to enjoy herself doing it. Then she saw Mitchell standing in the foyer with his cane.

"Shouldn't you bring your walker," she asked him warily.

He smiled. "I won't need it. If I need to, I'll lean on you. Natalie is already in the car." He moved slowly out of the door and towards limousine with Eva at his side. "By the way, you look gorgeous," he said as they approached the car.

The driver opened the door and Mitchell waited for her to get in first. She slid in the seat across from Natalie and her unknown escort. Mitchell handed her his cane and dropped his body in the seat beside her.

"So glad you could join us this evening, Eva," Natalie said mockingly, "I know your schedule is quite full."

Using the same tone, Eva replied, "It's a pleasure to see you too, Natalie, and I'm glad you won't be going alone tonight."

"It is a challenge to meet an eligible black man these days," Natalie said, crossing her legs, "Most of them are with white women or prowling around with cougars."

Mitchell interrupted their exchange. "Why don't you introduce us to your date, sweetheart?"

"Of course, Dad. This is Jonathan Ross; he's an executive at Bridgestone. Jonathan, this is my father, Mitchell Hamilton, and his wife Eva."

Eva nodded and Mitchell said, "Very nice to meet you, Jonathan."

"I'm surprised you don't know him, Eva," Natalie said, throwing more shade, "It's hard to find a young black man who hasn't made your acquaintance."

Eva smiled as she responded. "In my experience, people are more attracted to a sparkling personality instead of a disagreeable disposition. I guess I could give you a few pointers."

"Ladies, put away your weapons, we don't want to give Jonathan the wrong impression," Mitchell said, ending their verbal fencing match.

The limo dropped them off in front of Andrew Jackson Hall. Natalie and Jonathan went ahead saying they would rejoin them at dinner. Eva wished she could make a quick escape but she was tied to Mitchell's arm as he took his time up the stairs to the entrance. Thankfully, once they were inside, the escalators allowed him to conserve his energy. It was obvious that getting around on his own was physically draining. Eva didn't know why he insisted on coming.

What Mitchell knew and Eva didn't understand was that he had to keep moving, had to keep pushing, no matter how hard it was. It might not be as recognizable on the outside anymore but he was a still a worthy opponent. There was no way he was going to lie down and let death take him that easy.

Making their entrance into the ballroom, Mitchell balanced half of his weight on Eva's arm and the other half on his cane. He took this opportunity to remind her where she belonged as he steered her around the room mingling with friends and business associates.

Eva was embarrassed. She had never envisioned herself beside a frail old man. When she met Mitchell he was full of life and vitality. He used to dominate a room like this while she basked in the aura of his charisma. Now all she wanted was for him to find a place to sit down and leave her alone. The closer he held her the more she detested his presence, the sound of his voice, how he smelled, and his shaky grip on her arm. She felt like she wanted to scream.

"Hello Mitchell," one of his professional colleagues said, coming over to greet them."

"Good to see you, Stan," Mitchell replied. "How's the family."

"The kids are off in Europe somewhere spending my money and the wife is somewhere around here with a martini in her hand bad mouthing me."

Mitchell laughed and said, "I don't believe a word of it."

"Not every man is as lucky as you are," Stan said, smiling at Eva.

"No I don't guess they are," Mitchell said, glancing at his wife.

"Excuse me for a moment, gentlemen," Eva said sweetly, "I need to go to the powder room."

"Certainly, my dear," Mitchell said with a smile as he released her arm.

Eva rushed across the floor of the lobby into the restroom and past the attendant. Inside one of the stalls she braced herself with her hands pressed against the walls. She took a deep breath, blew it out, and began to relax. In the tiny space she felt free and didn't want to come out.

"Are you okay, miss," the attendant asked from outside the stall after ten minutes.

"Yes, I'm fine. I was feeling a bit queasy."

There wasn't any place for her to hide. She was being ridiculous. She had to pull herself together. It wouldn't be long before her behavior caused serious problems between her and Mitchell. Ultimately, she didn't want a divorce, she just wanted a time-out. She checked her make-up, smoothed her dress, and came out to be the dutiful wife.

"There you are, beautiful," Mitchell said when she found him seated at their table. "I'm happy to see you aren't having that stomach upset again."

"Oh no, honey," she lied, "I'm having a wonderful time."

Later in the evening her stomach truly did turn and do backflips when she found herself trapped on the dance floor with Mitchell barely able to shuffle his feet.

***

It was a few days before In Earnest would be open for business. Eva had a crew come in and do a final clean-up and the new shop looked spectacular. She had bought an antique wood door for the entrance that set the place off with an air of class and distinction. When the sign went up Ernest thought his chest would burst open with happiness. No more dust in the corners. No more chipped paint. No more calendars of naked women, and no more dodging bullets.

He had spent most of the previous week trying to figure out what personnel he would need for the spa. He had decided he would start off with another barber, one massage therapist, one nail technician, and a receptionist while he established a customer base. He would have preferred to have them all salaried on his payroll but that would mean he would have to provide a benefits package with insurance, and that was too much to take on with his budget.

He wanted to serve a diverse group of clientele so he'd

hired a diverse staff. The barber was a white female named Jayne, she was tall and slim, almost six feet, and looked like a model for Vogue, but she could cut hair better than most guys he had seen. He scouted her out at a salon in Cool Springs Mall. The massage therapist was a white male from Miami named Erik, he was the beach/body builder type and very laidback, but he had a long resume and good references. The nail technician he hired, Halina, was originally from the Philippines. She was pretty and petite, spoke with a strong accent, but she knew her craft. The last person he hired was Carla, she would be the receptionist. She was Latino with long dark hair that hung below her waist. She reminded him of hot peppers. She had spark and zest, she talked fast, and walked like she was dancing. She would be the extra spice he needed to welcome his customers.

Now that his opening was approaching he was thinking more about what Vince had told him. He hadn't said anything about it to Eva yet but now that he was in a position where he didn't need her help he felt more secure about ending the extra-curricular activities at the house in Brentwood. It was also time for him to patch up things with Rochelle. The two of them not speaking had gone on long enough and it wasn't good for the kids to be caught in between their conflict.

Ernest had also been so busy with the finishing touches on the shop and meeting with his new personnel that he hadn't been able to sit with his mama during her dialysis all week. Even though he knew she wouldn't respond, he texted Rochelle that he was going by his mama's house to check on her before he went home.

He could tell his mama was worn out because she usually heard him drive up and opened the door before he knocked. He let himself in with his key and found her half asleep in the living room watching *Family Feud.*

"What's up, Mama," he said, bending down to kiss her on the cheek.

"Hey there, child," she said, perking up. "It's good to see you."

"Are you feeling okay, you look tired," he said, sitting down next to her.

"The clinic got me today. I'm drained dry."

"Did you eat anything?"

"Yeah, I stopped and got a plate at Mary's on my way home."

"I'm going to get you some vegetables and fruit tomorrow. You should be eating healthier instead of that barbecue all the time."

"I'm fine, don't worry about me. How are things coming along with your new place?"

"It's looking good. I'm getting excited about the opening."

"That's good, Ernest. You know Rochelle called me today. She said y'all are having some problems. She's thinking about putting you out of the house."

"I've tried to talk to her, Mama, but she's not listening."

Sheila shook her head in dismay. "Maybe you don't need to talk so much and take your behind home at a decent hour every night."

"It don't make any difference. When I'm home she still has an attitude."

"She says some woman keeps calling the house looking for you. That she had the nerve to tell her to give you the message that she'll be waiting."

"I know I made some mistakes in the past but Rochelle never let it go. She's been accusing me for ten years when

I was straight. If I step out it's because she pushes me out there."

"So it's her fault if you can't keep it in your pants," Sheila said, raising her voice.

Ernest shook his hands in front of him with frustration. "She's mad all the time, whether I come home or not. It's nothing I can do about it."

"This is a shame. Between the children and you building up your business, you two have so much to share and be happy about. It don't make no sense."

"You're right, Mama," he said, looking out the window. "It don't make sense."

Chapter Eleven

It was opening day for the In Earnest Gentlemen's Spa, the day that Ernest had dreamed about, the day that he had risked everything to get, and he could count his supporters on one hand. There was his mama of course, Vince, Leon, and then Eva. Rochelle was still fuming about Eva and the new shop, feeling he had done both to spite her. She left the house early to drop Rhianna off at school and take E.J. to the daycare. Ernest had asked her to let the negativity go and invited her to come to the opening but she refused. Why should she go there pretending things were great between them when they weren't, at least as far as she was concerned.

Too nervous to eat any breakfast, Ernest went by his mama's to pick her up. Leon would be there later after he opened King Cut.

"This is it, Mama," Ernest said, brimming with excitement when they crossed the street from where they parked.

Sheila felt happy tears begin to tingle in her eyes when she saw the sign outside. "I'm so proud of you, Ernest. I didn't know it was going to be this fancy."

"We're going to be in first-class from now on, Mama," he

said, unlocking the door and flicking on the lights. "Let me give you a tour and show you my office."

Ernest gave her a walk through the shop, the manicure room, the massage area, the steam room, and his office, where he turned on his smooth jazz playlist to air over the intercom. Sheila was overwhelmed with the style and elegance of the spa. She almost couldn't believe her child had put it all together. It was much more than she had expected.

"This is so nice. I should have brought my camera to show everybody at the clinic tomorrow. I won't be able to describe how fabulous it is."

"I'll take some for you to show them with your phone in a few minutes," Ernest said, putting on one of the crisp white smocks he'd ordered for his staff with the name 'In Earnest' embroidered on it.

Then they heard a bell chime, letting them know the entrance door had been opened. Ernest rushed to the front with Sheila trailing behind him. They got to the front just as Carla soared in and made her way around to the back of the receptionist desk like she was on roller skates.

"Good morning, Mr. Shaw," she said, bursting with energy, "I hope I'm not late for opening day."

"No, you're right on time," Ernest said, smiling and loving her enthusiasm. "I just got here a few minutes ago. By the way, Carla, this is my mother, Sheila Shaw. Mama, this is Carla. She's the receptionist for the shop."

"Oh, it's a pleasure to meet you, Mrs. Shaw," Carla said, coming from the back of the reception area to give her a hug. "You have a great son here."

"I think so," Sheila said, smiling back at her. "Nice to meet you."

Ernest led Sheila over to his work station in the center. She sat down in the chair of the extra station by the window while he showed her all of his new equipment. Carla put on one of the white smocks Ernest had given her while she bounced to a lively salsa beat in her head and then she took her place behind the tall counter just beyond the door entrance.

Jayne and Halina were the next to arrive, chatting and walking in the door together.

"Good morning, ladies," Ernest said, greeting them. "It's good to see you both energized and ready to work."

"I'm really excited about the opening today," Jayne said, heading to the third work station. "I hope we get a good crowd, I can definitely use the money." "I'm with you on that," Ernest added, giving her a high five. "Ladies, I'd like to introduce you to my mother, Sheila Shaw," he said turning towards Sheila.

"Hello, Miss Shaw," Jayne said, shaking her hand, "It's good to meet you. This is a big day for all of us."

"Yes it is," Sheila said kindly, looking up at her.

"My pleasure, ma'am," Halina said, taking her hand with a slight bow. "I'll give you a manicure today."

"You don't have to do that," Sheila said, "I'm just happy to be here."

Halina smiled back at her and said, "Come back anytime."

Jayne got busy re-arranging her station and Halina went to the area just off the main room where the mani/pedi chairs were located. The door opened again and it was two employees from Panache Catering with the food. Ernest thought it would be a nice gesture to welcome his guests and clientele with bite-size hors d' oeuvres and champagne for the grand opening. Carla showed them where to set up.

It was about fifteen minutes before 11:00, opening time, when Erik sauntered in.

"You guys didn't start without me did you," he said, grinning like he was the guest of honor.

"We were about to," Carla snapped with her accent show-ing, "Did you forget to set your alarm or something?"

"Sorry about that, Ms. Carla, I'll be the consummate pro-fessional from here on out," Erik said, humoring her.

Ernest tapped his glass with a pair of scissors. "The top of the hour is about to arrive so I want to say a few words. Everybody grab a glass of champagne." He paused for a mo-ment while they got glasses and gathered around him. "First of all I want to thank you all for joining me on this new business venture. We are all in agreement with the level of professionalism that we want to exemplify here. Represent yourselves well, people. I know I have a good team with all of you. Here's to a successful opening and making 'In Earnest' the most esteemed and prosperous Gentlemen's Spa on the planet."

They all raised their glasses and cheerfully drank to his toast. Sheila felt like clapping. She hadn't fully understood what Ernest had been telling her about his dream but now that she could see it in real life she knew why he had taken the risks. He didn't belong on a side street in a ghetto strip mall barber shop. He was bigger than that. He knew it, and now everybody else would know it too.

Vince came through the door at 11:00 on the dot with two of the Titan football players behind him.

"I told you, E, I'm the first cut," Vince said with open arms.

"Sit in my chair, man," Ernest said after giving him a bear hug, "You're long overdue."

"I'm not going to argue with you," Vince said, sitting down. "We're here to get everything you have to offer in this camp."

"Now that's what I'm talking about," Ernest said, smiling as he reached for a drape to put around him.

One of the football players sat in Jayne's chair and the other followed Carla out to Halina's station for a mani/pedi.

"Hey there, Miss Sheila," Vince said, noticing her across the room near the refreshments. "How are you doing?"

"I'm doing fine, Vincent," Sheila told him. "How's your mama doing?"

"She's doing all right," Vince answered while Ernest placed the paper strip around his neck.

The two mothers had been close until Vince got drafted and moved his mom out of the duplex next door years ago. Eileen was glad to go. The two of them lost touch.

"Tell her I asked about her," Sheila said wistfully. Who would have thought their two boys would have come this far.

A steady stream of customers rolled in the shop while Ernest worked on Vince's cut and shave. Some had come in to check out the new place but quite a few wanted to get haircuts. It didn't take long for the chairs in the waiting area to fill up and a line formed that circled around the hors d' oeuvres table. The champagne kept the customers relaxed but Ernest was wishing that he had hired more help. Long waits are bad for business. He was about to get stressed and then Leon walked in.

He stopped at the door to take it all in before he made his way over to Ernest's station.

"You stepping in high cotton aren't you, man?" Leon said, giving him the brother man handshake and bumping right shoulders, "Congratulations, man, I'm loving this."

"Thanks, man, you're right on time," Ernest said, slightly frazzled. "I could use some extra help around here today."

Leon threw his hands out to the side. "You know I'm here for you, E. What do you need?"

"There's a smock in the bottom drawer at that first station. Put it on and do what you do."

"Nothing but a word," Leon said. He found the smock, put it on, and took a minute to see where everything was located. Then he told Ernest, "Let's do it."

Ernest motioned to Carla to send the next customer over to the first chair where Leon was waiting with a drape in his hand.

"That was a smooth move," Jayne said in a low voice so only he could hear.

The buzz of the clippers blended in the hum of the conversations and the melody of the music playing in the background. Ernest couldn't have asked for more as he finished up with Vince's cut and shave. He handed him a mirror so he could see his handiwork.

"Now everything is back on point," Ernest said, joking with him, "You were looking like Bigfoot when you walked in here."

Vince chuckled, admiring the work, "You worked your magic again. Now I need to get a rubdown. The guys and I worked out before we came."

"Carla will show you where to go," Ernest said, taking off his drape.

Before he started on the next client, Ernest went over to his mama who was sitting quietly near the refreshments. Her having to go to dialysis every other day was always in the back of his mind even though she never complained.

"Mama, you can go lie down in my office if you get tired," he whispered to her.

"No time soon," she said with a smile. "I'm enjoying sitting here and watching you."

Sheila felt like she was in heaven. There wasn't another thing she could ask God for. Seeing her son in his fine place of business, in authority, conducting himself with dignity and respect, was all a mother could ever want for her son.

For the next three hours traffic was brisk in the shop. It turned out to be a lifesaver that Ernest had food there because no one had time to stop for lunch. More of those who initially were just curious discovered that the atmosphere was so relaxing that they stayed and patronized the services of one of the staff. Just observing all the activity got Sheila tired after a while and she reluctantly agreed to take a rest in the office.

The door chimed so much that Ernest had stopped looking every time, it only slowed him down. Besides, Carla was handling the door and the order of service like a pro.

"Excuse me," Andrea exclaimed, walking over to Ernest and catching him by surprise. "Damn, E, this is all that."

"Thanks, lil sis, I didn't see you come in," he said, putting one arm around her and giving her a side hug. "I'm glad you stopped by."

"You know I was coming to check you out," Andrea said, scanning his set up. "I wanted to bring my man by but his funds might be a little low and I'm not paying for him. Maybe he can get a job shining shoes in here," she said, teasing.

"Don't even start clowning me, girl," Ernest said, laughing.

"I can't stay but a minute. I'm booked all afternoon but let me check out the food."

"Help yourself," Ernest said. He knew she couldn't pass up some free food.

Then the bell chimed again and it was Eva sashaying through the door like she owned the place. She went straight over to Ernest and kissed him on the lips. Andrea's mouth was full of food but that didn't stop her jaw from dropping. Ernest was thoroughly irritated by the gesture. He didn't care for her public display but he played it off, moving on the other side of his chair to put some distance between them.

"Congratulations," she said full of enthusiam, "It looks

like you've got a hit on your hands. I told you this was a hot spot."

He nodded and answered without looking at her. "You know the story, location, location, location."

Eva giggled, got herself a glass of champagne, and proceeded to introduce herself to Jayne who was working on a client.

Andrea couldn't believe it. She had feelings of loyalty towards Ernest for helping her out and being like a brother to her, but according to 'girl code' she didn't have a choice. She put down her plate and casually walked out to the front sidewalk of the spa and called Rochelle.

"Girl, you need to bring your behind down here ASAP. Miss Thang is walking around here like's she's the first lady."

"Oh hell no," Rochelle fussed, "I'm on my way down there."

"You know I would stay and help you beat that ass but I got to go make some money," Andrea said, peeping through the front window.

"Don't worry, I got this," Rochelle assured her. "Thanks for looking out."

***

Thirty minutes later, Rochelle stormed in the door of In Earnest with E.J. on her hip. Leon saw her first and from the look on her face, he knew that Andrea had called her and gave her the 411. Luckily, Eva was still playing hostess, making her introductions, and was in the massage room with Erik. Leon tapped Ernest on the shoulder and quickly eased towards the direction of the massage area to intercept Eva and diffuse the situation before the time bomb went off. Ordinarily, Ernest would have done some finishing touches on the cut he was working on, instead he handed him a mirror, and removed his drape.

Rochelle stomped over to the receptionist desk.

"Who are you?" Rochelle asked Carla angrily.

Carla was slightly confused but she was unperturbed. "I'm Carla. How can I help you?"

Before Rochelle could answer, Ernest grabbed E.J., swooped her up, and guided her back to his office. She was about to unleash a barrage of curses on him but seeing her mother-in-law lying on the sofa caused her to hold back.

"You know who I'm looking for," she said angrily to Ernest, "Where is she?"

"You need to calm down," he answered in a lower volume, hoping she would follow suit.

"Don't tell me to calm down. I heard that bitch was in here."

E.J., upset by her tone, started whimpering and leaned his head on Ernest's shoulder. The noise in the room woke Sheila up.

"You see I'm in here working my ass off," Ernest said, hoping to calm her down. "I'm trying to handle my business."

"Oh no, I'm not falling for that," Rochelle protested, "Something is up."

"There's nothing going on here," Ernest told her.

"Then why did you ask her to come here?" Rochelle demanded.

"I didn't ask anybody to be here except you and my mama. This is my opening day. You should be able to support that. I don't need any extra drama."

Rochelle didn't know how to react. Truth be told she didn't want to cause problems for Ernest. From what little she'd seen, the new shop looked really nice. Plus, Miss Sheila was there watching and she wasn't about to be disrespectful in her presence. On the other hand, she needed to put whoever this ho' was in her place.

Sheila was disorientated when the arguing first woke her up. After a minute or two she had figured out what was going on. She swung her feet to the floor and said, "Chelle, can you take me home? I'm not feeling good. I guess I've been here long enough."

Rochelle was immediately concerned. "Sure, Miss Sheila," she said, helping her stand.

Nothing was wrong with Sheila except she knew she had to get Rochelle out of there before she made a scene and ruined Ernest's big day. She gingerly walked to the front praying that the cause of the blow-up would stay out of sight. Ernest still holding his son walked them out to Rochelle's car.

"I'll talk to you later," Ernest said to Sheila after he fastened E.J. in his car seat.

Rochelle rolled her eyes at him and said, "So will I."

Ernest hurried back in the shop where there were three customers waiting.

"We'll be right with you," he said to them politely before going back to his office.

He reached in the right hand bottom draw of his desk for the pint of Hennessey he had there. He took off the cap and took a swig to settle his blood pressure. He put the bottle back, popped one of the mints from his pocket in his mouth, and was about to leave when the door opened and Eva walked in.

"You didn't knock," he said, still irritated with her.

"Why should I?" she said, moving close until their bodies touched.

"Because this is my office and I deserve that courtesy," he said, stepping aside of her. "I wouldn't come to your office and disrespect you."

"Maybe it's time we got some things straight," she said, leaning back on his desk.

"Absolutely," he said, "First, I have to ask you to leave. This is where I work. It's serious business for me."

"Are you forgetting that I made all of this possible?"

"What you have to remember is that you connected me to the company where I borrowed money. I'm paying my own bills."

"Meet me at the house this evening," Eva said, slightly peeved, "We have a lot to talk about."

Ernest shook his head no. "You can see my hands are full today, I have customers waiting."

"Be there," she said in a commanding tone.

Ernest walked out and held the door until she followed him out. He locked it behind them and went to his work station. Eva watched him as he draped his next customer. Every time she thought she had him broken in, he would buck up again. No problem, she liked a rebellious horse. They gave a more exciting ride. She would let him know who held the reigns later.

***

"I'm sorry about cussing in front of you, Miss Sheila," Rochelle said as she drove onto the interstate. "We're still going through some problems. He keeps on disrespecting me. I can't deal with it anymore."

"Woman to woman, Chelle, you've got to make up your mind what you want. If you don't want my son no more, then end it. If you do, end all that bickering about everything."

"He's the one out here running the streets and playing me," Rochelle complained.

"Child, the truth is you never forgave him for what happened over ten years ago. You've been trying to punish him over it for so long, even when he was doing right, and you're only driving him away. He's never going to leave his children but you'll be miserable in that house with him if you don't decide what kind of wife you gonna be."

"How can you say that, Miss Sheila? From what I heard you didn't try to stay with Ernest's daddy when he did you wrong."

"What are you talking about?" Sheila exclaimed. "How was I going to stay with him, he already had a wife and kids. I did what I had to do."

"Most men ain't right, even your son. I'm not going to be nobody's fool," Rochelle spouted, getting off on Metrocenter exit.

Sheila patted her foot against the floorboard of the car with exasperation.

"Child, you being a fool right now," she told Rochelle. "You about to let another woman break up your marriage. He don't want her. She's the one chasing him. Every time you push him out there she's waiting to catch him. Ernest ain't perfect and you ain't either. You don't have to kiss his ass, just be smart and meet him halfway."

"How can I be with somebody I can't trust?"

"He couldn't get you to trust him for ten years. So you probably not ever gonna trust him. That's your problem. Why should the whole house suffer because you don't want to be happy? Think about your children for a change."

Rochelle was tired of taking the blame for everything. It wasn't her fault that he couldn't be faithful. She didn't say anything else until they pulled up to the curb in front of the duplex.

"I hope you feel better," she said, "Do you need me to do anything for you."

"No, I'm fine. You go on home and relax yourself."

Rochelle stared out the front windshield while Sheila got out and opened the back door to give E.J. a kiss.

"What am I supposed to do, just let it go?" she asked in frustration while Sheila said goodbye to the baby.

"Start off listening for a change. Stop trying to fix it. Let it work itself out." Then she shut the door and walked into the house.

***

This should have been an evening to celebrate. It had been an extraordinary day. Ernest had accomplished a goal that he had dreamed about for a long time. He smiled to himself when he recalled how happy and proud his mama had been. The opening was a great success, they had taken in much more than he had expected. Vince and his guys dropping $300 each on services got the day off to a good start. His new team hadn't missed a beat but it was Leon who had really come through for him. Not only did he help them keep the patrons flowing, he kept a bomb from blowing the place up when he got Eva out of Rochelle's line of fire.

Pushing the door open of his own house, Ernest didn't know what to expect. He could hear the TV playing in the den. He peeped in the room and saw the kids lounging together on the couch.

"Hey, Daddy," Rhonda said, glancing his way for a second.

"Hey, Daddy," Rhianna said, echoing her big sister as usual.

E.J, sitting between them gave him a big toothy smile and went back to playing with his toy cell phone. Ernest tread softly towards the kitchen. With all the knives in there it could be dangerous. He peered through the doorway and saw Rochelle sitting calmly at the table. There was a plate of food and a beer waiting at his place on the table.

"Are you hungry?" she asked without changing her blank expression.

"I'm starving," he answered, sitting down next to her.

He ate several bites wondering how long it would be before she started her tongue-lashing. He didn't know how in the hell he had gotten caught between two women who wanted to control him like a puppet on a string. Certain things he had to put up with from Rochelle, she was his wife, but Eva, he didn't owe her anything. He ate a few more bites while Rochelle was still quietly staring at him. She had decided to take his mother's advice.

Ernest drank some of the beer and pushed the plate away. He looked her in the eyes. "Do you want us to stay together?"

She looked down at the half-eaten plate. "Yes, I do."

Ernest reached over and took her hand. "For the past ten years you didn't believe me but I wasn't with any other women. The woman who called here is the same woman at the shop that Andrea called you about. I met her at the bank after my first business loan application was denied. She helped me get the loan at the bank where her husband is the head nigga in charge. Some things happened between us that shouldn't have, partly because you and I weren't on the same page, and mostly because I thought she would help me secure the loan. I don't have any feelings for her and I don't want to be with her. This is where I want to be, with you, and with our kids."

"So you want me to forget about what happened with her and forgive you?" Rochelle said hopelessly, feeling it was too much to ask.

"It sounds bad when you say it like that, baby, but for ten years I took the heat from you for no reason. That was tough. I'm not going to see her anymore. I promise you that. I want us to start fresh."

Sheila's words from earlier in the car replayed in her head. She could raise hell every day and it wouldn't change a thing.

"I don't even know how to tell you how much you hurt me but I still love you, Ernest. I'll try to get past this but if I catch her at the shop again, I'll kill that bitch."

Ernest's phone vibrated and he looked at the number.

"This is her calling me now," he said, trying to be open and honest with his wife. "She's been blowing up my phone for the last hour."

"Turn it off," Rochelle insisted.

"I would but my mama might call."

"I'm getting you a new phone tomorrow."

Ernest nodded. "Thanks, baby, and thanks for listening."

"Don't stay up too late, you look tired," Rochelle said, standing up to leave. "I'll be sleeping in our bed if you don't mind."

"Isn't that where you belong?" he asked, grinning at her.

"We both do," she said on her way out of the kitchen.

Ernest went into the den and told his girls goodnight and picked up E.J. He gave his son a bath, read him *Cat in a Hat*, and put him to bed. Down the hall he went into their bedroom and closed the door behind him. Rochelle was lying naked on the bed in the light from the TV. He took off his clothes and lay on top of her. He kissed her neck, kissed her mouth, closed his eyes, and then Eva's face appeared. It threw him for a minute. He turned on the lamp on the night stand and stared into Rochelle's eyes. He needed to see her face. She smiled at him. The attention made her feel sexy. His phone still on the kitchen table vibrated again and again.

Chapter Twelve

Pacing across the foyer of the Brentwood model home in black strappy Jimmy Choo heels and a black negligée, Eva kept calling Ernest's number every five minutes.

"Where is he?" she shouted in the empty house, "What is taking him so long?"

In between her phone calls to him her own phone kept ringing. Each time she hoped it was Ernest but twice it was calls from Mitchell. She didn't answer, she would deal with him later, after she put Ernest in his place and then in between her legs on the fresh sheets in the master bedroom. Then she started getting calls from Natalie.

"What the hell is wrong with everybody?" she screamed in exasperation.

She drank a glass of wine to calm her nerves and sat down to wait in the living room. She dozed off and woke up at twenty minutes before eleven o'clock. Looking at her watch with disgust she realized Ernest wasn't coming. She clomped into the bedroom and put her clothes back on. She was backing out of the garage when her phone rang again.

"Dammit," she said, seeing it was Natalie calling again.

"What does she want?" She shook her head and answered the call.

"Hello," she said, sounding agitated.

"Where are you?" Natalie demanded. "I've been calling you for two hours."

"I'm on my way home. What's so important?"

"My father," Natalie hollered, "He's in St. Thomas hospital."

Eva was stunned. "What happened?"

"He collapsed at the house. He tried to call you before he called me but you didn't give a rat's ass about answering."

"I'll be there in a half hour," Eva said, pressing the end button on her phone.

Her temple began to throb. She was already stressed over Ernest ignoring her and now this. She took a deep breath to compose herself as she sped along the interstate. When she got to the Mid-town emergency room they informed her that Mitchell had been transferred to Neuroscience on the sixth floor, room 617.

Eva stared at the numbers above the closed elevator door and watched them going higher oblivious to the woman who stood beside her. Her nerves were wrecked as she tried to prepare herself for the unknown. She got off the elevator and followed the room numbers as they increased, hating the hospital smell of medicines and disinfectants that filled the air. When she got to room 617, his name was scribbled across the door on a small dry marker board. She pushed the door open and walked in. Mitchell observed her as she approached him. Natalie was with him sitting in a chair next to the bed.

"Well look who decided to drop by," Natalie said, her mouth dripping with sarcasm.

Eva ignored her, put down her handbag, and leaned over the side of the bed. She squeezed Mitchell's left hand with one hand and rubbed him across the forehead with the other.

"What happened, honey, how are you?" she asked him tenderly.

"I'm not sure," Mitchell answered, somewhat confused. "I got up from the dinner table and my legs just gave out under me. I couldn't pull myself back up. Loretta had gone home for the day. I tried to call you but you didn't answer. Then I called Natalie to come over and she and Jonathan brought me here to the Emergency."

"I'm so sorry, dear," she said sympathetically, kissing him on the cheek. "I was at a dinner meeting with a client and had my phone on silent. Are you in any pain?"

"I wish I was, I can barely feel my legs," he said, looking down at them. "They just feel numb, like they're asleep."

"Have you talked to the doctors?" Eva asked, looking at Natalie.

"Not yet," Natalie told her. "They're going to monitor his vitals overnight and his doctor will be here in the morning after they run some more tests. Now that you're finally here I guess we can go home and get some rest."

Natalie stood up to give Mitchell a hug.

"Thanks, sweetheart," Mitchell said to her, "Where's Jonathan?"

"He's out in the waiting room," Natalie answered, putting on her jacket.

"Tell him I appreciate his helping out," Eva told her as she was leaving.

She scowled at Eva and said, "Call me, Daddy, if you need anything."

"Are you comfortable?" Eva asked Mitchell when the door closed.

"Yes, I'm fine. Don't worry about me," he replied. "I didn't mean to alarm you. I can see you're pretty disturbed."

"I didn't know what to expect."

"That chair over there leans all the way back. Go on and lay down, we both need to rest."

Eva sat down in the chair, let her feet up, and closed her eyes. She couldn't decide if she was relieved or disappointed with Mitchell being relatively okay. She didn't wish any harm to him but her life would be so much simpler if he would have dropped dead. She had feelings for him but he was no longer the man she married. She was starting to feel like a prisoner on lock-down and she wanted out.

***

The door swung open and Dr. Gannon, Mitchell's neurologist, swirled in like a tornado.

"Good morning Mr. Hamilton and Mrs. Hamilton I presume," he said, switching on the lights. "I want to discuss the results of the tests with you." He paused as Mitchell pushed the button on the railing that raised the head of the bed to a sitting position. Eva also sat up and lowered the lift on her chair. "The good news, Mr. Hamilton is that you did not suffer a heart attack or a stroke. Neurologically you're good too, there weren't any seizures."

"So what's going on with my legs?" Mitchell asked anxiously.

Dr. Gannon pulled back the sheets and examined his legs. "There has been noticeable deterioration in the amount of muscle tissue in your legs. Let's try some out-patient rehabilitation to see if we can strengthen what's there. In the meantime, as a precaution, I want you to use a wheelchair," he said, nodding towards the one in the corner of the room. "It's also a good idea to have safety rails and guards installed in your bathroom and shower. A bad fall can precipitate other problems that we need to avoid."

"Is there any reason for me to stay in here in the hospital?" Mitchell asked impatiently.

"I don't think you need to rush yourself," Eva interjected, feeling sorry for him, "Give it a day to be sure you're all right."

"Not at all, Mr. Hamilton, you can go home if you like," Dr. Gannon said supportively. "I don't blame you, with such a beautiful wife I wouldn't want to stay here either. The nurse will be in with your rehab schedule and your release papers in a little while."

"Thank you, doctor," Mitchell said.

"Take care," Dr. Gannon replied, shaking his hand and leaving as quickly as he had come in.

"That's what I thought. It's nothing they can do," Mitchell said, looking at the ceiling.

Eva got up and stood by the bed. "What can I do?" she asked sympathetically, "Can I get you anything?"

"Help me get dressed. There's no sense in me lying in this bed."

"Don't you think we ought to wait for the nurse?" Eva asked with concern.

"For what reason," he snapped, "She's not going home with us."

Eva sighed. "Do you want to take a shower?"

"No," he said curtly, "I'll clean up in my own bathroom when I get home."

Eva got his clothes out of the closet. He put on his undershirt and shirt by himself. She helped him into his boxers, put on his socks, and helped him put on his pants. He tied his tie and slid his arms into his suitcoat. When the nurse came in he was poised in the wheelchair and ready to roll.

The nurse went over some instructions from the doctor with them, gave him his schedule with the rehab clinic, and explained the terms of his release. She also gave them directions to Williams Supply where they would pick up Mitchell's wheelchair.

"Do either of you have any questions?" the nurse asked.

Eva shook her head and Mitchell said, "No, we'll be fine."

"Okay, you can bring your car around to the front entrance," the nurse said to Eva.

Eva put on a fake smile and said, "All right, I'll meet you all there in a few minutes."

Mitchell might have been eager to get home but Eva needed more time to get her mind wrapped around the situation. Driving out of the parking car garage she resisted an impulse to keep driving and never look back. When she circled into the hospital turnaround she could see the nurse standing behind Mitchell at the front entrance. She pulled up beside them, got out, and opened the front passenger side door. The nurse pushed the wheelchair close to the car and helped Mitchell get inside.

"Thank you for your help," Eva said, closing his door and going around to the driver's side.

The nurse waved goodbye. "You're welcome. Good luck to you."

It was only four blocks to William Supply Co. Mitchell insisted on waiting in the car while Eva went inside. Twenty minutes later she came out and popped the trunk for the representative who put the wheelchair in the back. Neither she nor Mitchell spoke on the ride home.

***

It was lunchtime when Eva parked the car at the front door of the house. She opened the trunk and pulled out the wheelchair. She spread it, unlocked it, and rolled it to the open car door. Mitchell stood up and then eased back down into the chair. Before Eva could do anything else, Natalie popped out of the front door, grabbed the handles, and pushed her father inside. Eva closed the car door and followed them in.

"Loretta has some lunch prepared for you, Daddy," Natalie said, pushing him into the dining room, "Have you eaten?"

"No we haven't," he answered, "I don't have a big appetite but I do want to take this opportunity to talk with you and Eva." Natalie was about to move his chair from the table when he said, "I'd rather sit in my chair, sweetheart, my legs aren't totally useless.

Natalie watched him protectively as he moved from the wheelchair to his chair at the head of the table. Then she took the seat next to him opposite of Eva. Loretta came in and filled the table with Cobb salad, clam chowder, and roast beef sandwiches.

"I'm glad to see you back home, sir," she said before she left the room.

Eva made a plate of food for Mitchell and then one for herself. She ate in silence paying no attention to the darts that Natalie's eyes were throwing in her direction. Mitchell finished his bowl of soup and took a few bites of his sandwich before he began to talk.

"Lately I've been detecting some tension between the two most important women in my life and that's not something I want to continue. It really disturbs me. I want us all to respect and care for one another, we are family."

"I apologize for my behavior, Daddy," Natalie said, "It is not my intention to upset you but there are reasons for my animosity towards Eva."

Eva stared back at Natalie and thought, "Who did she think she was coming for her?"

Mitchell rested his hand on top of Natalie's and said, "I love you dearly, sweetheart, and I appreciate your concern for me, however, Eva and I need some time and space to adjust to the new circumstances in our lives."

"I'll back up for your sake, Daddy," Natalie said, getting up from the table. Then she glared at Eva, "Trust and know that I'm not going to close my eyes and if you do anything to hurt my father I'm coming for you."

Eva smiled as she watched her plod out of the room. If Mitchell hadn't been there she would have shown that girl a side of her that she would regret seeing. She was definitely too deep in their personal business.

When Mitchell heard the door shut, he turned the conversation to Eva. "There are some important decisions for me to make at this point. I'm going to need your support while I figure these things out."

"You have that, Mitchell," Eva assured him, rubbing on his arm.

"Dr. Gannon has me scheduled for two weeks of daily physical therapy. I would like for you to be there with me. When it's over I think it would be a good time for us to get away."

Eva took a large gulp from her glass of lemonade to swallow the words in her mouth. There was some language there she was sure Mitchell didn't want to hear. Being that he had just gotten home from the hospital, he deserved some extra consideration.

"I know this is a very difficult time for you so I'll do my best to be there with you in physical therapy," she said carefully. "However, taking a vacation afterwards would be hard for me to manage. I have several irons in the fire that I can't leave right now."

"There's much we can't control in this life, Eva. What I'm grateful for is the good fortune that money is not an issue. I'm sure whatever you have going on it can wait. If you never sold another piece of property it wouldn't matter to me. I can provide for you."

"You're asking too much from me, Mitchell. You want me to push my business to the side and drop everything I'm doing."

"I'm your husband and you're my wife, in sickness and in health. That's what it means to be in a marriage. There was no way I could have known that I would be in the predicament I find myself in. If you were in my shoes I would do whatever you needed from me."

Eva had understood the terms of her marriage at the outset, but things had changed, and now it seemed like he was altering the agreement. She didn't know what he required of her or if she was able to fulfill his expectations.

"Let's take it one day at a time," she said, unwilling to agree to his requests. "This is a lot to absorb all at once."

Mitchell grabbed her left hand and squeezed it. Eva winced from the pain of her wedding ring pressing against her fingers.

"Certainly, my dear," he said lovingly, "That's all any of us can do."

***

Over the next week, Mitchell worked his agenda and kept Eva occupied at his side or behind him pushing his wheelchair. She detested every minute of it. In all her dreams and fantasies she had pictured herself with a handsome man, a wealthy man, a powerful man, even an older man, but never once had she imagined herself with a man in a wheelchair. At the end of the first week of physical therapy she was on the verge of losing her mind. She couldn't stand breathing the same air as Mitchell, morning, noon, and night. The only time she was out of his sight was in the bathroom. Behind that door she had sent numerous text messages to Earnest that he had not bothered to answer.

On the first day of his second week in therapy Eva excused herself and went out to take a walk across the street in Centennial Park. She found a picnic bench, sat down, and called Ernest.

"Hello," Rochelle rudely replied on the other end.

"Who is this?" Eva said, taken aback.

"Who are you trying to call," Rochelle snapped back.

"I'm trying to reach Ernest Shaw."

"Well this is Rochelle Shaw, his wife. What do you want?"

"I need to speak to him," Eva said with authority.

"Well you'll have to give him the message through me," Rochelle declared. "This is my phone now."

"Tell him to call Eva Hamilton; I need to speak with him about a business matter."

"I bet you do but you can forget about that," Rochelle said nastily. "You're messing with the wrong one. Your business with my husband is done, bitch. Go find another home to wreck before you wreck yourself."

Eva pressed the word end to hang up the call wishing she could literally slam the phone in Rochelle's country-ass face. She considered calling In Earnest but by now Mitchell would be looking for her. She hurried back across the street to the rehab clinic. She had one more week and then after that Mitchell would be off her back and she would let Ernest and his little wife know who the boss is.

***

Eva and Mitchell had both been stewing for two days. The fire under the pot was on high and the contents were about to boil over. She had been the dutiful wife and supported him as he requested. She had conducted her business by phone and computer from the house with the help of her agents. There wasn't any more she could do. Now that he was done with his physical therapy she was ready to get back to her life, and that's exactly what she planned to do after dinner. She took her shower and instead of joining Mitchell in their sitting room in her lounge wear, she put on some slacks and a light sweater with matching cardigan.

"Where are you going?" Mitchell asked when he saw her dressed.

"I'm going out," she said offhandedly.

Mitchell got angry. "I'd rather you didn't."

"I'm sorry about that, Mitchell, but I'm going. I'm not going to be held in this house like a prisoner anymore."

"You had lost your perspective, Eva. It was necessary for me to remind you that you are a married woman."

"Married is one thing, joined at the hip is another. I've got some business to take care of."

"So what priority do you have that is above caring for your husband?"

"I didn't sign up to be your caretaker. If I wanted to play nurse maid I would have had a baby. You have got to let me breathe."

"Is that what they're calling it now?" he asked, enraged. "You're jeopardizing our marriage for what, some wannabe. What's wrong with you? You're practically old enough to be his mother."

"And you're old enough to be my father," she countered back.

"There's only so much I will tolerate, Eva."

"That goes for the both of us," she said, storming out of the room.

Chapter Thirteen

The more than two weeks without Eva tracking him down had been a reprieve for Ernest. He had been able to concentrate on his businesses without any distractions. He had been able to spend time with his mama while she was at dialysis. He was beginning to feel at peace again. Rochelle was really trying hard to work things out at home. His crew at King Cut was beginning to accept his decision to open In Earnest. It was all good for a change, so good that he didn't notice the white Mercedes trailing him.

He had started going by King Cut at the end of day on Tuesdays to see how things were operating after he closed up the new shop. He didn't need to though, Leon was holding it down and it was running like clockwork. The truth was he missed working with them. They were like family.

The blinds were closed but he saw all their cars in the parking lot when he pulled in. Leon's car was in his old spot so he parked at the end of the row. When he got to the door he could see Leon was sweeping up so he tapped on the glass with his keys to get his attention.

"What's up, E," Leon said cheerfully, unlocking the door for him.

"It's all you," Ernest said, coming inside.

Jeff and Andrea were over in the waiting area playing Tonk for a dollar a game.

"There he is, big money," Jeff said, turning around and grinning. "Come on and play a few hands, put some of them cold greens on the table."

"I would but I don't feel like emptying your pockets tonight," Ernest joked.

"Leave him alone, Jeff, he got three rents and a mortgage to pay," Andrea said, teasing him.

"You got that right," Ernest added. "It ain't no joke."

"You'll be all right, E, you got a sweet spot over there," Leon said, emptying the dust pan of hair in the trash. "When the smoke clears you'll be on easy street."

Ernest nodded. "I've been trying to get there for a long time. I can't afford to make another wrong turn."

Then the bell on the door rang again. Leon hadn't locked it. They all turned to see who had come in. Eva stood there in the middle of the entrance waiting for Ernest to come over and give her a proper greeting. He hesitated, and then sighed, realizing his short winning streak had come to end. He drug his feet to the door while Leon, Jeff, and Andrea watched as if it was a dramatic scene from *12 Years a Slave*.

Eva spoke first. "You haven't been returning my calls again. I thought we were past that."

"Look, Eva, I'm a busy man. I've got family and a business to take care of. Why are you out here stalking me? What do you want?"

"You know damn well what I want?" she hissed.

He shook his head. "That's not happening."

"I invested a lot in you and this relationship."

"This wasn't a relationship," he said, wondering if she had lost her mind. "We fucked a few times, and now it's over.

We were just two people giving each other what they needed for a minute. No delusions about a future and no emotions involved."

"It's not that simple, lover," Eva smirked. "Don't you know I own you?"

"You're crazy, lady. Nobody owns me, not even my mama."

"For your information, lover, the deal you made was not only with Pinnacle Financial. Only half of the money was a loan. The line of credit came from me. I'm your partner, half owner of In Earnest."

Ernest closed his eyes to visualize the terms of the loan. He didn't see her name on the document. She had to be lying.

"I bought half of your loan from the bank," she said, seeing his confusion.

"I don't see how you could do that without me agreeing to that."

"Then let this be a lesson for you. Portions of loans are transferred every day without the borrower's permission. You'll be notified within 14 days."

Ernest stood there speechless, too pissed to speak. He had been played.

"I'd be happy to come by your house and explain things to your wife," Eva said, taunting him. "She didn't seem to know her place."

"No that's not going to happen," Ernest said, trying to keep from strangling her.

"Should I give her a call on the phone?" Eva asked haughtily.

"Eva, you're coming at me wrong right now and I promise you, you don't want to do that. You are not about to disrespect my home by calling my house. I'm not about to let you or anybody else destroy my family."

"All you have to do is give me what I want or give me my money," she said simply.

"Look, bitch," Jeff interrupted, walking over to them, "If you just need a good fuck I can take care of you. You don't need to come around here going off on nobody."

"Say the word, E, and I'll beat her ass down, right here right now," Andrea said, taking off her earrings and coming towards them.

"I got this," Ernest said, holding up his arm.

"Think about it and call me," Eva said, turning to leave. "And I don't enjoy waiting."

Leon locked the door as soon as she was out. "That broad is out of her mind," he said, watching Eva walk to her car.

Andrea went back to the table and picked up her cards. "I don't know what you did to her, E, but it got her running around the hood in the dark about to get an ass-whooping."

"Ain't this some shit," Jeff said, sitting down and picking up his hand, "I thought you said you were leaving all the drama. It looks like you the one bringing it back in here."

Ernest didn't respond. What could he say? Jeff was right.

***

Mitchell got up early, dressed for work, and called his driver. It was a new day and it was more than a bright sun that had opened his eyes. Eva's cruel words had made it clear that closing the door to the outside world hadn't solved his problem. In fact, isolating her had only aggravated the situation. He didn't get where he was by avoiding the competition, he faced them head on, and that's exactly what he planned to do today. He ate the light breakfast that Loretta had prepared for him, wheeled himself out to the car with his new chair, and gave his driver the address.

From the tinted window in the back he gazed at the line of cars in traffic and wondered if all the rushing ever got anybody to the place where they were totally happy. At this point in his life he was beginning to believe that complete happiness didn't exist. When he'd first met Eva he thought that they could be happy together. Over the years they had shared many good times. Yet, when the see-saw of life brought him down as an older man he never thought it would come to this. She was openly humiliating him and he couldn't fight back. Why kick a man when he's down. The time when he could have let her go and have her easily replaced by another was past.

The car stopped and his driver got out and helped him back into his wheelchair. Mitchell paused outside and gazed at the façade of In Earnest Gentlemen's Spa. It was stylish and contemporary. Someone coming out opened the entrance door and held it open for him. He thanked them for their kind gesture and rolled himself inside up to the receptionist's desk.

"How may we help you today?" Carla asked, greeting him with a smile.

"I'm not quite sure," Mitchell responded, "I'd like to talk with the proprietor first."

"No problem, you can wait here and Mr. Shaw will be with you shortly."

"Thank you, miss," Mitchell said, rolling his chair to the end of her desk.

Mitchell was in full view of the barbers. He would have known who Ernest was even if the other barber were not a white female. There was no mystery as to why Eva would be attracted to him; he was handsome, fit and well-built. The question was the unusual effect he had on her. Mitchell had been able to tolerate her other dalliances but this man was different. He continued to stare at Ernest as he worked. He had to admit he was skillful, working similar to an artist as his hands and his tools seemed to become one. In a way he reminded Mitchell of himself when he was a younger man, strong, confident, and invincible. He too had conquered his share of beautiful women.

Tired of looking at the man who had taken over his wife, Mitchell stared down at his legs pensively. Nobody had prepared him to grow old and feeble. No one had told him that you explode in your prime like a flash of light and then you quietly fade out of it. It was only a few months ago that he stood sturdy and steadfast on his own feet. Then he would have walked over to Ernest and confronted him face to face.

His pulse started to race when he saw Ernest walking towards him.

"What services can we provide for you today, sir?" Ernest asked him graciously.

Mitchell answered him in a hushed tone. "Can we speak in private?"

"Absolutely," Ernest said, thinking it must have something to with his handicap. "We can talk in my office." He wasn't sure if he should assist the gentleman so he walked at a slower pace for him to follow. "I'm sure we can accommodate any special needs that you may have," Ernest said once they were in his office.

"I hope so," Mitchell said, looking at him. "I'm interested in what you have to offer."

"We can do whatever you need, sir, massage, manicure, or pedicure. I can personally start you off with a cut and shave."

Mitchell leaned his elbows on his chair and folded his hands. "Mr. Shaw, what I really need is for you to stop providing services for my wife."

Ernest had a moment of confusion but it passed quickly as he assessed the situation. He slowly, one inch at a time, backed away from Mitchell and eased down into his chair with his hand on his straight razor. He didn't know what this man was capable of and he didn't want to have to hurt him.

"It's possible that you have me confused with someone else," Ernest said.

"I'm Mitchell Hamilton, Eva is my wife."

"How can I help you, sir?" Earnest asked, unsure of how he should respond.

"As I said before, I want you to stop seeing her."

"Mr. Hamilton, I'm not going to insult your intelligence and lie to you. The mere fact that you are here says that you are aware of some dealings that your wife and I may have had. I want to assure you that you don't have me to worry about. The association between us has concluded."

"From where I sit, I have a hard time believing that. She's seems to be very involved with you."

"Sir, I have a wife and children of my own. The only connection I have with Eva now is purely business. Anything else was a mistake that won't be repeated. I can promise you that."

"That's all I came to hear," Mitchell said, pushing the lever on his wheelchair and rolling out the open door of the office.

Ernest reached for the bottle of Hennessey in his desk. He had gotten himself in some off-the-wall situations in his life but this one was driving him to drink.

Chapter
Fourteen

Ernest sat tapping his fingers on the counter at the bar in Sambuca Restaurant. The vibrations made small waves in his drink while he waited for Vince to meet him there. His right foot soon joined in the rhythm as it bounced against the rung of his stool. Ernest was deep in thought, straining his brain for a way to come up with the money to pay Eva back. If he were to be really honest with himself, he would have to admit that he knew from the beginning that the deal with Eva was suspect. At the time he didn't care about the consequences because as far as he was concerned it was his way out of no way. Old folks always say be careful what you ask for because you don't know who might give it to you. Needless to say he had a major disaster on his hands. In his world, a storm had raged, the earth had shaken, and fires had burned. Now it was time for damage control.

He looked down at his watch. It was after seven o' clock. He and Rochelle were on better terms for the time being so he made a quick call to keep it that way.

"Hey, babe," he said after she answered, "I'm going to catch up with Vince tonight before I stop by my mama's. I need to see where I can raise some money."

She sighed heavily. "All right, do whatever you have to do to cut ties with that crazy bitch. I'm not trying to go to jail over this mess."

"I don't want you to worry about this. I'll take care of it. Keep thinking pleasant thoughts about you and me, and the kids."

She laughed. "I will, at the same time I'm loading my gun."

Ernest saw Vince walk in the door. "Okay, babe," he chuckled, "I'll see you later."

"What's going on, man?" Vince said, bumping fists as he sat down.

The bartender came over. "What can I get for you?"

"The same," Vince said, motioning towards Ernest's glass.

"I need to make something happen real quick," Ernest said urgently, "I've got to get in some of those high stakes games you know about. Poker or black jack, it doesn't matter. "

Vince's brow wrinkled with concern. "You having money problems, bro, what's up?"

"It's my problem. I just need you to get me in a game," Ernest said, shrugging his shoulders.

"You don't get in those games, man, not unless you can afford to lose."

"I won't lose, I can't lose."

"You don't know that, E. Everybody's playing to win."

"I don't have a choice," Ernest answered hopelessly.

"Yeah, you do. We go way back, E. You covered for me many times and I'll do the same for you. Whatever you need, I got you."

The bartender returned with Vince's drink. Vince gave him a twenty dollar bill and told him to keep the change. Then he took a big swallow and waited.

Ernest exhaled and leaned back against the barstool. "It's about the loan for the new shop. Eva owns half of it. She's sweating me and I need to get her off my back."

"I thought you had her playing for your team."

"I don't know what the fuck is going on, man. I've been with some thirsty chicks but this is over the top."

"She's a freak, man. What's so bad about that?"

"I regret the whole thing now, but I got to tell you, she was hot. She's out of her mind though. I thought the situation with her was bad enough and then her husband came by the shop today."

"Oh shit, that's deep," Vince said, taking another swallow of his drink.

"At first I thought it was gonna get real ugly. The dude was in a wheelchair."

Vince laughed. "Man, I can see you on the news now; barber kills man in wheelchair with straight razor after sleeping with his wife."

"That's not even funny," Ernest said, keeping a straight face. "He was cool though, asked me to leave her alone. I let him know that was not a problem for me."

"So how much is it gonna cost to get her off your jock?"

"About 250K."

"When do you want it?" Vince asked without hesitation.

"By the end the week."

"Consider it done."

"Thanks, man. I'll get it back to you," Ernest said, shaking his hand in gratitude.

"No worries. Now can a man get another drink in this place?" Vince asked signaling the bartender.

***

Sheila was sitting in the living room watching TV with Buttons in her lap when Ernest came by to check on her. He bent over and kissed her on the cheek like he always did.

"You're out late," Sheila said, patting the seat on the sofa beside her.

"I'm on my way in," he said, sitting beside her. "I just stopped by for a minute to make sure you're doing okay."

"I'm hanging in there. How about you?" she asked, looking deep in his face for any hint of a problem.

"Working nonstop but I'm not complaining."

"That's good," she said, stroking Button's head. "I've been missing my grandkids. I haven't seen them in more than a week."

"I'll pick you up on Sunday. We'll go to church together and then get something to eat."

"All right then, I'll look forward to that," Sheila said, grinning with relief. "Things must be better between you and Rochelle."

"Yeah, they are. We're doing good."

"That's good to hear. Don't mess it up, Ernest."

"I won't," he said, staring toward the TV.

"So, how is that friend of yours doing who got mixed up with that woman?" Sheila asked, sensing something else was on his mind.

"She turned into some kind of fatal attraction. She was blowing up his phone, stalking him, and now she's threatening to shut him down if he won't keep giving her the sex or pay her back the money she loaned him."

"Sounds like he's between a rock and a hard place," Sheila said, shaking her head. "What's he going to do?"

"He's got it under control. He's going to get the money he owes her from a friend."

"Uh-huh, I feel sorry for him. It's a tough lesson to learn. You don't get something for nothing in this world no matter who you are."

"It'll be in his past before the week is out."

"Maybe, maybe not. If she's used to getting what she wants she won't let it go so easy. You can't tear a piece of meat from a hungry dog without a fight. Ain't that right, Buttons," she said petting the top of her dog's head.

"It's not that serious, Mama. When she gets her money back she can buy some more meat."

"I hope you're right for his sake," Sheila said, looking back at the TV.

Ernest stood up. "He's got it under control."

"All right, well, go on home before you get Rochelle riled up again."

"Okay, Mama, I'm out. I love you," he said, kissing her forehead.

She reached for his hand, squeezed it, and let it go. "You're my heart, Ernest."

***

On Thursday, Vince had come through with the money like he said. On Friday morning Ernest had the cashier's check. He called Eva and asked her to meet him for dinner at Ruth Kris. He thought about asking her to come by In Earnest but it wasn't his style to have a bunch of folks in his business and private affairs. What he wanted was a public place to discourage her from making any kind of scene. He thought the restaurant was a fitting choice because that was where they started out on this venture or misadventure. That was where it should end, bringing them full circle where he could get off this crazy merry-go-round/roller coaster ride.

Eva, on the other hand was on a whole other vibe. She thought the invitation was him coming to his senses and realizing that she was the partner he needed in business and in bed. She had planned to arrive at the restaurant early where she could get a cocktail to relax before he got there. Instead, she was surprised to see him already seated at the bar nursing a drink.

"You've got a head start," she said, slowly rubbing his back. "You'll have to give me a chance to catch up."

"Our table is ready," he said, standing up. "We'll sit down, get you a drink, relax, eat, and clear the air."

Eva smiled, "The beginnings of a lovely evening."

At the table Ernest pulled out a chair for her to sit and then sat across from her. He avoided eye contact by keeping his eye on the waiter until he came over to the table.

"Can I start you off with something to drink?" the waiter asked, glancing back and forth between them.

"I'm good, the lady will have a merlot," Ernest said dryly.

The waiter nodded and left the table.

"I'm really glad you called," Eva said pleasantly, "You had me worried for a minute."

"No worries," Ernest said, looking down at his hands. "Things went a little left field between us and that wasn't my intention. I have to give you props for helping me get the loan to move forward on opening the spa."

"I believed in your vision," Eva said, reaching across the table to touch his hand.

Ernest eased his hands back and said, "I want to thank you for everything you've done and repay you for the portion of the loan that you personally put up through Hamilton Realty."

Eva bristled and shifted in her chair. "Wait a minute. Are you trying to buy me out?"

"It's me returning your money," he said calmly, "Things got out of hand and I think it's best we settle our business on good terms."

"Oh hell no," Eva shouted, pounding her fist on the table just when the waiter came back with the wine. "You're not about to brush me off like a piece of dirt."

The waiter put down the glass and the bottle and rushed away from the table.

Still calm, Ernest said, "I'm doing what you asked, Eva. I'm giving you your money back."

"That's not what I wanted," Eva said, sounding hurt. "You can keep the money. I want us to be together. I want you to leave your wife. I'll leave my husband."

"I'm sorry," he said, trying to sooth her, "That can't happen."

"We can do whatever we want," she said desperately, "Come out to the house with me. I'll make you forget you have a wife. She's basic and boring. You and I think alike."

Ernest shook his head weary of the conversation. No matter what he said, she didn't get it. He didn't know what to say to get through to her.

So he told her, "Your husband came to see me."

Eva was taken aback for a moment. "What are you talking about?"

"He asked me to stop seeing you. It's the best thing for us to do. We both have a lot to lose. Take the check and move on."

"There's something else you need to know," Eva said haughtily, ripping up the check. "This doesn't end until I say so. I may only own half of In Earnest but I own the entire building you're leasing. Franklin Property Management Company manages several properties for me. I can close you down with one word whenever I choose to do so."

"I have a lease agreement and it is legit," Ernest argued back.

"Not if I decide to sell the building and I won't stop there. I'll destroy that pitiful family of yours before I'm done."

"You're crazy bitch, I'll kill you first," Ernest shouted at her.

All the eyes in the restaurant were fixed on their table.

The manager, already alerted by the waiter of the volatile situation was heading over to them.

"Is everything okay?" the manager asked in a hushed voice.

"Why are you making me act like this?" Eva begged, ignoring the manager, "All I want is to be with you."

Ernest didn't respond. He got up from the table with so much force that he knocked his chair over onto the floor and stormed out with the whole room staring at him.

Eva was angry too, but not at Ernest. She was blaming Mitchell for coming between them. Her mind was made up, her marriage was over. As much as she wanted to run out of the restaurant after Ernest to make him listen to reason, somebody else had moved to the top of her list. She placed a fifty dollar bill on the table, checked her face in her make-up mirror, reapplied her lipstick, and then coolly strutted out of Ruth Kris and handed the valet her ticket.

***

Eva didn't care that Natalie was there when she marched into Mitchell's study after she got home. There weren't any more secrets to keep among them at this point. Seeing her enraged face, Natalie moved from the leather couch where she was reading a magazine to stand protectively beside her father.

"Have you been following me?" Eva demanded, staring down at Mitchell behind his desk.

"Yes I have," he answered simply.

"How dare you put a tab on me like I'm some child," she protested.

"Possibly because you were behaving as irresponsibly as a child," he replied.

"I'm no child, I'm a grown woman. I don't need you or anybody else tracking me down and inserting themselves in my business."

"I respect your business affairs, Eva, but what you were doing with that barber doesn't meet the qualifications."

"You can't judge me, Mitchell, your record isn't clean," Eva retorted, "You're pathetic, trying to control somebody when you've lost control of yourself."

"No, my dear, that's what has happened to you. At first you were embarrassing me, now you're embarrassing yourself."

"What happened, Eva?" Natalie added with a smirk. "Did he give you your walking papers?"

"He couldn't if he wanted to," Eva snapped back.

"Well, well, well," Natalie said, mocking her, "I'm shocked. Someone actually penetrated that Teflon exterior. Now you can taste the bitterness of rejection for yourself."

The confrontation was making Eva more enraged. It was a good thing she didn't have a weapon or both of them would be lying on the floor.

"I refuse to stay here another night, I'm done," Eva yelled, "I'm tired of pretending."

"Good riddance," Natalie said, happy to hear it.

"Eva, if you walk out that door you'll be sorry," Mitchell said. "Don't make me do something I don't want to do."

"Like what, you're so weak I could probably kill you with my bare hands," Eva spat at him. "I won't even waste my time. You're already half-dead."

Then she turned to leave. Natalie started to charge towards her but Mitchell grabbed her by the arm.

"Let her go," he said coolly, "I'll handle this."

"Get rid of her, Daddy. You don't have to give her anything. She's not giving you anything."

For Mitchell, it wasn't about love or money anymore. This was a contest of wills and he didn't like to lose.

"In due time, sweetheart," he said, pondering his next move.

***

Ernest was too fired up to go home. In his experience anger was contagious and he didn't want to pass this on to Rochelle. He drove down Buchanan Street to King Cut. He was drawn to it, the simplicity of the rules in the hood. "Don't start nothing, won't be nothing. If you start it, I'll finish it." That was his frame of mind. He wanted to change it but he couldn't. He didn't want to do wrong but what alternative did he have? Why was it always kill or be killed? Why was it every time a black man tries to take a step forward, somebody is there to either push him back or pull him back.

Leon was in the barber shop sweeping up as usual. He saw Ernest pull in and unlocked the door for him to come in.

"From the look on your face I'm afraid to ask," Leon said as Ernest walked past him in the doorway, "Have you done it or about to do it?"

"Not yet but I don't see a way around it," Ernest said, dropping down in his barber chair.

"What exactly are we talking about here?" Leon asked, facing him.

"That fucking bitch won't let go. She's gonna make me cut her loose for real, man."

"Slow up, E," Leon said, leaning the broom against the wall and getting a liquor bottle from the bottom drawer of his work station. He poured Ernest a shot into a paper cup from the water cooler. "Let's think about this."

"There's nothing to think about," Ernest said, emptying the cup, "She wants to take everything I got from me, shut down the spa, and break up my family."

Leon was grateful that Ernest's cell phone rang. He needed a minute to text Vince and get his own thoughts together.

It was Sheila calling. Her left eye was jumping. That only

happened when her son was in some kind of trouble. It was a warning sign.

"Hey, Mama," Ernest asked, worried. "You okay, you need anything?"

"No, I'm all right. I just thought I was going to see you today."

"I wanted to get over to the clinic this morning but Friday is our busiest day."

"Where are you?" she asked, worried.

"At King Cut with Leon."

"Are you coming by here later?"

"No, I'll probably go on home in a few."

"Okay, son, don't stay out too late."

"I won't. I'll be over there in the morning. Love you, Mama."

"You're my heart, Ernest," she said before she hung up.

"Thanks for the shot, man," Ernest said, standing up. "I got to go."

"Listen, Ernest. If you need something done about your problem, let me know. You don't need to get your hands dirty. You got mouths to feed and your mama to take care of."

"It's my problem, I'll handle it."

Leon watched him drive off. He stood in the door long after the sound of the car engine had trailed off. He was still standing there when Vince got there. He told Vince that Ernest looked like his back was against the wall. Vince got back in his car and called him on the phone.

"Where are you, E?" he asked, trying not to sound concerned.

"Nowhere, man."

"So what happened?"

"She didn't want the money. She wants to fuck me over."

"Go home, E. I'm down for you. Don't worry about it. I

can take care of it."

"I'm past worrying about it, man."

"Let me do this for you, bro."

"It's not worth it, man. I don't want nobody cleaning up my mess but me."

***

Eva relaxed in the Jacuzzi of her suite at the Renaissance Hotel. Finally leaving Mitchell was a burden off her mind, she could breathe again. She had been smothered for so long. She should have done it sooner. No longer his captive bird she would be able to fly again. She had her freedom. She and Ernest could be together after all. When she got his text message she was relieved and content. She had fought him hard, used every advantage, broken all the rules, but now she was victorious. When he got there she would make him forget all the arguments and harsh words that had been spoken.

Under the luxurious bubbles of the hot water all the tensions of the week seeped out from her pores with any other impurities, leaving her refreshed. She closed her eyes and leaned her head back against the edge of the tub. She rubbed her hands along her body, from her breasts to the heat between her legs, thinking of the night to come, and imagining his touch. She smiled mischievously to herself when she heard her hotel door open. She was already near her climax.

Fifteen

A staid police officer stood outside the luxury hotel suite door with the hysterical housekeeper and the panic-stricken hotel manager. Inside, the suite buzzed with commotion as crime scene investigators searched every inch of the room, lifted fingerprints, and photographed the victim as the scene was processed. The medical examiner gently shifted the body to determine the preliminary cause of death. It was a gruesome sight, a horror you might see staged in a haunted house. A gaping wound, trails of blood, and a body submerged in a bath of blood.

A black male accompanied by a white female, both wearing badges, exited the elevator on the penthouse floor and approached the suite. The hotel manager, who looked like Barney Fife and was just as nervous, was doing his best to calm down the crying housekeeper.

The black male nodded to the officer and then spoke to the hotel manager.

"Hello, sir, this is Detective Meyers and I'm Detective Wilson," he informed them. "We're the investigators assigned to this case. A few things we need to know at the start is who was the person that found the body."

"My name is Bob Beasley, and this is Anna, one of our housekeepers, she found the body," the hotel manager replied, pointing to the woman heaving in his arms. "She came in to clean the room this morning, walked in the bathroom and saw her there. She started screaming and a guest across the hall heard the uproar and called the front desk. I called 911 before I came up."

"Do you know who the victim is?" Dt. Meyers asked, pulling a small writing tablet out of her pocket to take notes.

"Her name is Eva Hamilton," the hotel manager said, "She checked in last night without a reservation, said she would be here for an indefinite stay, and wanted one of the top suites."

"Looks like her stay is going to be a lot shorter than she thought," Wilson said, "Was she a regular at this hotel?"

"No, I don't remember seeing her before," Beasley answered, shaking his head.

"Do you know if she came in alone?" Dt. Meyers asked as she quickly wrote notes.

"The front desk said she was alone," Beasley said, "She registered for the room in only her name, but this is a hotel not a prison, we can't say who came to visit her. However, she did request two room keys."

"Do you know if she went into the hotel bar?" Wilson asked, wondering if she met someone there.

"No, she went straight up to her room as far as we know?" the hotel manager said.

"She was definitely expecting company," Wilson added, thinking about the second room key.

"Have you checked the surveillance camera in the lobby?" Meyers asked, still writing.

"We've only had time for a quick check," Beasley answered.

"From your first glance, did it show anyone suspicious or out of place?" Meyers asked.

"There wasn't anyone on it who wasn't a registered guest," Beasley said hurriedly. "I hope we can wrap this up as quietly as possible. We have two conventions this weekend and this kind of business would be a bit unsavory for our arriving guests."

"We'll try to be out of your hair before long but this isn't something you can keep quiet from the media," Meyers told him as she and Wilson entered the hotel room.

***

Dt. Rodney Wilson and Dt. Megan Meyers have been partners with the Nashville Police Department for six years. Each had persistently climbed the rickety ladder of promotions to become detectives. Wilson, because he thought it barbaric to go around town ready to shoot somebody at the drop of a hat, and Megan, because it was all about the Benjamin's and higher rank. Their initial loathing of each other gradually transformed over the years into a working relationship built on trust, respect, and tolerance. More like family than friends, they were the domineering older brother and competing younger sister who would have never associated if nature had not thrust them together.

Rodney was a tall dark-skinned black man with the beginnings of a receding hairline. He always wore a suit and tie, and the cliché detective trench coat in the fall and winter months. With thick glasses and an overbite that stuck out so far he couldn't close his mouth, he was the quintessential nerd in school who knew all the answers. He'd grown up in a middle-class family, graduated from college with a degree in criminal justice, and married the girl two doors down before he applied to the Metro Nashville Police Department. He scored exceptionally high on the Civil Service Exam and joined the force in 1991. He divorced when he was still in his blues, his marriage being the first casualty of his career in law enforcement, after which he decided there was no room on the ladder of success for a wife. He continued to test high to move his way up through the ranks of the department.

Megan was a rough-around-the-edges tough white girl. Average height with dirty blonde hair and pale blue eyes, she was considered attractive, but was more of a tomboy than a cheerleader. She was always in blue jeans that she dressed up with button down shirts and blazers. Raised poor in a trailer park, her way out of that dead end was joining the military after high school. She applied to the police academy after her second tour in Iraq. She studied her ass off but her scores on the exam to make detective were marginal. The reward for being a hard ass patrolling the housing projects for several years gave her the extra boost she needed to make the cut. She was single, never married, although not by choice. Her biggest challenge was finding a guy who was more of a man than she was.

***

The processing of the crime scene was almost complete when Wilson and Meyers walked in. With all the forensic evidence retrieved the medical examiner, Sy Altman, was preparing to remove the body.

"How's it going, Sy?" Wilson asked, coming in to view the murder scene.

"All in a day's work," Sy answered.

Side by side in the bathroom, only a few feet from the body, the detectives watched as the level of the bloody water slowly receded in the bath tub.

"She's gorgeous," Dt. Wilson said, morbidly admiring the body. "If I would have met her last night none of this would have gone down."

"She looks high maintenance," Dt. Meyers said, taking

notice of her styled hair, flawless make-up, and manicured nails.

"That's what money will do for you," one of the CSI team interjected, handing Dt. Wilson her wallet and ID. "She's married to Mitchell Hamilton, a high society banker at Pinnacle Financial."

Dt. Wilson chuckled. "With a body like that he should have kept her on a short leash."

"You're sick, Rodney, the woman is dead," Meyers said, frowning at him.

"So what do we got, Sy?" Wilson asked the medical examiner, ignoring her remark.

"From what I can tell it was one single cut to the carotid artery with a sharp narrow blade by a right-handed perp and she bled out."

"I can't believe there's no sign of a struggle," Meyers commented at the passive position of the body. "Could it be a suicide?"

"No way," Sy said, "It's a homicide, and they left with the murder weapon."

"She obviously didn't see it coming from the smile frozen on her face," Wilson said.

"What is your estimate about the time of death?" Meyers asked Sy.

Sy stepped back and watched as two of his crew lifted the body out of the tub.

"Rigor is already decreasing so I would say between ten and twelve hours," he said.

"So you're saying between 11:00 and 1:00 roughly," Meyers said, making a note of it on her notepad.

"Pretty much, we'll know more when I get the contents of the stomach and after the toxicology report," Sy said, motioning for his crew to zip up the body bag.

Dt. Wilson walked out of the bathroom into the bedroom followed by his partner.

"The room looks clean," he told her, "Everything is still in its place, her purse, money, credit cards, and jewelry. We can rule out a robbery. There's no doubt she knew the killer."

"Why are you so sure that she knew who it was?" Megan asked, interested.

"Either she didn't hear the culprit or she knew they were in the room and she was comfortable with that. She didn't even splash water on the bathroom floor."

Wilson squinted his eyes as they traveled around the room again looking for something out of place, a shadow, anything, but there was nothing. Meyers watched him and waited. Then she jerked her head to one side signaling Wilson to follow her.

"Time to go drop this bomb on Mr. Hamilton," she said.

Wilson nodded. "Being that he's not here and she planned to stay for a while, this probably won't be the first bomb dropped on him lately."

***

The detectives pulled up to the address on the victim's driver's license just before noon.

"That hotel suite was nice but I don't think I would leave this place to stay there," Meyers said, looking at the grandness of the Hamilton Estate.

"She probably had her reasons and they probably got her killed," Wilson said offhandedly, parking their car in the turnaround.

Meyers rang the doorbell peering through the glass, a Latina woman wearing a light blue uniform dress and flowered apron approached the door.

"May I help you?" Loretta asked guardedly when she opened the door, wondering who they were and what they wanted. The fact that she was an illegal always made her nervous when strangers came knocking.

"Yes," Wilson responded, "I'm Dt. Wilson and this is Dt. Meyers, we're with the Nashville Police Department. We would like to speak with Mr. Mitchell Hamilton."

"Please, come in," Loretta said avoiding eye contact and widening the narrow space between the door for them to step inside. She led them to the living room. "Just one moment, wait here," she said, leaving them there. She hurried into the dining room where Mitchell and Natalie were about to have lunch. "Mr. Hamilton, there are two detectives here to see you," she said anxiously, interrupting their conversation.

"What is this about?" he asked her suspiciously.

"I don't know, sir, they're waiting in the living room," she answered, worried.

Mitchell got up from the table and sat in his wheelchair. Then Natalie rushed over to him.

"Relax, Daddy," she said as she took the back handles of the chair and pushed him out of the dining room. Loretta followed close behind them.

"I'm Mitchell Hamilton," he said to the detectives as they entered the living room.

Both Wilson and Meyers were surprised to see the older wheelchair bound man come into the room.

"Hello there, Mr. Hamilton," Wilson said, "I'm Detective Wilson and this is my partner, Detective Meyers. Unfortunately, we are here with bad news for you, sir. I'm sorry to have to tell you that your wife, Eva Hamilton, was killed last night."

Mitchell's body went limp as if his backbone had been snatched away. If he wasn't sitting in the wheelchair he may have fallen to the ground. Natalie's face showed no expression at all as she held on tight to the wheelchair handles.

Loretta standing behind them screamed, "Oh my God," and covered her mouth.

"What happened to her?" Mitchell asked solemnly, gazing down at the intricate design of the rug underneath him.

"She was found in a bath tub at the Renaissance Hotel with her throat cut," Meyers said.

"Do you know who is responsible?" he asked, looking up at them. "Was this a robbery?"

"No, we don't know who did it, and nothing was taken," Wilson answered. "I know it's a bad time for you but we need to ask you some questions."

"You'll have to come back another time," Natalie protested, "Can't you see my father is ill."

"I'm sorry but the sooner we get through this the sooner we can catch the person who killed your mother," Meyers insisted.

"She wasn't my mother," Natalie spat out like she was insulted.

"Please excuse my daughter," Mitchell interrupted, "She's very protective of me. I'll answer your questions. I want to help find whoever did this awful thing to my wife."

Loretta fidgeted behind them. "Can I get you all something to drink, coffee, water, or anything?" she asked, searching for a reason to leave the room.

"Coffee would be great," Wilson said. "What I'd like to do is talk to Mr. Hamilton alone. Dt. Meyers will get any other information you two might have."

Natalie hesitated feeling they didn't have any right to tell her where to go in her house.

"It's all right, Natalie dear, I'm fine," Mitchell said to get her to acquiesce.

Natalie was not happy about the request but she left the room without any complaints and went back to the dining room. She sat down at the table and continued to eat the salad that she had started on as if nothing had happened. Dt. Meyer joined her at the table while Loretta got the coffee for Mitchell and Dt. Wilson. A minute later with the tray of coffee in her hand, Loretta hurried back into the living room. She sat the tray down on the table between Mitchell and Wilson, left hastily, passed through the dining room, and went back into the kitchen.

"I gather you weren't very fond of your stepmother," Meyers said to Natalie.

Natalie finished crunching on a crouton before she answered. She didn't know why this no-class white woman was disturbing her lunch, it was totally disrespectful.

"You're right, I never liked her," Natalie said, sipping from a glass of mint tea.

"Why not?" Meyers asked frankly, observing Natalie and thinking she might have had a reason to want to see the victim dead.

"She wasn't loyal and she thought too much of herself."

"By that do you mean she was unfaithful to your father?"

"She was a whore," Natalie blurted out.

"Strong language," Meyers said, surprised at her candidness.

"I'm sure you've heard worse in your line of business, detective."

"Would you know of anyone who would want to hurt your step-mother?" Meyers asked.

"Nobody, except for maybe a jealous girlfriend or wife," Natalie said sarcastically.

"Just for the record, Miss Hamilton, where were you last night?"

"I was here having dinner with my father when Eva came in. She said she was tired of being saddled with a cripple and then she left. I stayed here until my father went to bed, then I went by a friend's apartment where I spent the night."

"You mind if I ask the name of your friend?" Meyers asked, jotting notes in her tablet.

"I do," Natalie replied defiantly, "His name is Jonathan Ross."

"Sorry for the inconvenience," Meyers said, frowning.

Natalie ignored her. She couldn't stand white women who thought the world revolved around them.

***

"This is good coffee, thank you," Wilson said after taking a big gulp. "I know this might sound inappropriate right now but this is a very beautiful home that you have out here." Mitchell nodded but didn't respond. "I don't mean to be blunt, sir, but did your wife have any enemies that would have wanted to kill her?"

"None that I know of," Mitchell said, rubbing his forehead. "However, she was a shrewd business woman which always creates competition and jealousies."

"Are there any rivalries with other companies or employees at her company that may have an ax to grind?"

Mitchell shook his head. "None that she discussed with me."

"When was the last time you saw your wife, Mr. Hamilton?"

"Last evening, she left after dinner."

"Did she say where she was going?"

"No she didn't."

"How long were you and your wife married?"

"Almost eight years," Mitchell answered, reflecting back.

Wilson paused for a moment. "I hope you don't mind my asking but were you in the wheelchair when you met?"

"No I wasn't. I was diagnosed with a degenerative disease

about a year ago; my legs began weakening more in the last six months."

"Did your illness create problems in your marriage, like in the bedroom?" Wilson asked, less from a formal inquiry standpoint but more to satisfy his crude curiosity. "I couldn't help but notice how attractive she was."

"Are you married, detective?"

"I'm divorced, sir."

"I'm sure that wasn't only because of problems in the bedroom," Mitchell said, defensively. "The only thing you need to know is that my wife and I were very much in love."

Wilson volleyed back. "If that's true, why was she spending the night in a hotel room?"

"We had an argument last night. She left to cool off."

"I don't mean to be rude but the way it looked to me she was trying to heat things up with somebody else. Do you know who that person might have been?"

"I wouldn't know anything about that, detective."

"Please understand, Mr. Hamilton, I have to ask if you were home all evening after the argument with your wife?"

"Yes I was, my housekeeper, Loretta, can verify that."

"Did your wife have any close friends that we can talk to?"

"Not really, she wasn't what you would call a social butterfly; she was more of a workaholic."

"Thank you, sir, for your cooperation at a time like this. I'm truly sorry for your loss."

"Thank you, detective," Mitchell said, rolling his chair away towards the huge picture window.

Wilson drained his cup of coffee and went back towards the dining room to join Meyers. She met him in the hallway on her way out. Loretta lingered at the side kitchen door while they whispered back and forth between themselves.

"I don't think we'll get any more info here today," Wilson said, "We can get more of the story from the housekeeper at the station. I doubt if she'll have much to say with them looking down her throat."

"We'll be leaving now," Meyers said turning back to Loretta.

She moved ahead of them through the foyer to show them to the door.

Wilson handed her one of his cards when she opened the door. "We'll be in touch. Feel free to call us if there's anything you know that can help us find Mrs. Hamilton's killer."

"I don't know anything," Loretta said, closing the door behind them.

Chapter Sixteen

"Well Megan, looks like your nine-times-out-of-ten theory about the jealous husband being the killer won't hold water this time," Wilson said once they were in the car. "I don't think he could pull it off running around in that wheelchair."

"I said there is always one exception but don't cross him off the list too fast," Meyers smirked, "I'll bet you twenty dollars he still had something to do with it."

"I don't mind taking your money," he chuckled. "You've got your wires crossed if you think he could have rolled up on her without her knowing it."

"Where there's a will there's a way. Besides, the daughter said our lady wasn't keeping it all in the family; she liked to spread it around. Rule number one: when you find a motive you find the killer, and that's enough of a motive."

"Don't hate on our lady. With a body like that what was she supposed to do with a crippled husband? I can't blame her if she tipped out every now and then. It's too bad we couldn't have met under better circumstances. She'd be cooling it at my house instead of the morgue."

"Stop your fantasy, Rodney, the marriage vows say in sickness and in health."

"You're the one who needs a dose of reality. Things change for one or both in a marriage and then it's over. There's no such thing as happily ever after."

"Just because you never found it doesn't mean it doesn't exit."

Wilson rolled his eyes up in his head. "Which one do you want me to pull out for you, Megan, my crying towel or my violin?"

"Shut up," Megan said, speeding out of the turnaround. "Anyway, if she was leaving him, he might have decided he wasn't going to pay any alimony. Being that he's loaded, that might have added up to a small fortune, no doubt enough to kill over."

"That's a white man thang," Rodney laughed, "They don't believe in divorce, till death do us part because I'm not parting with my money."

"At least white men aren't afraid to commit."

Wilson smirked. "Commit what, fraud, adultery, or murder in the first degree?"

"Turn up the radio, I'm tired of listening to your mouth," Megan said, tuning him out.

***

Without much more to go on until the forensics report came in, the detectives headed over to Eva's real estate office. Their hope was her employees or agents might have some information on possible rivals or who she associated with in her off hours.

"Now this is upscale," Rodney said, admiring the real estate office in Maryland Farms.

"She was obviously making some real money of her own," Megan said, getting out of the car.

Rodney nodded. "Oh, yeah, with the price of property in this city, I'm sure she was."

"I wouldn't know about that, I'm still renting," Megan said curtly.

Rodney pulled the heavy brass-handled door open of Hamilton Realty. As soon as he and Megan walked in, a short balding white guy wearing a plaid suit with a yellow shirt and baby-girl pink tie rushed up to them with his hands extended.

"Hello, welcome to Hamilton Realty," the guy said, smiling. "I'm Steve Flowers and I can find whatever you're looking for at a price you'll love."

"I hope you can," Megan said, taking one of his hands and shaking it.

"Is Mrs. Hamilton available?" Rodney said, cutting in, "We were told that she's the one we should talk to."

"Honestly, you two, work with me," Steve said slightly whispering. "I can get you a better deal. You didn't hear it from me but she's a killer, she'll cut your throat in a heartbeat."

"Funny you should say that, Mr. Flowers," Wilson said, "Eva Hamilton was killed last night. I'm Detective Wilson and this is Detective Meyers. We're the investigators on the case."

"OMG, that's horrible," Steve said frantically, grabbing his face with his hands in shock, "Simply unbelievable."

"Would you have any idea why someone would want to hurt Eva Hamilton?" Meyers asked.

"I have no idea," Steve said, having regained his composure. "I'm not one to listen or spread gossip but I do know that she was indulging in some extra-curricular activities in the marriage department. I never saw her with anybody but I've overheard a few phone conversations, and she kept a listing in Brentwood that she wouldn't allow me to show. It may have been some sort of love nest for her."

"Is there anyone else working here at the office?" Meyers asked, looking around.

"Not in the last year," Steve answered hastily, "Our administrative assistant was only a temp. Eva was a little hard to work with. I'm the only agent she had left."

"Interesting, can you show us where her office is?" Wilson said.

"Follow me," Steve said as he led them back to her office.

They went in and closed the door with Steve still on the other side; he would have his chance to run through it later. On the surface nothing seemed out of place. Rodney went through her desk drawers to satisfy his growing curiosity about Eva but there was nothing in them, no dirty books or magazines, no racy lingerie, and no sex DVD.

"It doesn't look like there's anything revealing in here," he told Megan.

"Maybe her laptop has something interesting to tell," Megan said, unhooking the cord from the wall and placing it under her arm.

After another quick look around they turned out the light and left.

"Come back if you're ever in the market for a house," Steve yelled cheerily behind them on their way out.

"Mr. Flowers sure wasn't broken up over the news," Megan said, getting back in the driver's seat. "She must not have believed in sharing the wealth with him."

"He's just a hater because she was everything he wanted to be and got more dick than he did."

"I don't know why you're being so hostile and taking this personally. You didn't even know the victim."

"Now I won't get that chance," he said quietly, "Maybe that's why I'm so hostile."

***

Ernest stopped in mid-sentence when he heard her name and hesitated for only a few brief seconds when he saw Eva's face appear on the afternoon TV news report. It was just long enough for his clippers to linger on the head of his client and cause him to make his first slip-up on a head in eleven years. His hands started to shake for two reasons, the horror of his error on his patron's head and Eva's face smiling back at him. Then his belly started to bubble like he had taken a strong laxative.

Jayne who had been listening to him followed his focus to the TV screen. "Oh my God," she shrieked, "Isn't that your business partner they're talking about?"

"She wasn't my partner," Ernest answered sedately, "She was an associate, my real estate agent."

"Pardon me," Jayne said, sensing irritation in his tone. "Whenever she came in here she walked through the place like she owned it."

Ernest ignored her remark and went back to repairing the handiwork on his client. Jayne let it go and put her attention back on her customer's haircut.

"I can't believe they found her dead in a hotel room," Carla remarked as the news report continued, "That is so sad."

"Me either," Ernest said, "That's crazy."

"I wonder what happened to her," Jayne said, finishing up with her client and removing his drape. "They didn't say if she committed suicide, had a heart attack, or if somebody killed her."

"It was probably drugs," Carla said, standing up and walking around to get a better view of the TV. "There have been a lot of people who have overdosed on meds in hotel rooms, Anna Nicole Smith, Whitney Houston, and even Heath Ledger."

Ernest rubbed his temple with his left hand and covered his mouth. Panic was growing in his stomach making him sick. He felt his guts would spill out from the top and the bottom.

"Sorry for all the drama," Ernest said to his client when he was done struggling with his cut, "Get yourself a manicure or pedicure, it's on the house."

"Thank you," the man said, pleased with the offer and unaware of the mishap. "I appreciate that."

"Cover for me," Ernest told Jayne, taking off his smock.

"Are you okay?" she asked, concerned. "You look terrible."

"I need to go to the restroom," he said, hurrying down the hall to his private bathroom.

Having emptied his insides, Ernest stared back in the mirror at his reflection. It was real, it wasn't a dream. Eva was dead. He had to be prepared for the fallout. For months he had been compromising himself to hold onto his new business and now that he was unconstrained he didn't know what was about to happen. Surely all of his decisions were coming back to haunt him. He should have known the first time he saw Eva that nothing good would come out of getting in bed with her, figuratively or literally. He needed to rally his people and get their stories in line before the police came knocking.

He went into his office and called Vince. "Hey man, I need to holler at you."

"I was already on my way over there."

"Meet me at the park, man, at the back of the pond."

"Okay, I'll be there in fifteen."

Ernest left through the rear door. He didn't want to have to look or speak to anybody. He didn't want them to see that he was flustered or have to dodge any more questions about his connection to Eva. Inside the car his knuckles gripped the steering wheel tightly as he drove, all the while commanding his brain to get a hold of his emotions. Ten years ago none of this would have fazed him but the aloofness of his youth was gone, he had so much to lose now. He had to pull it together.

At the rear of the park he saw Vince leaning against his car near a huge walnut tree. Gold, faded green, and burnt orange leaves drifted in the wind and on the ground beside him. Ernest parked on the street and walked across the grass to where his friend was waiting. They just looked at each other without saying anything. Then Ernest kicked one of the green walnut seeds hard and it flew into the pond.

Vince took off his sunshades before he spoke. "What's the deal, man?"

"That's what I'm asking you, Vince? I told you I would handle it."

"I told you I had your back."

Ernest shook his head in dismay. "There's a good chance this could blow up in my face. I needed more time."

"So what went down, bro?" Vince asked frankly.

Ernest looked at him puzzled. "I don't know, that's why I called you. You did something that could bring us both down."

"Are you for real? You know me better than that. I wouldn't do anything to hurt you, we're closer than family, man."

"No doubt," Ernest replied.

Ernest smoothed his mustache and rubbed the short stubble on his chin while he concentrated. He stared at the ground near his feet and around the car searching for a pattern in all the half-crushed and whole nut seeds that lay on the ground under the tree while his thoughts ran a circle in his head. Nothing was making sense.

Vince stared at him. Then he asked, "Where did you go last night?"

"Come on, man, you know me."

"Hell yeah I do, that's why I'm asking."

"I bought a bottle and got drunk."

"Then what?"

"That's all I can tell you."

"Are you saying that you were with me at my place?" Vince said, offering him an alibi.

"I don't know what I'm saying."

"Well you need to figure it out and soon," Vince said, frustrated with him for being evasive. They had been through too much together for him to be tripping like this. He put his shades back on and said, "I've got to go."

Standing under the tree Ernest watched Vince drive off. Two more nut seeds fell from the tree after a shift in the winds. He kicked one of them into the leaves piled on the grass and shook his head. There had never been any secrets between him and Vince but for some reason he couldn't tell him he'd woken up in his car this morning at the Spa with a massive hangover and that he wasn't sure where he had been. He hadn't even gone home last night. What was even stranger was that Rochelle hadn't called to curse him out.

His cell phone vibrated in the jacket pocket against his chest shocking him back to reality. He pulled it out and saw 'Mama" at the top of the screen. He slid his fingers across the flashing light to answer.

"Hey, Mama," he said, trying to sound normal.

Sheila didn't bother to pretend. "Ernest I need you to get over here right now," she said seriously.

"I'm on my way," he said without asking any questions.

He figured he knew her reason but it didn't matter whether she had one or not. He needed to be there, the only place where things made sense.

***

Ernest could hear Buttons barking on the other side of the door when he turned the key in the lock. She stopped when she saw it was him and stood up on her hind legs for him to rub her head. He slid his fingers through the soft puff of hair on top of her head and massaged her little skull. Sensitive to his mood and melancholy she tightened her paws around his leg. Thankful for the small amount of comfort and solace she offered he picked her up and carried her into the living room where he heard the TV playing.

"Sit down, Ernest, where have you been? Why haven't you been answering your phone?" she scolded as soon as he walked in.

Ernest sat down on the sofa next to her and Buttons crawled over into Sheila's lap.

"I've been out of it," he answered. "I had too much to drink last night."

"Have you seen the news? That woman who loaned you the money was found dead. They're saying she was murdered."

"I didn't kill her, Mama," he said emotionally, trying to convince himself as well as his mama.

"I know that, child. I raised you," she said, patting him on the leg. "I just don't want the cops to give you any trouble. They might come around asking questions. Where were you last night? I called Rochelle this morning and she said you didn't come home."

"I don't know, Mama. I got drunk. I don't have an alibi."

"Child, yes you do. Anybody ask you; tell them you were here with me. I'll say I was sick after my dialysis and you came to sit with me."

"I can't get you involved in my problems."

"Whatever problem you have, son, I'm already involved. I'm your mama."

"Okay, mama," he said, standing up. "I got to go home. I'm sure Rochelle has been waiting all night to go off on me."

"All right, but remember what I told you if anybody asks."

"I will. I love you, Mama."

"You're my heart, Ernest."

***

Ernest eased the front door open feeling like an intruder in his own house, mainly because he didn't know what to expect. It had been nearly 36 hours since he had seen his family. Inside the den he saw Rhianna watching TV while E.J. played with a handheld video game beside her.

"Hey, Daddy," she said, running over to give him a hug.

E.J. followed suit squealing "Daddy" and Ernest picked him up.

"Where your sister?" he asked.

Rhianna shrugged her shoulders. "She went to the movies with some of her friends."

"Where's your mama?" Ernest asked cautiously, peering into the kitchen doorway.

"She's downstairs washing clothes," Rhianna said, going back to her TV show.

Ernest bent over to put his son back on the floor but E.J. kept a tight grip on his daddy's neck with his pudgy arms, not wanting to be put down. Ernest bounced him playfully as he walked down the stairs to laundry room. He stood there for a moment watching Rochelle fold towels until she felt his gaze and looked back at him.

"It's good to see you're alive," she said cynically.

"I overdid it last night. I'm sorry. When I woke up at my mama's it was time to open up the shop. I cleaned up, drove over there and went to work."

"You could have called," she said dryly, reaching for another towel.

"My phone didn't ring either," he said, throwing the accusation back at her.

"Why don't you put E.J. on his scooter, we need to talk."

Ernest slid the long legs of his toddler over the seat of his mini motorcycle and smiled as he watched him pedal across the floor.

"I guess you heard the news about Eva," he said, moving closer to Rochelle.

"Yeah I did. I'm surprised the cops haven't come here knocking yet."

"I didn't have anything to do with that, Chelle," he said, holding his hands up.

"Save all that for the police. We need to get our stories straight."

"What do you mean?" he asked, taken aback.

"I need you to say we were together before you went over to your mama's house."

"Why do you need me to do that?" he asked suspiciously.

"I went out looking for your last night."

"Why didn't you just call me?"

"Because that slut called me and said you were meeting her for dinner and for me not to wait up for you. Then later on she kept calling the house for you and then she stopped. You didn't come home so I thought you were with her."

"Where did you go?" Ernest asked, scared of what her answer might be.

"I drove by the spa first and then I drove down Broadway trying to find you."

"I was at the light on 8th Avenue when I saw her car pull up beside me. Andrea told me she drove a white Mercedes. When the light turned green I followed her. She pulled up to the valet parking at the Renaissance Hotel. I parked across the street and I waited for you to show up."

"Did you go inside the hotel," Ernest asked, holding his breath.

"No, I stayed in the car where I could see the door."

"Dammit, Chelle, I hope you didn't say anything to her.

"No I didn't. I started thinking about the whole thing and I left. If you wanted to be with her it was nothing I could do about it."

"Not even kill her?" he asked, gauging her reaction.

"She wasn't worth me losing my children," she said, grabbing another towel. "Was she worth you losing yours?"

"You don't even have to ask," Ernest said, wrapping his arms around her.

Chapter
Seventeen

"What did the report from the lab say?" Rodney asked Megan, getting into the car with two large smoking cups of coffee.

"We didn't get much," she answered with a sigh. "Tapes from monitored exits at the hotel didn't give any suspects. There were 13 sets of prints picked up in the room but no matches."

"That sucks. The Medical Examiner says that the murder weapon was a thin sharp blade, probably a scalpel, straight razor, or even a box cutter," Rodney said.

"That could be the doctor, the barber, or who knows who," she said, throwing her hands up.

"Did you get any leads or anything interesting from her laptop?" he asked with raised eyebrows.

"I spent my whole Sunday going through all of her business transactions and I didn't see anything that threw up a red flag," Megan answered, taking a sip of the hot brew.

"I may have something we can go on," Rodney said, sounding superior after her null report. "There were quite a few calls and personal text messages to a number listed to Ernest Shaw. Urgent messages if you get my drift."

"So what do you have on him? I know you ran his name already," Megan said, hating the way he always dragged out anything he thought was significant.

"Some petty stuff as a juvenile, nothing lately. He owns a barbershop on Buchanan Street, King Cut, and he recently opened up a Gentlemen's Spa in the Gulch."

Megan nodded. "Sounds like a man with a head for business."

"I don't doubt it," Rodney laughed, recalling some of the text messages. "It depends on which head you're talking about. Hamilton Realty holds the lease for the building and his loan was from Pinnacle Financial."

"So that's why you're showing your teeth this morning," Megan said, nodding, "You think you're on to something."

"Most definitely, partner," he said, "Based on the texts, he was the one she was waiting for."

Megan turned the key and started the engine. "I guess it's time to make a visit to the spa."

"Not yet, let's go by King Cut first," Rodney said slyly, "Somebody there might not be too happy about his recent good fortune and be willing to have a conversation."

"You might be getting ahead of yourself thinking he's your man," she warned, "Keep an open mind or you might miss something."

Megan was talking to the breeze that blew in from the crack in her window, or may as well have been. Her partner wasn't listening. One look at Ernest was all it took; Rodney had made up his mind that he was guilty. It wasn't because of a hunch or a psychic inclination; it was jealousy pure and simple. He was jealous of the youth Ernest still had and the women he got because of it. He was always talking about haters but he was one of them.

***

Rodney and Megan pulled into the parking lot at King Cut. It was late afternoon, around 4:00 but the sun was still up. On the corner a few guys hung outside the liquor store trying to hustle up enough to buy a bottle for the evening.

"I can't understand what a woman like her would even be doing in this neighborhood," Wilson said, scanning the litter covered block from the refuse of an overturned trashcan.

"Maybe we're about to find out," Megan told him, getting out of their car, although she really didn't think so. She was almost certain it was going to be a dry run. Even she knew that people around here believed snitches get stitches, and they definitely didn't like cops. She suspected it was just a ruse by Rodney to get Ernest to squirm before they confronted him. Unlike her partner, she preferred to catch her suspects completely off guard.

"I knew they would be here sooner or later," Leon said, looking out of the cracked glass of the front window held together with clear tape. "Ain't nobody been by here to ask questions about who killed Pee Wee's cousin but here they come for that rich bitch who got what she deserved."

"You better cap that before they throw your wrists together, Leon," Andrea said, "They don't care if they get the right nigger, they'll take anybody."

"You got that right," Jeff said, turning down the radio.

The bell on the door rang as it opened. Two guys waiting for their turn in one of the barbers' chairs got up and left. They probably had warrants and didn't want to get caught up.

"What services are you here for today?" Leon asked politely as they stepped in. "Sir, you look like you could use a line and a shape-up."

"I do white hair," Andrea said, speaking up before he could

respond, "Once you go black you'll never go back to your old salon."

"Thanks for the offers," Rodney said, running his hand over his hair, "But we're here for another reason. This is Dt. Meyers and I'm Dt. Wilson with the Nashville Police Department." He flashed them his badge. "We're investigating the murder of a woman at the Renaissance Hotel last Friday. Her name was Eva Hamilton. This address was in her GPS."

It got quiet throughout the shop. You could hear the drops of water from the leaky faucet as they hit the bottom of the first wash bowl. The detectives looked around the room hoping to make eye contact with someone but nobody in there would meet their gaze.

"This is her picture," Megan said, holding up a photograph.

"I've seen her before," Leon volunteered, "She came in here once, said she was in real estate."

"Did she have any connection or business with anybody working here?" Wilson asked.

Leon shook his head. "I did her eyebrows a couple of times, that's it."

"Are you sure she didn't have another reason for coming back?" Megan insinuated.

"I do an excellent job, I can hook you up in no time," Leon said, smiling.

"No thanks, maybe another day," Megan replied.

"Maybe she just felt like slumming every now and then," Jeff told them.

"She was a real thirsty chick," Andrea added, "She was always trying to hook up with somebody else's man when she came in here."

Wilson ignored Andrea's remarked. "What was her

relationship with the owner here, and where is he by the way?"

"How should we know?" Jeff hollered at them, "Why don't you tell us, you're the ones doing the investigating. If that woman would have come back around here in that white Mercedes you wouldn't have found her in no hotel downtown that's for sure."

"Why is that?" Wilson asked.

"Let's just say she didn't have a nice personality with our regulars."

Wilson didn't like Jeff's attitude. He needed to learn some respect. He suspected that if he searched his work area he would have reason enough to drag him down to the Justice Center. He moved closer to Jeff's station.

"Is that right?" he asked, staring him in the eyes.

"I don't guess there's a need for us to thank you all for your help," Megan said, tapping Wilson on the shoulder and turning towards the door to leave.

"Like I said, girlfriend, I can hook you up whenever you're ready," Andrea joked.

Back in the car Megan told Rodney, "Looks like your pretty lady had a bunch of folks waiting in line to take her out, and I don't mean to lunch."

"The world is full of haters, that's all I can tell you," he said, staring back at the broken glass on the front window.

***

Megan was getting annoyed on the drive to Pinnacle Financial. She didn't like Rodney's strategy of circling his prey, unnerving him with the knowledge he was being hunted. She preferred a more direct approach. She thought they should stop wasting time and go question Ernest Shaw. After all he was their prime suspect as far as she was concerned, especially after a call had come in about a guy matching his description threatening to kill Eva Hamilton at the Ruth Kris restaurant. Still, Rodney wanted to question some of the employees at Pinnacle and then go back to Mr. Hamilton about his wife's activities within the company. His tactic was to eliminate all the other possibilities before he threw out his net. In his experience, not being meticulous in the investigation always leads to mistakes.

They caught the elevator up to the executive floor and walked past the receptionist as if they were being expected. They passed an older woman in a dark red suit walking ahead of them in the hallway of glass windows.

"Can I help you find someone?" she asked curiously, seeing they were unescorted.

"Yes we're detectives with the Nashville Police Department," Megan said, opening up her blazer so the woman could check out her badge.

"Oh, you're here to see Mr. Hamilton," the woman said, "I'll show you to his office."

"No, that won't be necessary," Rodney said, surprised that Mr. Hamilton would be back on the job before his wife was buried. "If you would point us in that direction I'm sure we'll be able to find it."

"Of course," the woman answered, "It's down this long hallway and to your left. It's the last door at the end."

"Thank you," Megan said with a smile.

"Certainly, this is so sad and shocking for all of us," the woman said sincerely. "I don't know who would do such a thing. No place is safe from robbers these days."

Megan walked ahead of Rodney down the long corridor lined with impressionist paintings. Just as they approached the executive office suite at the end of the hall, another woman dressed in forest green and somewhat younger than the other, exited the door. She smiled as she passed them. Rodney stretched forward to grasp the edge of the door before it closed. They walked in the office unannounced and saw the wheelchair unoccupied and to their surprise Mitchell Hamilton was standing at the side of his desk taking in his panoramic view of downtown.

"Mr. Hamilton," Megan said, clearing her throat to get his attention. "We're sorry to disturb you but we had a few more questions."

"Hello, detectives," he said, turning around. "What do you need to know?"

Megan said the first thing in her head. "I didn't know you were able to move about without the use of your chair."

"I'm not cripple, Dt. Meyers, I have a degenerative disease," Mitchell said nonchalantly, "My legs are weak from time to time but I haven't completely lost the use of them."

"That's interesting, it completely blows my theory," Megan said pensively.

"What theory are you speaking of?" Mitchell asked her.

"I never considered you as a suspect in your wife's murder because of your physical condition."

Mitchell pulled the large tufted leather chair out from his desk and sat down. "Don't worry, detective, your theory is still intact. I would never do anything to hurt my wife. I loved her."

"Would an affair with a younger man have changed things between you?" Rodney asked, hating his unflappable manner and wanting to get a rise out of him.

"I'm not a possessive man," Mitchell answered coolly. "I have never been monogamous nor did I expect my wife to be."

Rodney was entirely put off by Mitchell's cavalier demeanor. There had to be some anger or sadness somewhere in this man. His wife was murdered. He kept pushing hoping to press one of Mitchell's buttons to release his true feelings.

"Were you aware that your wife was seeing another man recently?" Wilson asked, "It seems that they were close enough that she would co-sign a loan with him."

Mitchell was still unruffled. "My wife worked here for several years as a loan officer. She retained her authority to approve loans here without it being reported to me. However, I make it my business to know what loans from this company are approved."

"Did you and your wife have any discussions or arguments about her relationship with this man?" Rodney asked, getting frustrated.

"She knew how I felt on the subject."

"And how was that, Mr. Hamilton?" Megan asked.

Mitchell swiveled from side to side in his chair. "I told her to end it. Furthermore, I don't really want to talk about it anymore. I'm sure that you two can respect that."

"Certainly we can," Megan said, backing up to leave.

"I hope you don't mind my saying so but you don't seem to be saddened by your wife's death," Rodney said, probing deeper into their relationship.

"I am deeply hurt by what happened to my wife, I cared for her very much," Mitchell said, turning away from their judging eyes. "Not to mention, I've lived long enough to know that shedding tears doesn't change things."

"We'll finish this at another time," Wilson said at the door.

Jayne kept glancing at Ernest out of the side of her eye. Something was wrong. He seemed out of sorts to her. It made her feel like she was watching a candle burning down to its end. When the shop first opened she got a kick out of watching him work. He was a master hair groomer whose haircuts and shaves were kin to art. Now he was preoccupied and the haircuts lacked his usual inspiration.

"I'm starting to think you're in mourning over that woman that was killed," Jayne said, half-teasing Ernest. "You might need to fill that third booth if you're slowing down."

Ernest knew she was right except he wasn't in mourning, he was worrying. Leon had called last night to give him a heads-up after two detectives had come by King Cut, a black man and a white woman asking questions about his relationship with Eva. With that on his mind he wasn't able to concentrate on his clients and the walk-ins were having longer waits. He was distracted by every car that rolled down 12th Ave.

"It's this stomach virus, I can't seem to shake it," Ernest told her.

"You need to do a colon cleanse," Carla said, joining in the conversation. "It will get all the bad toxins out of your system."

"I think I'll just let nature run its course," he said, wincing at the thought.

"It's all natural," Carla said, "I can bring you a bottle of the one I use when I get clogged up."

"I'm not clogged up," he said, "I haven't been able to keep anything down."

"You probably need to eat something bland, like white rice. It'll give you some energy too," Jayne advised him, "Some vegetable soup is good for that too."

"I'll get some for lunch," Ernest lied, knowing he wouldn't.

He didn't want anything to eat. He had been dreading the inevitable questioning that was coming and not only was it driving him crazy, it was driving him to drink. He had taken a shot that morning before anyone had arrived to settle down and if his jumpiness was becoming noticeable it must be time for another.

He was finishing up a shave when a tall black man in a trench coat accompanied by a petite white woman walked into the shop. He wasn't surprised. He knew exactly who they were from Leon's description. He was wondering what had taken them so long to come knocking. They spoke to Carla and then took a seat in the waiting area. He felt the heat of their eyes glaring at his every move and it was making him perspire. He took a deep breath and exhaled to relax. He refused to allow them to make him uncomfortable in his own place of business.

Megan was captivated by his attention to detail as he worked. She couldn't help but be impressed by the way he handled the straight razor around the neck of his patron. The possibility that it could have been the murder weapon was not lost on her. Despite that, she could plainly see the attraction that drew Eva Hamilton to him. He definitely hit the gym and he was sexy, but there was something under the good-looking façade that spiked her curiosity. He had an aura that gave her the impression that so much about him was unseen, that there was the possibility of finding something of value hidden below. She wanted to dig deeper, inspired by an urge of optimism that makes one dig for oil, gold, or diamonds.

Rodney disliked Ernest from the moment he saw him. He hated guys like him. It seemed like they didn't have to try at anything. Women always threw things at them: food and shelter, money, unrequited love, and their bodies, for nothing more than a grin of approval. He scowled as he watched Ernest slide his blade under the chin of the unsuspecting man in the chair. He visualized him slicing the beautiful Eva's throat without a word and walking away. Rodney fought the impulse to jump across the room and punch him in the face before he slapped the handcuffs on him. In due time, he would have the satisfaction of taking his freedom away for the life he took.

Sweat dripped down Ernest's back but he played it cool as he led his customer over to Carla at the receptionist desk to check out.

"Those two sitting on the end would like to talk with you privately," Carla said to him with her voice just above a whisper.

"Sure, no problem," he said pleasantly as he made eye contact with them. He beckoned them with his hand. "We can talk in my office."

Ernest held the door for them to walk in, took off his smock, hung it on the coat rack, and motioned for them to sit down in the chairs beside his desk.

Megan spoke first. "Mr. Shaw, I'm Dt. Megan Myers and this is my partner, Dt. Wilson. We're investigating the murder of Eva Hamilton."

Megan waited for a reaction from Ernest but he just looked back at her without any.

After a few seconds Ernest asked, "How can I help you?"

"I couldn't help but notice how skilled you are with the straight-razor," Megan said, staring.

"It's a tool of the trade," he replied casually.

"The victim was sliced with a blade just like that," Rodney said accusingly.

Ernest looked at him calmly and said, "I wouldn't know anything about that."

Rodney snapped back. "You were one of the last people to see her alive. You were seen arguing with her at Ruth Kris restaurant."

"We had a business disagreement, that's it," Ernest said, maintaining his composure.

"Where'd you go after that?" Rodney asked.

"I went by my other shop. Then I stopped by Donk's and had a few drinks to chill. After about an hour I went by my mother's house to check on her. She's sick and wasn't feeling well so I stayed the night with her."

Rodney shook his head in disgust, not believing a word of what Ernest had said. "We've gone through Eva Hamilton's business records and found that she was part owner of this place and your landlord," he said smugly, growing weary of Ernest's arrogant behavior.

"Correction, detective, it was a loan, and I make monthly payments for the lease on this place."

"What was your relationship with Mrs. Hamilton?" Megan asked, taking over. "From the text messages between you it seems that you two had a personal relationship."

"Things went further than they should have between us a few times but there was no relationship," Ernest answered.

"Were you aware that she had left her husband?" Rodney asked.

"No I wasn't," Ernest said, hiding his surprise that she had gone that far, "Probably because that wouldn't have anything to do with me. Maybe her husband hired someone to kill her."

Rodney continued. "She texted you and asked you to meet her at the Renaissance, Mr. Shaw."

Ernest was getting antsy but he managed to stay relaxed. "If you have her phone you can see that she did that many times. I ignored most of them."

"You responded that night and told her that you would be there," Rodney said.

Ernest hesitated before he answered. "That's not true, I never texted her back."

Megan was puzzled. "Do you mind if I take a look at your cell phone?"

"No, not at all," Ernest said, reaching in his pocket and handing her his phone.

Megan checked his messages. "Is this a new phone, Mr. Shaw?"

"Yes it is. I've had it about a month."

"Where is your old phone?" Rodney asked, skeptical of his whole story.

"It's probably at my house somewhere," Ernest said, getting irritated. "What difference does it make?"

"Just curious," Megan said, realizing that the text message that went to Eva was from the other phone and may not have been made by Ernest. "Was your wife aware of your 'relationship' with Mrs. Hamilton?"

"Mrs. Hamilton called my wife a couple of times and

they had words. I assured my wife that she didn't have anything to worry about."

"Maybe she didn't take your word for it," Rodney remarked.

Ernest responded angrily. "Whatever, it's between me and my wife."

"Do you mind if we look around here and take a look at your car?" Megan asked.

"Yes I do mind. I'm running a business here."

"We can get a warrant," Rodney added.

"Then that's what you need to do, detective," Ernest said, standing and moving to the door, "I need to get back to my clientele."

"We'll be back," Rodney said, following him out of the office.

Ernest led them all the way to the front door and opened it. "Thanks for dropping by," he said sarcastically.

Rodney turned up his nose in a grimace on the way out. The whole thing stank. He knew Ernest was connected to the murder but he didn't have enough to arrest him. They needed the murder weapon and for all he knew Ernest had it under the man's nose shaving him with it while they looked on.

"We need a search warrant for both of his shops, his house, and his car," Rodney said as soon as the door closed behind them.

"Yeah, but we don't have probable cause yet," Megan said, "We need more to go on. We can't even place him at the scene."

"Then we need to request the tower dings around the hotel and get detailed call records dialed and received by the victim," Rodney said. "Hopefully that will give us a break."

"In the meantime we need to talk with Mrs. Shaw about his alibi," Megan said once they were in the car. "Right now there's no telling who killed this lady."

***

Megan twisted her lips and grunted when they pulled up to the curb in front of the Shaw home in South Nashville. She was impressed yet again with their prime suspect. It was a quiet street in Melrose. His house and lawn were well maintained. For some reason she couldn't put a profile together that said who he was. He was neither a ghetto thug nor a wanna-be-white. He seemed to be a contradiction to everything they knew about him. Was he the street hustler or the successful businessman, the tough guy or the loving father, the unfaithful spouse or a dedicated husband, King Cut or In Earnest Gentlemen Spa?

She stood in front of the dark-stained lead glass door while Rodney rang the doorbell. She was surprised again when Rochelle appeared in the doorway. She was a no-doubt-about-it home girl with her large eyelashes, blonde-dipped weave, over-sized earrings, leopard top and tight black leggings.

"Yes?" Rochelle demanded as she flung the door open with her left hand on her hip as if she had been rudely interrupted.

"Are you Rochelle Shaw?" Megan asked.

"Yes I am. Who are you?" Rochelle asked impatiently.

"I'm Dt. Meyers and this is Dt. Wilson. We're investigating the murder of Eva Hamilton."

Rochelle rolled her eyes and sucked her teeth. "Why are you here?" she asked defiantly.

Rodney was about to lose his temper when Megan answered politely. "We have some questions to ask you related to the case. May we come in?"

Rochelle stepped to the side for them to come in. She stood outside of the living room with her arms folded and didn't offer them a seat. She wanted them out of her house before Rhonda and Rhianna got home from school.

Rodney, highly irritated with her attitude and feeling disrespected wanted to put her in her place said, "Your husband is the prime suspect in the murder of Eva Hamilton and now seeing your behavior I'm thinking you might have had a hand in the crime with him."

"You have a lot of nerve coming up in my house and criticizing my behavior," Rochelle said, unperturbed by his comment. Her family had enough dealings with the cops for her to learn that if they had anything on you they didn't even bother to talk to you.

"We know you had some heated conversations with the victim," Rodney said.

Rochelle rolled her eyes. "She was the one calling me constantly, trying to tear up my family, and take what's mine."

"So you're saying you had a reason to want her dead?" Rodney replied.

"Ernest didn't want that old hag," Rochelle said, shaking her head no, "He kept telling her that but she wouldn't back off."

"Maybe that's what he wanted you to think," Rodney said, disputing her. "He told us that he didn't come home Friday night."

"So what," Rochelle snarled.

"Was that a normal occurrence?" Meyers asked to clarify their relationship.

"No it wasn't, not that it's any of your business," Rochelle said, frowning.

"By the way, Mrs. Shaw, where were you last Friday night?" Rodney asked.

"I was here at home with my children."

"I bet you were," Rodney added, being facetious.

Rochelle turned up her nose at him.

"We spoke to your husband at In Earnest earlier," Megan

said, "He mentioned that you have his old cell phone."

"It's around here somewhere," Rochelle said, shrugging her shoulders.

"We'd like to see it if you don't mind," Megan asked.

Rochelle curled her lip and frowned again before she turned and left the room. First she went into their bedroom where she thought she had placed it, but it wasn't in her nightstand. Then she checked in Ernest's nightstand. It wasn't there either. She looked in their closet and in the drawers in the bathroom. She took her cell phone out of her pocket and dialed the number. She didn't hear it ring. That's when she wondered if Ernest had taken it back. She was about to throw a hissy fit but she stopped herself. She wasn't about to start tripping over it, the bitch was dead and she wasn't coming back as far she was concerned.

She walked back out to where the detectives were waiting.

"I'm sorry but I can't find the phone," Rochelle told them indifferently.

"All right, Mrs. Shaw," Rodney said as if he didn't believe her. "Why don't you keep looking, we'll be back."

Rochelle opened the door for them to leave and then contained the urge to slam the door behind them. They were not going to piss her off and ruin her new outlook. She was determined to better herself on the inside and on the outside. She was going to be a better mother, a better wife, and a better person. She even planned to take some computer classes at Nashville Tech after the holidays.

"I didn't believe a word she said," Rodney said as they walked to the car. "That was bullshit about not being able to find that phone. She's probably hiding it."

Megan chuckled at his agitation. "Don't sweat it. Next we'll talk to his mother and then we'll go get that search warrant."

***

The dog barked on the other side of the door for nearly a minute with her yelps reaching a higher pitch as she warned them to go away but the detectives kept knocking. Through the slight opening between the drapes that hung across the front window, Meyers and Wilson could see the lights of the TV. Standing on the stoop waiting, Megan wondered why Ernest would allow his mother to stay in this modest duplex in such a rough neighborhood while he stayed in the upscale quaint area of Melrose.

"Who is it?" they heard his mother ask from the other side of the door.

"It's the police ma'am," Megan answered, holding her badge up to the peep hole. "Can we speak with you please?"

Sheila unlocked the door and cracked it open. Then Buttons began to jump and jeer at the detectives, growling between her barks.

"Hold on a minute, let me put Buttons in my room," Sheila said slowly in the dim light, "She doesn't like strangers in the house."

She gently pushed the door back shut and Wilson and Meyers waited another minute or two while Sheila took Buttons to her bedroom. They saw the front light turn on outside and then the door opened again.

"Come on in," Sheila said, opening the door wider.

She was wearing a magenta velour housecoat and slippers in the same color. Her thick black hair with streaks of gray was pulled back in a rubber band. Rodney was surprised at how attractive she was. Ernest had mentioned she was sick so he'd thought she would have been much older. He figured she wasn't much older than he was.

"Mrs. Shaw," he said, "I'm Dt. Wilson and this is Dt. Meyers. We are investigating the murder of Eva Hamilton."

"It's Miss Shaw," Sheila said, cutting him off. "I've seen that story on the news but I don't know how I can help you."

"The victim was an associate of your son, Ernest Shaw." Megan said, "We just have a few questions to ask you."

Sheila hunched her shoulders and said, "All right."

Looking somewhat weak, she led them into the living room taking small measured steps.

"Please have a seat," she said, sitting down on the sofa, turning the end table light on, and turning down the TV volume with the remote.

Megan sat down across from her on the leather loveseat on the other side of the coffee table and took a pen and notepad out of her jacket pocket. Rodney still wearing his trench overcoat squeezed in beside her.

"Miss Shaw, did you ever meet Eva Hamilton?" Megan asked, starting off the questions.

"No, I didn't."

"Did your son ever mention anything about her to you?" Rodney asked next.

"No he didn't," Sheila answered abruptly, "What does she have to do with my son?"

Megan skipped over Sheila's question. "Miss Shaw, do you know where your son was last Friday night?"

"Yes I do," Sheila said, getting defensive. "I called him at the shop before he closed up like I always do. He asked me how my day was and I told him it was a bad one. He said he would be by in an hour or so."

"Are you sure it was on Friday?" Megan asked.

"Of course, I go to the dialysis clinic every Monday, Wednesday, and Friday," Sheila said. "It gets me sick sometimes."

"What time did he get here?" Wilson asked,

"It was just after 10:00, the news hadn't been on too

long," Sheila said, looking towards the TV as she recalled the time. "After the news, we watched a movie and we both fell asleep here in the living room."

Then there was a lull. Neither detective asked another question. Buttons began to whimper between barks in the bedroom. Sheila scooted to the edge of the couch. Rodney let out a big sigh in frustration before he stood up. He knew they couldn't easily dispute her story without more proof. Megan put her notepad back in her pocket and got up.

"Sorry for disturbing you, Miss Shaw," Megan said, "We'll come back if we need anything more from you."

"All right," Sheila said, slowly leading them to the door, "I hope you don't think Ernest had anything to do with that woman getting killed."

"He was one of the last people to see her alive," Rodney said, turning back to face her.

"I don't know about that," Sheila said warily, "All I know is that he didn't kill her."

"Take care, Miss. Shaw," Megan said, walking out.

"Bye, detectives," Sheila said as she shut the door.

The front door light went out and Buttons' barking stopped.

"So what do you think?" Megan asked her partner when they were back in the car.

"No clue, although it wouldn't surprise me if a mother lied to protect her son. We're going to have to place him in that hotel before we can arrest him."

"Either him or one of the others," Megan said, reminding him they still had three other suspects.

Chapter
Nineteen

The search warrants for King Cut, In Earnest, Ernest's house and car, yielded nothing, no murder weapon or blood evidence. The forensics report from the hotel room hadn't provided any clues either. The case was growing colder without any substantial evidence until they sorted through the cell phone hits downtown in the vicinity of the Renaissance Hotel. That's when it got complicated. The list was longer than they had suspected it would be. There was Mitchell Hamilton, Natalie Hamilton, Vince Taylor, Ernest Shaw, and Rochelle Shaw.

"We're going to have to take this all the way back where we started," Megan said to her partner, "We still don't have anything. We going to have to put the pressure on and hope one of them slips up."

"You're right but first call and have the Hamilton housekeeper come down here for questioning," Rodney said. "She knows a lot more than she's telling."

***

"I really don't know why you asked me to come down here, Dt. Wilson," Loretta said, sounding distressed as she sat across the table from Megan and Rodney. "I don't know anything about Miss Eva's killing."

"Relax, Miss Lopez," Rodney said softly, trying to soothe her nervousness. "We just want to ask you a few things about the relationship between Mr. and Mrs. Hamilton."

Loretta moved her head from side to side. "I don't pry and I don't judge. I do my job. I mind my own business."

"We only have a few questions about that night," he said, leaning in closer.

"All I know is that Miss Eva came in the house after Mr. Hamilton and Miss Natalie had finished having their dinner. She was hopping mad with Mr. Hamilton about something. They had words and then she went up to her room, packed a few things, and left."

"Did you happen to overhear the conversation between Eva and Mr. Hamilton?"

"No, it was behind closed doors but I could hear raised voices."

"Do you know if Mr. Hamilton or Natalie went out that evening?"

"On Friday nights I usually go out to the movies with my sister. Miss Natalie left about the same time I did. I didn't come back until the next morning."

"So you don't know if Mr. Hamilton went out later?"

"No I don't."

Then Megan asked a question. "I've noticed that Mr. Hamilton doesn't use his wheelchair all the time. Is he able to drive or leave the house without it?"

Loretta wasn't about to give them any information about Mr. Hamilton. She owed him her loyalty. He had saved her from being deported.

"I'm not a doctor so I wouldn't know the details of his condition," Loretta said confidently, "He's never discussed that with me."

"Surely you've seen him walking through the house," Megan insisted. "You can tell how strong his legs are?"

"I've worked for Mr. Hamilton for almost 20 years. All I can tell you is that he is a very private man. He has treated me well. I do my job and stay to myself."

"All right, Miss Lopez, you can go," Rodney said, standing up. "We'll call you if we have any more questions."

Loretta nodded as she slipped her handbag onto her forearm and rushed out of the room.

"If she knew anything she wouldn't tell us," Rodney said, frustrated.

"I guess you can get good help after all," Megan laughed. "So what's your next move?"

"I think we need to pay a visit to Natalie Hamilton's office."

***

Natalie's cosmetic surgery office was located a couple of blocks away from St. Thomas Midtown Hospital on Patterson Street. Her father had made sure she had the funds to set up her practice in a prime space. Business looked good as Wilson and Meyers walked through a filled waiting room to speak with her receptionist.

"Please sign in and I'll be with you in a moment," the dark-haired model-type said with a smile.

"We don't have an appointment but we'd like to speak with Dr. Hamilton," Megan said, smiling back at her and flashing her badge.

"She's with a patient right now. Have a seat and I'll let her know you're here," the receptionist said, picking up the phone.

The detectives glanced around the waiting room meeting the stares of the patients who were wondering which one of them was the patient and what work they were there to get.

Megan found she was the object of a conversation between two black women giving her the side eye; they had obviously mistaken her and Rodney as a couple. She crossed her legs and leaned in closer to her partner just for the fun of it.

"The doctor can see you now," the receptionist called from the small opening in the window.

Megan gave a fake smile to the two black women as she got up and led Rodney through the door leading back past the examining rooms to the office area.

Natalie's office was as transparent and beautiful as she was. One whole wall was glass and her desk was made of glass and Plexiglas. She didn't give the impression of someone who wanted to hide anything.

"Are you two interested in getting some cosmetic work?" Natalie asked flippantly without getting up to greet them.

"Not today, Dr. Hamilton," Megan said, "We'd like a moment of your valuable time?"

"How long is this going to take? As you said my time is valuable."

"Not very long," Megan said, sitting down in front of her.

Natalie took a deep breath and said, "Let's get on with it, I have patients waiting."

"Getting right to the point," Rodney said, still standing. "Your cell phone was dinged in the area of the Renaissance Hotel on the night your step-mother was.., sorry, correction, your father's wife was killed."

"So what?" Natalie said, shrugging her shoulders."

"So did you pay her a visit in her hotel bathroom? Possibly use your skills with a scalpel to cut her throat?" Rodney said, hoping to provoke her.

Natalie laughed. "I may have been downtown, detectives, but I had no idea where Eva was or where she was staying. Had I known, I would have loved to play the lead of the heroine who slays the wicked witch in this fictional scenario that you're dreaming up."

"Still no sympathy for her, Dr. Hamilton," Rodney snarled, "That's mighty coldblooded of you."

"Why would you expect to receive something that you have never given?" Natalie asked without wavering.

"What about your father's loss?" Rodney asked, still pushing. "Doesn't that mean anything to you?"

Natalie shook her head no. "He's better off without her."

"You never said what you were doing downtown, doctor," Megan asked.

"I was with a friend at the Boogie Blues Bar having a drink," Natalie replied, standing up to signal their time was up. "I'm sure you'll be able to verify it. I ran a tab and paid with a credit card."

Wilson and Meyers walked out of her office without another word; there was nothing else to say. Natalie Hamilton wasn't the murderer. Megan would have loved it if she were the killer. She would have taken great pleasure in handcuffing her and taking her down to the station. Rodney couldn't have been more pleased. He admired the black women who got their act together, educated themselves, and were considered to be successes.

On their way out they passed through the waiting room and Megan gave the two women who had rolled their eyes at her another fake smile.

"My my, look who's letting their over-sensitive side show today," Rodney said, holding the door for her.

"I'm not the one wearing the chip on her shoulder," Megan said in her defense. "They were ragging on me as soon as we came in. Black women are always tripping on a white woman when she's with a black man. It takes two to get jungle fever."

Rodney laughed. "You're just pissed that Dr. Hamilton had an alibi."

"I should have known she didn't have anything to do with it. As arrogant as she is she probably would have told us if she did it and dared us to prove it."

"I kind of like that about her," Rodney chuckled. "Anyway that leaves us with four suspects, Vince Taylor, Mitchell Hamilton, Rochelle Shaw, and my personal favorite, Ernest Shaw."

***

The clientele at In Ernest was mixed, black, white, old, young, often high-end clients, and quite a few students. The only person he hadn't expected to see walk through the door was Bishop Rayburn. Leon had been cutting his hair before Ernest was born.

"Bishop, welcome, it's good to see you," Ernest said eagerly, extending his hand. "Are you here to look around or would you like a cut and shave."

Bishop grinned wide and looked around. "Well, I know I probably could use both but I'm too old to change. I'm gonna stay with the horse I've been riding with for 38 years. What other things can a man get done in here."

Ernest was relieved. The last thing he wanted to do was take a regular away from Leon, especially the Bishop. He still felt guilty about leaving King Cut.

"We can get you fixed up with a manicure and a neck and back massage," Ernest suggested. "It'll give you some time to unwind before you start working on your message for Sunday."

"That sounds fine, Ernest," Bishop said, "I want to support your new venture here."

When they were out of earshot of Carla and Jayne, Bishop pulled Ernest by the elbow.

"I know it takes a lot to run a business but I've been missing your face in church, son. Is everything all right with you and the family?"

Ernest suspected that Bishop probably had heard some gossip floating around King Cut.

"Yes, sir, everything is fine. I've been so busy getting this place running and Sunday is the only day I have to rest."

Bishop smiled. "You've got me in a corner on that one. I can't argue with resting on the Sabbath day, but you can come to the house of the Lord for an hour or so. You know I don't preach long."

"I guess it must be the choir holding us in there past kick-off," Ernest said, joking with him. "Come on let me introduce you to our manicurist."

Halina was thumbing through a magazine in the nail area. It had been a slow morning. When she saw a customer her face lit up.

"Halina, this is Bishop Rayburn, the pastor of my church," Ernest said, "Help him get rid of those rusty knuckles."

"Sure, sure," Halina said, guiding the Bishop into her chair.

"When you get done with him, take him back to see Erik for a massage."

"No problem," Halina said, rubbing the Bishop's hands

Ernest was walking away when the Bishop said, "I'm praying for you, Ernest."

"Thank you, sir," Ernest said, looking back at him.

***

Ernest had almost forgotten it was Friday. The hours had drug on so long they felt like two days. It had been a week since Eva was killed although it seemed more like a month. It had been a tough seven days and he didn't feel like he could keep functioning under the pressure. His nerves were shot. He'd rushed through his receipts at In Earnest and headed over to King Cut to talk with Leon. Everything he had was on the line. He needed to make some important decisions with the police hounding him.

Through the still cracked window he could see Jeff sitting in his chair doing something on his iPad, Leon cleaning his clippers, and Andrea curling her last client and running partner, Tasha. She had a standing appointment every Friday night before she and Andrea went out to hit the club. Ernest wanted to have a private conversation with Leon and Jeff so he sat in the parking lot to wait until she was done.

He leaned his head back against the headrest and relaxed for the first time of the day. His eyes drifted along the street up to the corner and then back to the barbershop. He couldn't believe that his life had completely blown up and then apart in less than a year's time. All of it was because of the woman he met at Third National Bank that day. "Why couldn't they have just approved my loan," he said to himself. "If they had I wouldn't even be in this predicament."

Twenty minutes later he watched as Andrea and Tasha came out of the door. He waited until they both had driven away and then he got out of his car. He didn't want either of them to see him. He knew that there were no secrets in the hood and the word on the street probably was that he'd knocked off this old broad who was trying to jack his new business.

"What's up, E," Jeff said when he saw Ernest walk in the door. "You look like you about ready to come back home."

"That's the one thing you never did understand, Jeff," Ernest said gruffly without looking at him, "This ain't your home, this is a place of business."

"Aw'ight, man, chill out," Jeff said, seeing he wasn't in a joking mood. "I didn't mean no harm. You know I got your back."

Ernest sat down at his former work station. "Man, it's cool, I'm not tripping. I just got a lot on my plate right now."

"Just tell us what you need," Leon said, sitting at his station beside him. "We got you."

"Y'all know the police are hassling me," Ernest said.

"That bitch got what she deserved," Jeff said.

"I'm thinking I might need to hire a lawyer before this is over," Ernest said, leaning his arms on his knees.

"Hold up on that," Leon said, "Don't hire nobody unless they charge you. It'll make you look like you got something to defend."

"That makes sense," Ernest said, thinking about it. "I really don't need the extra expense right now anyway. That's why I'm here. I've got a lot of financial ends I'm trying to hold together and this place is pulling me down."

Jeff started shaking his head. "Aw hell, here we go, I knew this was coming."

"Don't go there, Jeff, let the man talk," Leon said, cutting him off.

"I don't want to close this place but it's got to carry its own weight. To keep King Cut open I need to put another barber and another stylist in here because I need Leon over at In Earnest with me. I need somebody there I know I can trust."

"Nothing but a word and I'm there," Leon said.

"Hold on, E, what are you talking about?" Jeff asked, confused.

"I'm saying that I need you and Andrea to cut out the bullshit, stop selling weed, hosting card games, and handle your business, this business or I will have to shut this place down."

Jeff nodded. "Trust me, man. I can run this place for you. Don't even worry about it."

"I know you can but you got to keep it legit. That's no joke," Ernest said, "If they can't get me for this murder they might try to get me on some petty shit over here."

"I hear you, E," Jeff said. "We'll keep it straight."

"Can we drink to that," Leon said happily, reaching for the Hennessey bottle he kept in his bottom cabinet.

"I've been drinking too much lately, man," Ernest said, shaking his head no. "I've got to get my head together."

"What's going on with you?" Leon asked.

Ernest stared at the floor. "I don't know, man."

"Was it you?" Jeff asked just above a whisper.

"I dreamed about killing Eva several times in day dreams and nightmares. I know I wanted to take her out. The problem is, I was crazy drunk and I don't remember."

"That's messed up, man," Jeff said, "You should have let me handle that for you."

"I'm not trying to go to jail or have anybody close to me go down for something like that. I'm at a different place now."

"I feel for you, E," Jeff said sympathetically. "All this shit over some old pussy."

"Shut up, Jeff," Leon hollered, "You don't know what you talking about."

"It's cool," Ernest said to calm him down. "He ain't lying."

"So how was it, man? Was it worth the trouble?" Jeff asked, wanting to hear some dirt.

"I done told you about your mouth," Leon huffed.

"Go on and pour the liquor, Leon. What you waiting for?" Jeff said, ignoring his gripe.

"None of it was worth the trouble," Ernest said, sounding downcast. "You might as well pour one for me too."

Twenty

Vince's administrative assistant, Davita, timidly opened the door to his office suite. She usually buzzed him on the intercom for his appointments but for these visitors she thought she needed to give him a heads-up. He glanced up at her from his huge computer screen with a questioning look.

"There are two cops here to see you," she whispered.

"What's that about?" he asked, puzzled.

"They didn't say," she said, still whispering.

"Send them in," Vince said, closing the browser on his screen. He had played dumb with Davita but he had more than an idea of why the cops were there. He got up from his desk and sat down on the couch.

"Sorry to bother you, Mr. Taylor," Rodney said, marching in and standing in front of him. "I'm Dt. Wilson and this is Dt. Meyers."

Vince paused and looked at him and then at Meyers.

"Hello, detectives, what can I do for you?" he asked, acting oblivious.

Megan spoke up next. "We're investigating the murder of Eva Hamilton."

Vince kept looking at them like they were speaking another language.

Rodney took over again. "We understand that you are close friends with Ernest Shaw."

"Absolutely," Vince said, unconcerned, "We grew up together."

"It just so happens that Mr. Shaw was the last person to see the victim alive," Rodney said suggestively.

"You mean the last one that you know about," Vince said, challenging him.

"Were you aware of the relationship between your friend and Mrs. Hamilton?" Megan asked.

Vince knew they were on a fishing expedition and he wasn't about to take the bait.

"As far as I know there wasn't a relationship between them," he said plainly, "I'm sure you know my friend is a married man."

"You're playing games with us, Mr. Taylor," Rodney said, trying to contain his irritation. He hated guys like him, professional athletes who were handed the world on a silver platter just because they could run fast, jump high, or hit a ball with a stick.

"First off, I don't understand why you are here at my place of work?" Vince said, unintimidated by them, "You could have called and asked to see me."

"We're not here to cause problems for you," Megan said, "It's simply easier and more efficient for us to do our job if we go directly to the persons we need to speak with."

"Well, you're wasting your time because I don't know anything about the woman," Vince said, crossing his legs. "We never met."

"We know you and Ernest Shaw go way back. We know that you owe him an old favor. Maybe you just paid up."

"I don't know what you're talking about," Vince said calmly.

"We're talking about the large sum of money you gave to him on the day Eva Hamilton was murdered," Wilson said, leaning over the desk.

"As you said, he's my friend," Vince said, glaring at Rodney. "I was helping him with some expenses on his new business. I don't think there's a law against me helping a brother out."

"As long as that's all you did to help him out," Rodney sneered.

"First of all, why would Ernest want to kill the woman anyway?" Vince asked.

"Maybe she wouldn't take his money," Rodney said, folding his arms.

Vince shook his head. "If he was trying to give her money, why wouldn't she take it?"

Rodney was getting more agitated by the minute. He took a couple of steps back to resist the temptation to throw a punch. Megan sat down in a chair by the side of Vince and took out her notepad and a pen.

"Where were you last Friday night, Mr. Taylor?" she asked.

"Probably out at the Metro Sports Bar having a drink," he answered brusquely.

"We checked your phone records," she said, eyeing him, "We know that you were near the Renaissance Hotel around the time that the victim was killed."

Vince chuckled. "In case you hadn't notice, the Renaissance is in the heart of downtown Nashville not out in a field somewhere. There are thirty bars within a block around there."

"Why don't you tell us exactly where you were and who

you were with?" Megan asked with her pen poised to write.

"It's really not any of your business but I was at the Hilton with a lady friend."

"Does this lady friend have a name?" Megan asked.

"Yes she does, but under the circumstances I can't tell you that."

"That means you don't have an alibi, Mr. Taylor," Rodney interjected, "That makes you a suspect in the murder."

"Go down to the Hilton and talk with the manager. He'll vouch for my whereabouts in addition to several other people including the valet and room service. I'm sure I was caught on several security cameras."

"We'll do just that," Megan said, standing up to leave. She knew they weren't going to get anything out of Vince.

"Good luck on the game tomorrow," Rodney mentioned on the way out. "The way the Titans are playing you'll need it."

"Good luck to you too," Vince said to his back.

***

"Vince Taylor's story checks out. He's running around with the General Manager's wife," Rodney told Megan on Monday morning."

"Can't say I blame her," Megan said, pouring herself a cup of coffee. "The good news is that means we're down to three suspects, Mitchell Hamilton, Rochelle Shaw, and Ernest Shaw."

"Uh-huh, there's really only one and I'm slow walking that brother down. He should already feel me on his ass. Her blood is on his hands, I can feel it in my gut."

"No you don't," Megan laughed. "You're just mad he went to that place you never will."

"And who do you think you're kidding, Megan? You been

drooling over that hairdresser since you saw him."

"All that jealousy inside your belly is going to give you an ulcer," Megan said, sitting down at her desk across from him.

"Shaw's wife is a lot more jealous than I am," Rodney said, bumping his foot against the desk. "Don't forget her phone dinged in the area that night too. The two of them were probably in on it together."

Megan took a sip of the hot black coffee before she responded. "Please explain to me why Shaw would get his wife involved when he has access to who knows how many drug dealers and thugs who would knock the woman off for the fun of it."

"Passion, that's why," Rodney said, looking at her like she was from another planet. "Have you been so deprived and inexperienced that you've never felt that urge to do something totally out of your character? It's the intensity of emotion that is uncontrollable by your better judgement. It's obsession. It's the very thing that turns people into great lovers, stalkers, and even murderers."

"What is up with you today, professor," Megan joked, "You must have been up all night watching the Lifetime Channel or reading Psychology Today. I'm telling you the husband is the one with the motive and he can get around a lot better than he wants us to believe."

"I still can't believe that none of them showed up on the surveillance tapes," Rodney said as he unconsciously rubbed his lip over his overbite.

"We can take photos over there and see if anyone working there saw them in the hotel."

"It won't hurt but first let's pay Mr. Hamilton another visit?" Rodney proposed, "He forgot to mention that he left the house after their argument."

***

Mitchell sat motionless in his high-back executive chair staring at his wheelchair on the other side of the room. Among other things, it was something he couldn't come to terms with. Outwardly he appeared sedate but he was like a volcano with emotions that stirred beneath the surface threatening to erupt and spew over anyone that came near him. If he had been capable of crying he would have, except that was a luxury, a waste of time that he had put away when he was a young man. Now he was old, sick, and lonely.

He had barely held it together when Eva's family had come to him and requested that he release her body to them to be buried back in D.C. He had consented without thinking about it. He didn't care. At least that was what he thought until the pain began in his heart and radiated throughout his chest. It reminded him of the feelings he had for her, the way he felt before she became obsessed with Ernest Shaw. The humiliation was gone, it had passed away with her, and now he wanted her back.

Lost in his rumination, Mitchell jumped at the knock on the door.

"Who's there?" he shouted, regretting that he had sent his administrative assistant home for the day.

"It's Detectives Wilson and Meyers, sir," Rodney said through the door.

Mitchell's head fell back and he closed his eyes. These were the last two people he wanted to see. The salacious press on Eva's murder was hard enough to bear without them coming to his workplace and feeding the fire of office gossip.

"Come in, detectives," Mitchell said with a sigh.

"We're sorry to have to bother you again, sir," Megan said, "Except, you weren't completely honest with us when we took your statement at your home."

"What are you talking about?" Mitchell asked, annoyed with their continual prying into his private life.

"You forgot to mention the important detail that you left the house on the night your wife was murdered," Megan said accusingly.

"So what, that doesn't mean I killed her," Mitchell retorted.

"Your cell phone was dinged downtown near the Renaissance Hotel," Megan continued, "You were angry that she ran out on you. You followed her down there. You went up to her room, you sliced her throat, and you left her there bleeding to death."

"An interesting theory, detective," Mitchell said unperturbed, "Except there's not an ounce of truth in it. I did consider going after Eva, not to hurt her but to talk some sense into her. However, I changed my mind. My daughter, Natalie, has a temper. She rushed out of here behind Eva so I followed her to make sure she didn't do anything crazy. My driver trailed her all the way downtown, past the Vanderbilt Loews where I thought she would have gone. Natalie parked on 3rd Avenue where I saw her meet up with a friend. I called her a few minutes later to see if she had settled down. She was fine. After that I went back home. My security cameras will verify what time I got back home."

"Why didn't you mention that when we questioned you the first time?" Megan asked, puzzled.

"It's not that complex," Mitchell answered, "I couldn't chance implicating my daughter."

Megan put away her notebook. She may have just lost $20 but at least they were down to two suspects.

"We'll have to verify your story, Mr. Hamilton," Rodney said, hiding his pleasure, "If it checks out you have our apologies."

Chapter Twenty-One

Ernest was breathing easier than he had since In Earnest had opened. Having Leon there working with him was the missing link. The flow in the shop was smooth and he felt like he could relax. His biggest problem was the increasing number of women who wanted to come in the shop for their services, particularly for manicures and massages. He never turned away business but he wanted to keep it as a space basically for men.

"Turn the music up one notch," Leon said to Carla, hearing the jazz rendition of Marvin Gaye's *Sexual Healing* playing.

"I don't get it," Jayne said, complaining again, "This is Country Music USA, why can't we listen to country music or blue grass every now and then."

"Oh no," Leon said, chiming in. "As soon as we let you play country music, Carla is going to want to hear some salsa, Erik is going to want to hear some hard rock, and then

I don't know what Halina is going to want to listen to."

Ernest laughed hard. He couldn't remember the last time he laughed. It had to be months. It felt good in his throat and his chest, and to Leon it sounded good.

"I don't mind country," Ernest said, "If it's jazz we can play it. We play hip-hop jazz, pop jazz, R&B jazz, reggae jazz, old school jazz, new school jazz, and even jazz jazz. Find yourself some country jazz and it's on."

"And where am I supposed to find that?" Jayne asked.

"TSU's Homecoming is next week," Ernest told her, "If you can't find what you want, I guarantee one of the independent CD brothers will hook it up for you."

"I bet they would but I can't support bootlegging," Jayne answered back, "My man is a struggling singer trying to make it in the business."

"You just broke my heart," Leon said, teasing her. "I didn't know you already had a man. I was waiting for the right moment to ask you out on a date. I was gonna be Tarzan and you were going to be my Jane."

"I can give you a raincheck," Jayne laughed, "If it doesn't work out I'll take you up on that."

"That sounds fair to me," Leon said, agreeing.

Ernest laughed some more and said, "They say I changed, look at you, Leon. I thought your taste was for darker plumper meat."

Leon kept a straight face when he said, "A man can expand his horizons can't he?"

They laughed and joked some more until Vince walked in looking like a man on the run from the cops. He lingered across the room standing to the left of the receptionist desk with his hands in his blue jean pockets.

"What happened to your boys on Sunday?" Leon said, riding him about the Titans losing to the Redskins.

"It's not like it was a blow-out," Vince said in a serious tone, not wanting to talk about it.

"Excuse me one moment," Ernest said close to the ear of his client before he walked over to where Vince was.

"You look like you need a drink," Ernest said quietly, wondering what was wrong.

"Yeah I do," Vince answered, "You got a minute."

"Sure thing," Ernest said, "Let me finish up and we can grab a bite down the block."

Vince went back outside to wait. He wasn't in the mood for joshing about the team's loss.

When Ernest finished with his client he took off his smock, grabbed his leather jacket, and went out to catch up with Vince. A half block down the street, Vince was looking through a clothing boutique window.

"You want to grab a sandwich?" Ernest asked when he got there.

"Let's hit the Pub, you can get whatever you like in there. I only want a beer."

They walked the rest of the block and across the street to the Pub with their shoulders hunched against the chill in the wind. Inside they made their way to the bar and sat down.

"Two Yazoo on tap and a lamb burger," Ernest said to the bartender.

Vince looked down at the tile that resembled a chess board and said, "The cops came by to see me."

"Why would they come to see you?" Ernest asked curiously.

"They know about the money I gave you and they asked me if I killed Eva for you."

"Come on, man, that's ridiculous. Why would they think that?"

"I used my cellphone in the area on the night she was

killed. I was hooking up with a lady friend of mine at the Hilton. I got dinged."

"You got an alibi, man, don't worry about it."

"They can make real trouble for me. I was out with some-body who is off-limits. That alone could cost me my job. If they tie my name in the investigation I'm done. Suspicion is guilt in the NFL. If you didn't do it you should have."

"I'm sorry about all of this, man," Ernest said, wishing he could turn back time. "I should have listened to you and my mom."

The bartender sat the beers in front of them. "The sand-wich will be out in a few."

Ernest nodded to him.

"I'll deal with my end, E, but they're coming after you. They think you killed Eva."

The detectives hadn't been back around and Ernest had hoped they were satisfied with his alibi. Now he knew they were still on his case. He thought about everything he had being in jeopardy and then just like that, he was suffocating again.

***

Wednesday mornings were the best time for Ernest to be out of the shop. He didn't have many scheduled appoint-ments and Jayne and Leon could handle the walk-ins. Instead of going to the shop he went to the dialysis clinic. He hadn't seen his mother in a few days. To him it seemed like there weren't enough hours in the day and he was neglecting her.

He walked in the room filled with patients laid out in lounge chairs beside their machines. As many times as he had come to sit with her there he still couldn't get used to it. He saw his mama at the end of the row again with a blanket covering her legs. He stood there at the entrance for a mo-ment gazing at her and wondering what he could do so that she wouldn't have to come back here. Without an answer, he grabbed an extra chair and carried it in with him to sit beside her. She was half asleep when he smoothed a fly-away hair into place on the side of her face. She smiled and opened her eyes when she felt the warmth of his touch.

"Good morning, child," she said, glad to see him.

"Hey, Mama," he said, pulling his chair closer, "How you feeling."

"I'm doing okay," she said sleepily. "How's everybody?"

"The girls are busy, Rhianna got on the volleyball team and Rhonda is writing essays for her college applications. Rochelle is trying to decide what to dress E.J. up as for Halloween."

"You got to tell Rochelle to pick me up so I can see Rhianna play in one of her games. Y'all getting along pretty good?"

"Yeah, we just got a lot going on right now. It's you that I feel like I'm letting down."

"Put all that silly mess out of your mind. That's just the devil talking to you. You're a good son, Ernest, a good man, and I'm proud of you. You've got a beautiful family and you're a successful businessman."

"I want to take better care of you, Mama. I want to make everything all right for you like you did for me.

"What you talking about? You paying my rent and all my bills. There ain't nothing else for you to do. I'm getting my disability from Social Security. There ain't nothing else you can do."

"If you let me, I can give you a kidney. It tears me up seeing you hooked up to this machine."

"Stop it now," she said, getting upset. "This machine ain't killing me. It's a temporary thing. I'm on the list for a new kidney. God willing I won't have to do this for the rest of my life."

"All right, Mama, calm down. Don't get yourself all riled up."

"You're the one who needs to stop worrying so much," she said, snatching on the blanket. "You gonna give yourself high blood pressure."

"I'm done," he said, "We can talk about something else."

"Good," she told him, ready to change the subject. "What about your friend, how's things going on his place?"

"It's working out. The only thing is he's worried about the terms of his loan. He doesn't know if the papers he has are legit. The person who got him the loan had things so crossed up he doesn't know who he owes."

"My Lord, he needs to check on that as soon as he can."

"It's a touchy situation."

"Nothing he can do about that. He has to go to the company and get it straight."

"You're right, Mama."

"Tell me something I don't know," she said, laughing.

Ernest laughed too. "I guess I better get to work."

"I think so, you not making any money babysitting me."

He stood up leaned over and kissed her on the forehead. "I love you, Mama."

"You're my heart, Ernest. That much you know."

Ernest rubbed her knee on top of the blanket, grabbed the chair to return to the front, and left without looking back. It still hurt no matter what she said.

***

Ernest ran his hands over the phone in his pocket for the third time. He knew he couldn't put off making the call any longer with his business in limbo. He'd planned to call first thing that morning but the words to say to a man whose wife he'd had an affair with, and was suspected of murdering eluded him. There were no etiquette rules to refer to for this particular situation. He thought about apologizing but that seemed inappropriate. He wondered if he should limit his discussion to the business inquiry only. It was like touching a toe at the edge of the river wondering if it's too cold or if the current is too strong. The easiest way was to dive right in. He whipped out his phone and pushed in the number he'd gotten from Carla on the day Mitchell came into the shop.

"This is Mitchell Hamilton," the voice responded after two rings. "Hello, sir. This is Ernest Shaw. I would like to make an appointment to meet with you. There are some things I need to speak with you about concerning the loan I have with Pinnacle Financial."

Mitchell didn't answer right away. The call was completely unexpected. Why would the man who was still a suspect in the killing of his wife call him? What did he hope to gain? Yet Mitchell wanted to talk with him. There were things that he wanted to know as well.

"We do have some things to talk about, Mr. Shaw," Mitchell told him, "However, with the fascination surrounding the case around my office I would prefer to speak with you in private, preferably at my home."

"Certainly, sir, at your convenience," Ernest replied, thankful he had agreed to see him.

"Why don't you come by this evening around 8:00? My home address is on file with your receptionist."

"Thank you, sir, I'll be there."

***

Ernest reached for his jacket on his way out at the end of the day and suddenly it dawned on him. He was going to the house of the man who probably thought he murdered his wife. Why didn't he prefer to meet at a public place? Maybe this was some kind of set-up. Maybe he wanted revenge. Ernest rubbed his hand over his left-hand pocket and it was there, his straight-razor. On his way out he felt a chill, the temperature had fallen. He turned against the wind to lock the door and set the alarm to the shop. Then he buttoned his jacket and walked to his car. He got in and typed the address into his GPS.

He knew the street address was off Granny White Pike which wasn't that far away from the Gulch. He wouldn't have minded a longer drive where he could have had more time to get his words together. It was less than a half hour later when the robotic voice of the GPS said he had arrived at his destination, 914 Tyne Blvd.

It was an amazing tudor-style mansion. Landscaping lights accented the grand architecture and the meticulous garden around it. He pulled into the turnaround and parked near the entrance. The air of money seeped through his dash vents and filled his nostrils even before he got out of the car. He'd figured that Eva had been comfortable but this was the lap of luxury. He stopped his fretting about Mitchell Hamilton being a danger. If the man wanted to hurt him he wouldn't do it himself, he'd just hire somebody.

Ernest rang the doorbell and from the outside he could hear the loud chime. Through the leaded glass he saw a woman wearing an apron approaching the door.

"Good evening," Loretta said, narrowly opening the door.

"I'm Ernest Shaw," he said.

Before he could say anything else Loretta stepped to the side and said, "Please come in, Mr. Hamilton is expecting you."

Ernest stepped into the foyer and got an eyeful of what he had smelled outside.

Loretta held out her hands and said, "Let me take your jacket." Ernest slid it off his shoulders and gave it to her. She put it over one arm and said, "Follow me," leading him to the study.

Ernest was completely impressed with the winding wrought iron staircase and the immense chandelier at the top of the lofty ceiling. The scent of money hung heavy in the house like the velvet and satin drapes against the wall. He could almost taste it. Loretta stopped outside the open door of the study and motioned for him to go in. The room was covered in a rich medium-dark stained wood from the walls to the built-in book cases and to the fireplace. Mr. Hamilton sat with his thin legs crossed in a huge chair with thick cushions. He had a drink in his hand. As Ernest walked towards him, he heard the door close behind him.

"Mr. Shaw, you're right on time," Mitchell said, "Please have a seat."

Ernest sat down on the plush sofa to the left of him.

"Thank you for seeing me, sir, under the circumstances," Ernest said, nervously rubbing his hand over the arm of the couch.

"I must admit I wanted to speak with you as well, Mr. Shaw," Mitchell said, "Join me, pour yourself a libation."

Ernest scooted towards the end of the sofa and reached for the crystal decanter of brown liquid on the marble coffee table. He poured until the snifter sitting there was half-full. He took a sip. The aroma of the French brandy was rustic and smooth as silk in his mouth. After a pause he parted his lips to speak but Mitchell preceded him.

"Did you kill my wife?" he asked without sentiment, looking him dead in the eyes.

The bluntness of the question caught Ernest off guard. He couldn't tell the man what he didn't know. Blacking out wasn't an excuse or an alibi.

"No, sir, I didn't," he answered in the only way he could

and expect to continue with a congenial conversation.

"Why did you want to see me?" Mitchell asked just as candidly.

"Sir, it's strictly a business matter."

"I see. First, why don't you tell me how you met my wife?"

Ernest took a big swallow of the cognac.

"I met your wife the day I applied for a loan at Third National Bank. The loan had limited terms and she offered me complete financing at Pinnacle. Later I found that the loan may have been jointly held. In light of her death I need to clarify who owns the note."

"Are you saying that you weren't aware that my wife was part owner of your business?"

"There was no way I would have agreed to that, sir. I am the sole-proprietor of King Cut and I intended on being the sole-proprietor of In Earnest."

"I wouldn't have blamed you for wanting to use your relationship with her to achieve your business goals."

"With all due respect, sir, I wouldn't say there was a relationship between us. Things got out of control and I swear to you that nothing happened between Eva and I after you came to see me. I'm here because I want to repay the money that she put into my business."

Mitchell paused for a minute to think. He didn't have any reason or desire to maintain any personal connection to Ernest Shaw or his business. He knew better than the man sitting in front of him that Eva had lost her rationality over their liaison. He had seen her phone records and the texts between them. He wasn't sure if this man was innocent or guilty. Nevertheless, that would be for the police and the courts to decide and to punish.

"Mr. Shaw, I have already gone over the details of your loan agreement with Pinnacle and Hamilton Realty. I will have the loan refinanced with Pinnacle buying out the portion owned by my wife's realty company. There will be no other owner attached to your business besides yourself."

"Thank you, sir," Ernest said, breathing a sigh of relief. "I'm very sorry for any pain or upset that I may have caused you."

"Consider this portion of your problems solved," Mitchell said. "Is there anything else you want to discuss with me?"

"No, sir," Ernest said quietly.

"Then Loretta will see you out."

Ernest got up and left the room. Loretta was waiting just outside the door with his jacket in her hands.

"Thank you," he told her, putting it on.

Loretta escorted Ernest back to the foyer walking slightly ahead of him. She opened the door for him to leave and said, "God bless you," just loud enough for him to hear. He didn't look back and a moment later he heard the lock click behind him.

Inside his car he took another look at the magnificent estate. It didn't shine as bright as it did before he went in. It was hard for him to release a lifelong belief that wealth and its luxuries would guarantee him the happiness and satisfaction that he longed for. Seeing Mitchell Hamilton sad and alone in his big house with his housekeeper was proof of that. He drove out of the turnaround with a renewed determination to get closer to his family. That meant making things right with Rochelle.

***

"Why did you even come back," Rochelle shouted in his face as soon as Ernest stepped in the door. "Why don't you just pack your shit and go? You're hanging out more than you did when you were fucking that bitch."

"Come on, Chelle," Ernest said, not wanting to argue with her. "Give the kids a break."

"If you cared anything about them you would have been here for dinner."

"Baby, I want us to talk but I'm not going to put our kids through this bullshit again."

"So you're all self-righteous all of sudden," she said, mocking him.

Ernest went straight into their bedroom without taking off his jacket. He wanted to make things right with Rochelle but she wasn't making it easy and he refused to expose their children to their fights anymore. He could still hear Rochelle fussing through the door. He couldn't understand why she wanted the kids to hear all of that drama. He supposed that she probably wanted to humiliate him in front of them. He set on the edge of the bed wondering if it might be better if they gave themselves some time to cool off. It was bad enough that the police still considered him a suspect in Eva's murder.

He pulled his cell phone out of his pocket and called Vince. He didn't want to worry his mama, she had enough on her plate.

"What's up, E," Vince said, answering the phone.

"Hey, man, I need a place to crash for a few days. Rochelle is on my ass and won't let up."

"No problem, bro, you know that. I'm here."

"I'm on my way," Ernest said, hanging up.

Ernest was throwing some things in a duffle bag when Rochelle busted into the room.

"What do you think you're doing?" she asked, mad and shocked at the same time.

"I'm going over to Vince's crib for a couple of days. I think we both need some space right now. I'm under a lot of pressure."

"All the problems you're having you brought on yourself. I told you from the beginning we didn't need the second shop.

Chapter Twenty-one

We were doing fine."

"I'm not trying to argue over something in the past. I can't go back and change any of it."

"So that's your answer, to leave. I'm tired of raising these kids by myself."

"How in the hell do you think you would raise them if I was in this house all the time. Somebody has to get out here and make some money. Ain't nothing free out here."

Ernest zipped up the bag and moved towards the door.

"I stayed with you after all the shit you did to me and now you're going to leave me," Rochelle said in disbelief.

"I love you, Chelle, and I love our family. I know I was wrong for what I did but you're not perfect either."

"Go ahead and go. You ain't never here anyway," Rochelle shouted at his back.

Halfway to the door, Ernest wanted to back up and explain things to the kids. He wanted to tell them that everything would be okay but it would only make things worse if Rochelle came in there talking trash about him.

Ernest didn't feel like speeding along the interstate. He was tired of rushing and stressing about everything. He made a right on Franklin Road to take the long route to Vince's house. He needed to slow things down in his life. It seemed like as soon as he got one problem under control something else would get away from him. Now that he didn't have to worry about Mitchell Hamilton taking his business away from him, the police were still on his case, and no matter how he tried he couldn't make peace with Rochelle.

Chapter Twenty-Two

The murder of Eva Hamilton may have been pushed off the front page of the Tennessean but it hadn't been buried too deep in the newspaper. The constant speculation on the attractive socialite killed in one of the more prominent hotels of the city was a story that wouldn't die out that easily. It was the middle of the fall tourist season and the Nashville Police Department was feeling intense pressure from the mayor's office to close the case. The idea that a psychopath was roaming around downtown wasn't good for business. The Police Chief shifted the weight of the responsibility to his Captain and he dropped the burden on his detectives assigned to the case, Dt. Rodney Wilson and Dt. Megan Meyers.

Rodney walked into the office they shared with a frown on his face. With his lips resting above his teeth it looked more like he had eaten something that tasted horrible.

Megan knew the look and asked, "Now what?"

"They're turning the heat up on us. They want an arrest and this case wrapped up ASAP."

"Based on what?" Megan asked, throwing her hands up. "We don't have enough to arrest anybody. There wasn't a drop or thread of forensic evidence in the hotel room. We're stuck."

"Nobody wants to hear excuses," he said, cutting her off. "We're going to have to get something moving or we lose the case. I don't want to tarnish my record over this one."

"What options do we have, Rod? We aren't any closer to making an arrest than we were on the day we got this case."

"We've got to come up with something or it'll be our asses on the line."

"We only have two possible suspects left, the husband and wife."

Rodney paced back and forth thinking. "What we need is an eyewitness who can place one or both of them at the scene."

"We've already interviewed all the housekeeping staff, the bartenders in both of the bars, the kitchen staff, and the waiters and waitresses. Those that saw the victim said they didn't see anybody with her."

Rodney stood still. He had an idea. "We only asked them about the victim, we didn't ask them about seeing the other suspects in the hotel. They didn't have to come in together."

"All right, that makes sense to me," Megan said, mulling it over. "We can take pictures of Shaw and his wife over to the hotel and see if anybody recognizes them or saw them there on the night of the murder."

"I don't know why I didn't think of this before," Rodney said, hitting himself on the head in frustration.

"Let's get on it, the second shift has already started,"

Megan said, getting up from her desk with the case file in her hand. "What have we got to lose?"

Rodney snatched his trench coat off the back of his chair and followed Meyers out of the station to their car in a no-parking zone.

"Why is it you can't park the car in a legitimate space?" he asked her, shaking his head.

"Why should I?" she chuckled, "Haven't you heard, membership has its privileges."

"That's why I'm driving today," he said, moving to the driver's side, "I'm not going to be bothered with you running through red lights for the hell of it."

"The truth is we could probably walk over to the hotel quicker than it will take us to drive," she said, turning around and letting him have his way.

"I don't go anywhere without my transportation," Rodney said, starting up the car and pulling into the intersection.

Ten minutes later they were turning onto Commerce Street.

"Come on, Rod, I don't believe you're actually going to park in the hotel parking garage," Megan said, rolling her eyes up in her head.

"Yes I am," Rodney said, grabbing a parking ticket from the dispenser. "I know you're used to doing whatever you want but some of us have to keep it correct."

He found a space on level three and they caught the elevator up to the bridge that connected into the hotel.

Megan checked her watch. "If we split up we can get this done by dinner."

"What's the rush? Don't tell me you have plans for the weekend."

"I plan to pick up a pizza, a movie from the Redbox, and call it a night."

"Sounds like fun," Rodney said wryly, "I'll take the bars and restaurants."

"I guess that leaves me the lobby and the kitchen staff," Megan said with a sigh.

She caught the elevator down to the Commerce Street entrance. There were two attendants wearing matching blue blazers at the front desk, a black male and an Asian female.

"I'm here investigating the murder of Eva Hamilton," she said once she approached the desk. "Were either of you working that night?"

"I didn't work that night," the female attendant said.

"I worked the night it happened but I already spoke with you," the male attendant said, "I saw the lady but I didn't see anybody with her."

"I want to show you some pictures," Megan told him, reaching in her folder. "Do you remember seeing any of these people on that night?"

The black male attendant exhaled and held his hand out to take the pictures, he didn't like cops and he wasn't eager to help. Megan handed him the one of Ernest. It was clear by a raise of his eyebrows that he recognized the guy.

"I've seen him before," he said, handing her the picture back.

"Where did you see him?" Megan asked eagerly, hoping it was a lead.

"Not from the hotel. He cuts hair in a barbershop on Buchanan."

"You sure you didn't see him here in the hotel that night?" she asked, holding the picture up.

"Naw, I'm sure," the male attendant said.

"What about this one?" Megan asked, handing him a photo of Rochelle.

"Nope, I never saw her before," he responded, handing her the picture back.

Megan moved away to the side of the desk and called her partner. "Where are you?"

"I'm on my way down there," he said, "Nobody up here has seen them before."

"Same down here."

"Well this was a bust," he said, disappointed.

"Why don't you go and get the car," Megan said, looking through the front glass windows of the hotel. "I'll meet you out front." It suddenly occurred to her that they hadn't questioned the valet. She pushed her way through the revolving door where he was standing.

"Hi, I'm Dt. Myers," she said, flashing her badge, "I was wondering if you were working the night of that murder up on the penthouse floor."

"No, I'm sorry I wasn't," he answered with a shy grin.

Megan paused beside him to wait for Rodney to bring the car around but the brisk October wind blowing against the building mixing with rain urged her to go back inside. There was a tall lanky bell hop with short blonde hair standing inside the door when she came back in.

"Getting a little chilly?" he said, being friendly.

"Yeah, it is," she said, huddling her shoulders. "By the way, were you working on the night that the woman was murdered here?"

"Yeah, I was," he answered, animated. "That was crazy."

"I'm Dt. Meyers. I'm investigating that case. I have some photos I'd like you to take a look at and tell me if you remember seeing them here in the hotel that night."

"Sure, no problem," he said, bouncing on his feet.

He shook his head no at the first picture of Ernest.

"What about this one?" she said, showing him the picture of Rochelle.

"Yeah, I saw her that night," he said energetically,

recognizing her. "She was by herself. She looked like she was waiting for somebody."

Megan got a rush. It was the first decent lead they'd had. "Did you see her speak to anyone?"

"Nope, she just sat there and kept looking out the door," he said, pointing to chairs by the window.

"Did she get up to go to the restroom or the restaurant?"

"No, she didn't. I kind of kept an eye on her because she didn't check-in or anything. I thought it was kind of strange that she was just sitting there."

"How long did she sit there?"

He tilted his head to the side while he thought about and then said, "For about 45 minutes."

"Did you leave the lobby even for a minute during the time she was here?"

"Nope, I was here the whole time. She made a phone call around 10:00 and then she left."

Megan saw Rodney pull the car up to the curb. She asked the bellhop his name and number and wrote them in her notebook. He didn't know it but he was possibly the only witness to the crime.

"Thanks," she said, pushing the heavy door to leave. She pulled up the collar on her jacket and rushed over to the car. "I got lucky," she said, hurrying to close the door against the wind and rain.

"Oh, you found somebody to keep you company tonight," Rodney said flippantly.

"No, much better than that. The bellhop says he saw Rochelle Shaw in the hotel that night."

"You're kidding me," Rodney said with his eyes bucked wide.

"Not even a little bit. He said she looked like she was waiting for somebody, then she made a phone call and left after about an hour."

"Is that all he saw? Did he see Ernest Shaw?"

"No, he said he didn't see him."

"Well at least that's something," Rodney said, losing some of his exuberance. "Mrs. Shaw forgot to mention that when we questioned her. She told us that she was home all that evening."

"I guess it's time we paid the Shaw family another visit."

"I thought you were in a rush to get your pizza and a movie."

"That'll hold a little longer," Megan said, rubbing her hands together. "With the first break in this case I'm too excited to eat."

***

"Mama," Rhonda yelled on her way back out of the kitchen, "Those detectives who were here before are coming up the walk."

Rochelle jumped up from the sofa in the living room before they knocked. She was rushing to get to the door so quick that she stubbed her toe on the coffee table.

"Ouch," she griped as she hobbled to the door.

She opened it just wide enough to peer out.

"You remember us, Mrs. Shaw," Megan said, "I'm Dt. Meyers and this is Dt. Wilson. We need to ask you a few more questions."

"I don't know what else I can tell you," Rochelle said through the narrow opening.

"May we come in?" Megan asked.

"I'd rather you didn't. My kids are here."

"Isn't there a room where we can talk privately," Rodney said impatiently, "Or we can talk downtown at the police station."

Rochelle took a breath and pulled the door back and let them in. She turned around, led them into the living room, and sat back down on the sofa.

"So what do you want to know?" she asked with an edge.

Rodney started the questions. "When we last spoke about the night Eva Hamilton was murdered you told us that you were home all evening."

"That's right," Rochelle said, "What about it?"

"You lied," Megan said. "We showed a bellhop at the Renaissance Hotel a photo of you and he remembered seeing you."

Rochelle didn't respond at first. She crossed her legs and looked at her foot. She could almost see the throbbing in her big toe.

"Big deal, so what," she said, annoyed with their presence. "I went by there but I didn't have anything to do with killing her."

"So why were you there?" Megan asked.

"I saw a message in my husband's phone begging him to come and meet her there. He said he wasn't going to have anything else to do with her but I wanted to make sure for myself."

"Did you see him at the hotel," Rodney asked anxiously.

"No I didn't. I waited for a while, but after he didn't show up I left."

"Why didn't you tell us that before?" Megan asked.

"I didn't want him to know that I was checking up on him."

Rodney and Megan looked over at each other. They didn't know what to think.

"Would you mind coming down to the station and taking a polygraph test?" Rodney asked, not believing her explanation.

"It doesn't make me any difference, I'm not lying."

"In that case we'll see you at the Central Precinct, on James Robertson Parkway tomorrow. Make it there by 10:00 in the morning."

"Thanks for coming by," Rochelle said snidely, getting up to show them out.

She slammed the door behind them and stomped into her bedroom to call Ernest. She was hot, flaming mad like the fever in her toe. "How in the hell did she even get caught up in this shit," she wondered. She probably needed a lawyer. To make matters worse, after spending so many years worrying about Ernest she hadn't taken care of herself. She didn't even have her own money. She hated that she even had to call him after he was the one who walked out.

"Hello," he said, answering on the third ring.

"I wouldn't have called but we need to talk."

Ernest waited a few seconds for her to start talking. When she didn't he asked her, "What do you want to say?"

"Do we have to talk over the phone?" she asked with her anger taking over. "You should want to come and check on your kids anyway."

Ernest didn't want to aggravate the situation. "Are the kids okay?"

"Yeah, they're fine."

"All right, I'll be there in about 30 minutes."

***

Ernest wasn't sure whether to knock on the door or use his key. He never seemed to be able to do anything right as far as Rochelle was concerned. He thought about it for a second and then let himself in. This was where he lived and where he paid all the bills.

"Hey Daddy," Rhianna said, rushing out of the den to greet him when she saw him pass by the hallway.

"Hey, sweetie," he said, giving her a hug. "How are you?"

"Good," she said, swinging on his arm. "The police came by here earlier."

"They did. What did they want?" he asked after his heart skipped a beat.

"I don't know. They talked to Mama."

"Where's Rhonda and E.J.?"

"She's in her room and E.J. went to sleep already."

Ernest checked his watch. It wasn't that late. Rhianna could probably stay up a while longer. He turned around to walk her back to the den.

"Finish watching your show, sweetie, I'll be back. I need to talk to your mama for a minute."

"Are you leaving again?" she asked with an anxious look on her face.

"I don't want you worrying about me and your mama, sweetheart, we'll be fine."

Ernest was sincere in what he said to Rhianna. He was worrying enough for all of them. He went to the kitchen and got a beer out of the refrigerator before he headed to their bedroom to talk with Rochelle. When he walked in she was holding a bag of ice on her foot.

"What's going on?" he asked, "Rhianna said the police were here."

"It was those two detectives again."

"What did they want?"

"They found out I was at the Renaissance when your ho' got killed."

"What are you talking about?" Ernest said, totally con-fused. "You told me that you didn't go inside the hotel."

"I was looking for you and that bitch."

Ernest started to feel sick to his stomach. He sat down on the bed beside her. He tried to think but all he could concentrate on was the pattern of the bedspread. The black lines against the gold background were like a maze. He tried to follow the paths with his eyes to find a way out but he kept running into a wall.

Not knowing what to think he asked Rochelle the question. "Did you kill her?"

"How in the hell are you going to ask me if I killed her?" she screamed at him. "You're the one she was waiting for. You're the one who carries a razor. Did you kill her?"

"Did you see her or talk to her?" Ernest asked in a lower tone, needing to know what happened.

"No I didn't. Maybe if I did I would have killed her."

"What did you tell the police?" he asked, hoping she hadn't said much.

"The same thing I told you. They want me to take a lie detector test."

"When?"

"Tomorrow morning. That's why I called. Do I need to have a lawyer with me?"

"You don't have to take the polygraph if you don't want to. They can't make you."

"I don't have anything to hide," she said, rubbing her toe.

"Are you sure? If you get down there and they ask you about something and you lie, they'll be all over you."

"I'm not the one who lies," she said, meeting his gaze.

"Then you don't need a lawyer," he said, not wanting to argue.

"I don't need you either," Rochelle said with her temper rising again. "I'm sick of all of this."

She was frustrated and disappointed. The conversation wasn't going the way she had hoped it would. In the back of her mind she had hoped he would have hugged her when he got there or tried to comfort and reassure her. All he cared about was what she said to the police. He hadn't even asked her what happened to her toe.

"I'm sorry, Chelle."

"You sure are," she said angrily, "Why don't you pack the rest of your shit and get out."

Ernest got up from the bed and walked out of the bedroom, down the hallway, past the kitchen, to the den where Rhianna was standing with tears rolling down her face.

"I'm sorry, sweetie," he said, squeezing her shoulders. "It'll work out, I promise."

He wanted to stay and sit with her for a while, make all the tears go away, but he felt helpless. He locked the door behind him, got in his car, and drove back over to Vince's place.

Chapter Twenty-Three

"So where do you want to go from here?" Megan asked Rodney. "Rochelle Shaw passed her polygraph test. The bellhop says she came in, sat there, and then left. We don't have any evidence to contradict that."

"Looks like we're back to square one," he said, tapping his desk with a pencil. "I still think the boyfriend is our man. He was seen arguing with her and he was heard threatening her. I bet he cut her throat with the same razor he shaves with."

"We searched his house and both barber shops. All the razors and blades came up negative for the victim's DNA."

"He wouldn't be stupid enough to keep the murder weapon. Besides, his only alibi is his mother and that doesn't hold water with me. She'd say anything to save his ass."

"We still can't put him at the scene, no witnesses, no finger prints, and no forensic evidence."

"Without his mother covering for him, he can't prove he

wasn't there. His phone dinged within a mile of the hotel. My money still says he was there."

"That's not enough for the District Attorney," Megan reminded him, "We have to prove it."

"We just have to keep the pressure on him. Somebody somewhere saw him. We just have to find that person."

"How are you going to do that, Einstein?"

"It'll be easy if we can get the husband to offer an award for information."

"You're still assuming he had nothing to do with it. With the money he has he could have hired a professional hitman to take her out."

"Well, what do you suggest, miss-know-it-all?"

"Like you said, we need to keep the pressure on Ernest Shaw. I want to talk with him alone. He likes the ladies. I could try to get close to him, bluff him a little, and maybe get him to slip."

"I'm not going to talk you out of it but I am going to offer you a bit of advice, keep it clean. If you get down and dirty with this guy it'll kill the case."

"Get you head out of the gutter, Rod. I'm not that stupid."

"I think you're slightly crazy in love, Beyonce."

"If I am, at least it's not with a corpse."

"Ooh, the claws came out that time," Rodney sniggered, acting like he'd been scratched on his arm. "You may be further gone than I thought."

"Screw you, Rodney."

He laughed. "At least I'm available."

Megan got up, grabbed the pencil he was annoyingly tapping, and threw it at him. Then she put on her denim jacket and left. She walked down James Robertson Parkway in the frigid morning air to cool off. Rodney had pushed her buttons and she hated it when she let him get to her. What she hated even more was that it was true. She did have a crush on Ernest. She was curious about him and being lonely didn't help the situation. She had no intentions of crossing the line with him; she just wanted to see what made him tick.

***

Ernest got up early to have breakfast with his mother. It was something that had gotten harder to do since she started dialysis and In Earnest opened. The police investigation was still a pain in his ass and Rochelle was dogging his nerves but other than that things were starting to come together. After settling the questions about the financing of his shop the next thing on his agenda was to get his mama moved. He was determined to talk some sense into her this morning.

"Hurry on up," she called from the open door after he turned off the engine, "The food is getting cold."

"Good morning, Mama," he said, relieved to see her standing in the door with Buttons beside her like she used to.

"Uh-huh," she said as he ran up to the door. "You got me letting all my heat out."

Ernest inhaled deeply when he stepped in the house. "It smells good in here. I can't remember the last time I had some home cooking."

"We'll talk about that later," she said, patting him on the back. "Hang up your coat."

Buttons trotted behind Sheila and Ernest and followed them down the hall into the kitchen. "Oh snap, I can't believe you cooked homemade biscuits and sausage links," he said, pulling out his chair.

"Eat it while it's hot, I'm going to turn over some eggs."

"Sit down and eat with me, Mama, I want to talk to you about something."

"I will in a minute," she said, putting the syrup on the table. "Not everything you eat comes out of the microwave."

"Rochelle has her hands full with E.J. so she doesn't have time to cook," Ernest said, chewing on the sausage. "At least that's what she tells me."

"I spoiled you with a hot meal every day. You know, since I'm not working, all you have to do is call and tell me what you've got a taste for and I'll cook it for you."

"That's kind of what I want to talk to you about."

"Oh really, you want to give me the menu for Thanksgiving? You know I'm going to have everything you like."

"No, Mama, that's not what I was thinking. I want you to move. If you don't want to live with us then I'm going to get you a place near us."

Sheila put her hand on her hip and shook her head. "We have talked about this 100 times, child, I'm comfortable here."

"I know that but things have changed. Business is real good and I can afford to get you a place where it's safer. You don't need to be living out here by yourself."

"You don't need to go spending a bunch of money on a place for me. I don't want you wearing yourself out paying my bills. You have enough to do. Rhonda is getting ready to go to college next year."

"That's the reason I work so hard. I want to take care of my family. You being here and us out South is the thing that's wearing me out. Let's just look at some places. You might see something that you like."

"I'll think about it," she said, giving in a bit.

"You can think about it but my mind is made up. How do you think I feel? Vince moved his moms away from here 10 years ago. You deserve it." "All right," she said, tired of fussing about it. "If it means that much to you, I'll do it."

"Thank you, Jesus, at last," he said, throwing up his hands.

Ernest turned his attention back to the fluffy biscuits as he dipped one in syrup. Sheila made herself a plate, sat down to eat with him, and blessed her food.

"You mean to tell me things are going that good down there at your new place," Sheila said, passing a sausage to Buttons who was standing on her hind legs.

"Oh yeah, better than I expected. So many women come in I'm thinking about expanding. I still want to have a separate shop for the men."

"I guess times have changed. Everything is going unisex."

"Not really, men and women need some space from each other sometimes," he said pensively.

"Is that right," Sheila said, being matter-of-fact.

Ernest's demeanor changed and he put his fork down. "We're very different," he said.

Sheila knew the look. "Why would you say that?"

"I was talking to one of my clients the other day. He's been having a lot of problems at home. He's thinking divorce might be their best option but he doesn't want to hurt his kids."

"I'm sorry to hear that," Sheila sighed. "Did he tell you what was going on between them?"

"He said it was a combination of things."

"It would have to take a whole lot for him to give up his family."

"He's thinking that maybe they got together for the wrong reasons and no matter what they do it's not going to work."

Sheila nodded. "I can understand that. How long have he and his wife been together?"

"Since they were in high school."

"That's a lot of years to fight and then decide to give up. For some reason people think that when they're with somebody everyday is going to be roses and sunshine or else there's a problem. Nothing could be further from the truth. Happiness isn't something that is given to you. It's something you have to work for everyday."

"I think he's tired of fighting and I know how he feels. It gets old after a while."

"It couldn't have been all bad if he stayed with her that long."

"He probably stayed because of the kids."

"That's not enough to make him do it," Sheila insisted. "He still loves his wife. Kids can't make you stay with someone you don't love for that long. It ain't easy to live with somebody for a week if you don't care about them, much less year after year."

"People can get used to each other."

"Sure they can, and that's when they start taking each other for granted."

"Feelings change sometimes."

"That's true but if they've been together that long they care about each other more than they realize."

"Caring is real but it's not a substitute for being happy."

Sheila put her fork down. "Next time your client comes in tell him he should think long and hard before he does anything. Then he needs to talk to his wife."

"Thanks for the breakfast, Mama," Ernest said, wiping his mouth and getting up from the table. "Everything was right on time."

"Anytime, son, anytime," she said, shifting to the side of her chair.

He bent down and gave her a kiss. "Don't get up, finish your food. I'll call you. We can look for a place for you on Sunday."

"Okay, baby," she said with a smile.

He stopped to get his jacket out of the closet on his way out.

Chapter Twenty-three

"Don't forget to tell your friend what I said," Sheila yelled to him.

"I won't. Love you, Mama."

"You're my heart, Ernest."

In the car his phone whistled in his pocket. He pulled it out and saw he'd received a text message from Rochelle. All it said was, "I passed."

***

In Earnest was already open and clients were waiting when Ernest walked in. His energy was low after talking with Rochelle last night and the heavy breakfast wasn't helping at all.

"What's the deal with you this morning?" Carla joked, "Usually that's how you look at the end of the day."

"He must have been up all night," Jayne chimed in, "Since you look like that your wife must have a smile on her face."

"I wouldn't know," Ernest said, going straight to his work station.

"Okay Superman," Jayne teased. "She's still asleep."

Leon felt bad for him. He was the only one in the shop who knew what Ernest was dealing with. His mom was sick, his wife was giving him a hard time, and he was a murder suspect. That was a lot to weigh any man down.

"Go on back in your office and take a 20 minute power nap," Leon told him. "We got things covered out here."

"I think I will," Ernest said, picking up his jacket and heading to the back.

Carla noticed how slow he was walking. "If it's that bad, boss, Erik can give you a massage."

Ernest looked back at her and smiled. She knew good and well that under no circumstances was he about to let Erik give him a rubdown. He knew that some men swore by his massages but Ernest still wasn't comfortable with a man's hands on him.

Inside his office he closed the blinds to block out the morning sun and lay across the leather sofa. It was cool to his body at first but after a minute or two he relaxed and shut his eyes. He thought about his marriage, what his mama said to him, and how sad Rhianna looked when he left. He was thankful that Rochelle had been cleared of suspicion, even though that would shift the focus back on him. It probably would be easier to cut all ties with his family now instead of waiting until he was arrested. It would be cruel to keep going back and forth. Aside from all that, who would run his business if he were locked up. All of it was draining to think about.

He only realized that he had fallen asleep when he opened his eyes after feeling another presence in the room. In the dim light of the office he could see it was the female detective, Meyers, standing over him.

"Not feeling well today?" Megan asked.

"As a matter of fact I'm not at my best," he said, sliding his legs to the floor and sitting up. "What can I do for you?"

"I didn't know if you heard that your wife passed the polygraph test this morning."

"Yes, she told me."

"Would you consider volunteering to come down to the Justice Center and take a test to clear yourself?"

"Why would I do that?" he asked. "You don't have anything tying me to Eva's murder."

"I just thought that if you didn't have anything to hide you wouldn't mind taking the test."

"My history with the police wouldn't inspire me to do anything that extra."

"That's fine," she said casually, "I was just asking. Since I'm here, what are the chances of getting you to cut my hair?"

"I specialize in short cuts. Your hair is long. Jayne might be able to hook you up."

"I'll check with her another time. What I'd really like is to talk with you in a more relaxed atmosphere."

"More relaxed than this," he said, looking around, "What do you have in mind?"

Megan looked at her watch. "Could I offer you a late lunch?"

Ernest was puzzled as to why the detective investigating the murder case of which he was a suspect would want to buy him lunch. He figured it must be some kind of soft touch questioning scheme where they get him comfortable and he would inadvertently confess to the crime. Nonetheless he was curious. If he played it right, she would be the one who got relaxed and spilled her guts.

"I'm still trying to recover from the effects of a big breakfast this morning but I'd be glad to join you. How much time do you have?"

"I'm not in a rush," Megan said.

"We have all walk-ins on Saturdays," Ernest said, "I have all day."

"Grab your jacket then," Megan said with a smile, "Let's roll."

Leon almost choked on the gum he was chewing when he saw Ernest come through the shop and walk out with the detective. Jayne was laughing and talking with a client in her chair. Carla was enjoying another gentleman flirting with her at the receptionist desk. He was the only one who knew that they were after Ernest for a murder case. He couldn't help but wonder if they had something on him. Ernest was the son he never had. He took his phone out of his pocket and texted, "Are you cool?"

Ernest stood in front of the shop and waited for Megan to take the lead.

"If you don't mind I'd like to get out of the Gulch," she said, "It's a little ritzy for my paycheck."

"No problem," Ernest replied, going with the flow. "Where do you want to go?"

"I'll drive," she said, darting across the street between traffic.

Ernest waited for the light at the crosswalk. He knew better. Hitting her would be vehicular homicide, hitting him would be an accident. When he got to the car she was already inside with the motor running. He slid in the front seat and she sped down 12th Avenue.

Ernest looked out the window as she zoomed by the other cars. "So this is how it feels not to have to worry about getting stopped by a cop for speeding."

She sniggered at his comment. "What can I say, membership has its privileges."

Ernest didn't feel the need to make small talk so he checked out the sights on 12 South. No matter how many times he drove down this street he couldn't believe how much it had changed in the last few years. The only things that remained the same were the two blocks of projects between Edgehill Avenue and Wedgewood Avenue. Young whites had swarmed in like locusts taking over the whole area. He had to give them their props though; the new homes and businesses had brought new life and new money to the neighborhood. So much so that it had priced black folks out.

Megan made a left turn onto Woodmont Blvd where the steady and somewhat heavy traffic slowed her down. A couple of miles up, she turned into 100 Oaks Mall and parked out front of Logan's Roadhouse. Ernest chuckled to himself, thinking this place was more her style.

"Is this okay with you?" she asked as they walked to the entrance.

"Fine with me," he said, not caring one way or the other.

"How many in your party," the hostess wearing jeans and

black t-shirt asked when they walked into the restaurant.

"Two," Megan said.

Ernest followed them through a path strewn with peanut shells and crowded tables to a booth at the end.

"Your waiter will be right with you," she said before she left.

Megan grabbed a handful of peanuts from the can in the middle of the table. She cracked one and put it her mouth and then cracked another. She looked around the room as she chewed. A waiter came by, gave them menus, and took their drink order. They both ordered beer, she wanted Miller's, he wanted a Bud lite.

"So why are we here?" Ernest asked after the waiter left, tired of being in suspense.

"I want to get to know you better, Mr. Shaw," Megan said as she cracked another peanut. "Maybe after that I can give you the benefit of doubt."

Ernest nodded to himself. "What do you need to know?"

"How did you meet Eva Hamilton?"

"I was at the bank applying for a loan and the bank officer introduced us. She contacted me later about a loan and offered to be my real estate agent."

"Were you both instantly attracted to each other?"

"No it wasn't like that. It was strictly business but things went farther than they should have."

"So how did you get to the point where you threatened to kill her?"

"I was mad, I'll admit that, but it was nothing I would want to spend the rest of my life in jail over," Ernest answered, guessing that she was hunting for a motive.

"Maybe you can tell us something we don't know," Megan said, slightly frustrated.

"I can't tell you something that I don't know."

"We know she texted you the hotel and room number. She was waiting there for you."

"I never went there," Ernest said firmly.

"Why didn't you?" Megan asked with her tone becoming accusatory.

"I'm married. Getting with her was a mistake. I was done."

"Was she threatening to tell your wife about the affair?"

"My wife already knew."

"Mrs. Shaw doesn't seem like the type to forgive and forget."

"She's not."

"Is that why you're staying at Vince Taylor's house?"

"You're keeping tabs on me?"

"Of course we are, Mr. Shaw. You're still a murder suspect. My partner is convinced that you killed Eva Hamilton."

"Your partner is way off base."

"I told him that but he's not buying it. He says your mother is lying to protect you."

"Detective, I don't think we have any more to talk about," he said, agitated.

"I think we do, I'm on your side. Why don't we start with you calling me Megan?"

Ernest downed the rest of his beer. He could sense that this was some of the same bullshit he got into with Eva. "When did women get to be this scandalous," he wondered. He was hungry when Eva got him on the hook, this time he wasn't taking the bait.

Chapter Twenty-Four

Rochelle looked down the pew at her kids and their mixed emotions. Rhonda's mouth was twisted in anger waiting for a reason to curse somebody out and Rhianna's eyes were watery waiting for a reason to cry. E.J. was the only happy one in the bunch giggling as he sat playing a digital game on her iPad. Maybe it was her fault for putting them in the middle of her and Ernest's squabbles but why should she hide the truth from them. Her mama had never hid the truth about her father from her when he was doing his dirt.

Her first instinct was to skip church that morning when she saw how hard it was raining. The way it looked outside was the way she felt inside. She pushed on in spite of it hoping to get some peace of mind from the message but it wasn't happening as she squirmed restlessly in her seat. Bishop Rayburn was getting on her nerves preaching forgiveness and some 'he who is without sin casting the first stone' nonsense.

She knew she should have stayed in bed. Some people deserve a rock or two thrown at them. As far as she was concerned there is a difference in sin. She hadn't committed adultery and she hadn't killed anybody.

The sermon went on for another 30 minutes. Seated down front she could see Ernest's mama waving her hands and shouting amen to every word that came out of Bishop Rayburn's mouth. She couldn't wait until church was over so she could tell her about her son.

When the service finally ended Rochelle sent the girls to get their grandma while she rushed out to the car with E.J. She didn't want to talk to anybody. The last thing she needed was somebody asking her about Ernest. It was hard to keep a secret in North Nashville. She pulled the car up to the front of the stairs at the church entrance since it was still raining. She could see the girls were smiling as they hugged tightly to their Grandma under her umbrella. When they got into the car Rhianna put on her headphones.

"Rhonda says she's going to let her perm grow out so she doesn't have to worry about her hair getting wet," Sheila said as she folded up her umbrella.

"Since when?" Rochelle asked, sounding testy, "I just paid $80 for her to have it done."

"That was the last time, Mama," Rhonda said. "When the New Year comes in I'm going natural, and I'm going out for the basketball team when I get to UT Knoxville."

"Child, what are you talking about UT, you know we're all about TSU," Sheila said, joking with her.

"I wouldn't mind going there but I want to be on a winning team," Rhonda said.

"Once you get on the team, they'll start winning," Sheila told her.

The conversation between Rhonda and her Grandma lasted

all the way home. Once they were all in the house, they all fanned out in different directions, Rochelle to her bedroom, Sheila to the kitchen, Rhianna to the den, Rhonda out the back door, and E.J. to his playroom. Rochelle joined Sheila in the kitchen after she changed out of her Sunday clothes.

"Bishop Rayburn sure did preach this morning," Sheila said, already picking the green beans at the table.

"He always does," Rochelle said, sounding unimpressed.

"Where was Ernest this morning?" Sheila asked, "Did he have some work to do at the shop?"

"I wouldn't know," Rochelle answered smugly. "He hasn't been here since Tuesday."

Sheila tossed the green bean in her hand in the bowl with the ends still on it. "What in the world is that about? Where is he?"

"He says he's staying over Vince's house," Rochelle said with a doubting tone.

"I tell you the truth, this doesn't make no sense," Sheila said wearily, worn-out with the conflict between them. "What are y'all fighting about now?"

"It doesn't even matter. The problem is that he doesn't care about me or how I feel."

"You know that's not true, Chelle."

"Look at what he did, Miss Sheila, I can't keep going through this."

"If you can't forgive him, then leave him," Sheila said, reaching for another green bean.

"I wish it was that simple. I love him."

"I loved his daddy too, but I had to make a choice. If he couldn't be all mine, I didn't want to see him again."

"I've been with Ernest since I was Rhonda's age."

"I know that but trying to punish him for what he did everyday is no way to live. You're making yourself as miserable as he is.”

“So what am I supposed to do,” Miss Sheila, “Let him walk all over me?”

“I’m not saying that but this mess between you two has gone on long enough. It’s not good for the kids to be around this. Those girls have been through it, listening to all that fussing and fighting all their lives. It would be a shame to do the same to E.J. I would rather see y’all apart than to see that but that’s a decision you’re going to have to make. When you decide, make sure it’s what you want and not for your children.”

***

Megan had the Monday morning blahs when she got to work. She had given Ernest Shaw her card and asked him to call her but she hadn’t heard from him. She couldn’t really blame him; he probably thought it was some kind of set-up.

Rodney was kicked back with his feet on the desk drinking a cup of coffee.

“How was your weekend?” he joked, “I thought you were going to come in with your lover boy handcuffed behind you.”

“Save the jokes. I’m not in the mood,” Megan said, sitting down at her desk.

“I take it that you didn’t get anything out of him.”

“Nothing new, he still says he didn’t do it.”

“I told you it was a waste of time.”

“So what have you been working on?” Megan asked, turning the conversation back on him.

“It just so happens that I called Mr. Hamilton and asked him to come down here this morning. I have an idea I want to run by him.”

“Is this your plan to hit him up for some cash?”

“Do you have a better plan?” he asked her, looking over

the top of his glasses. "One thing I do know is that money talks and it makes people talk."

Megan smiled to herself when she saw Mitchell Hamilton come through the door in his wheelchair with Natalie Shaw pushing him.

"I think your plan just hit a snag," she said, making a quick exit.

Rodney followed the direction of her eyes and saw them coming towards him.

"Hello, Mr. Hamilton, I'm glad you could meet with me today," Rodney said, standing to shake his hand.

"I presume you have some information to tell me about my wife's murder," Mitchell said.

"Not exactly, sir. Please have a seat, Miss Hamilton," Rodney said, pulling another chair closer to the desk. "There's an avenue we haven't used yet to find the killer."

"What might that be?" Mitchell inquired.

"I think it would be helpful if we offered a reward for information that might lead to an arrest. It's the extra motivation to help potential witnesses come forward."

"If you ask me, we should offer the killer a reward," Natalie said, half-joking.

"Don't be horrible," Mitchell said, frowning at her. "If you don't mind I'd like to speak with Dt. Wilson alone."

Natalie stood up. "I don't mind at all," she said, strutting out of the office and taking a seat in the outer area.

"So what type of reward do you think is necessary?" Mitchell asked, squinting his eyes.

"I was thinking an amount between $10 thousand and $50 thousand might shake out quite a few tips for us."

Mitchell was dumbfounded. "Are you telling me that you have no idea who killed my wife?"

"No, sir, I know who killed her. I just can't prove it yet."

"And who might that be?" Mitchell asked, although he knew who Wilson suspected.

"His name is Ernest Shaw," Rodney said. "Do you know anything about him?"

Mitchell thought about Ernest coming by his home and then about the visit he made to In Earnest. Not once did the man say that he had feelings for Eva or that he had any desire to keep seeing her. On that day at the Spa, Mitchell had been prepared to offer him money not to see her, except his instincts told him that it wasn't necessary, the man didn't want to see her. Eva had been a victim of her own making. She had done the very thing Mitchell himself had considered doing, coercing another to pretend they love you.

"I can't say that I do," Mitchell answered after his recollection. "What makes you think he was the murderer?"

"She invited him to meet her there at the hotel. From her text messages she seemed quite taken with him, but witnesses heard him threaten to kill her at a restaurant earlier that evening. He had motive and opportunity. I just need some evidence or corroboration that ties him to the crime scene that I can present to the D.A in order to make an arrest."

Mitchell didn't bear Ernest Shaw any ill will. He knew Eva could push any man's buttons to make him want to kill her. After all she had even pushed his.

"It seems ironic, detective, that at one time you suspected me of killing my wife and now you ask for my help in doing your job," Mitchell said, staring Wilson in the eye. "Be that as it may, I'll offer a reward of $25 thousand."

"I really appreciate your cooperation on this," Rodney said, relieved. "I think this is going to give us the break that we need."

"I take comfort in the fact that if you don't get a conviction,

I'm not out of anything," Mitchell said, wheeling himself out to where Natalie was waiting.

***

Ernest was still staying at Vince's house but they barely saw each other with their crazy schedules. Ernest was working twelve hour days at In Earnest and Vince liked to travel with the Titans on away games. It was a by-week for the team and Vince was chilling on the couch in front of the TV with one of his lady friends. When she saw Ernest, she jumped up like a jack in the box, said a few words to Vince, and made a quick exit.

"I'm sorry, man," Ernest said, "Did I come at a bad time."

"No, man, don't worry about it. She's just spooked. She's still married and paranoid about anybody seeing us together."

"If I can tell you anything, let it go, man. Look at me. You can get anybody you want."

"I'm crazy about her, E. You know me, I was doing my thing but she got under my skin."

"Then she should leave her man, get out there and do this in the open."

"She needs some time."

"You're tripping. She could have left him this morning, yesterday or last week. Cut her off until she comes correct."

"Is that what you're going to do?" Vice asked, switching the conversation to him and Rochelle.

"I don't know but I'm going to have to get out of your way regardless."

"Now you're tripping, this house is big enough for the both of us."

"It's cool but I'm about to move my mama anyway."

"How did you get her to agree to that?"

"It wasn't easy. I told her running back and forth was wearing me out," Ernest sighed, dropping down on the other side of the couch.

"You sound beat," Vince said, laughing. "Your ass is getting out of shape."

"I haven't worked out in over a month. Between the shop, Mama, Rochelle, the kids, and the cops on my ass, I don't have time. I've lost some weight too. I barely have time to eat."

"I don't know how anybody can look flabby as hell and have lost weight."

Ernest had to laugh too. "Me either but it's possible."

That's when the game ended and the local news came on with the anchor beginning with a news update. "Crime Stoppers is offering a $25 thousand cash reward for information leading to the arrest and conviction of the suspect or suspects in the murder of Eva Hamilton at the Renaissance Hotel in September."

Ernest just stared at the TV screen speechless.

"You know what that means don't you, bro," Vince said, watching him.

"Hell yeah, they're coming after me. They're looking for anybody who'll come forward and finger me for a payout."

"What do you want to do about it?"

"There's nothing I can do," Ernest said, holding his head in his hands.

"That's messed up, man."

"The whole thing was messed up. That's why I'm telling you, man, get your hand out of the cookie jar before you get caught. Ain't no pussy that good, trust me."

"I hear you, man," Vince said, feeling bad for his friend.

Ernest's head began to pound. It was his brain on overload. Something had to give soon or it was going to explode. He needed some rest. His phone rang just as he stood up. He saw the name and answered it.

"Hey, Mama," he said, trying to sound upbeat. "I was going to call you but I thought you had gone to bed already."

"No, I'm still up. Buttons wanted me to let her out."

Ernest threw his hand up to Vince as he left the room. "How'd your treatment go today, are you feeling all right."

"I'm doing fine. It's you I'm worried about."

"Me, you don't need to worry about me."

"I didn't see you at church yesterday."

"I had a lot of paperwork to catch up on."

"I had dinner with Rochelle and the kids. She said you walked out."

"She threw me out or I walked out, it doesn't make any difference. We can't live together right now. I don't know what she wants from me but I need somebody who can support me. Me and Chelle aren't on the same team right now."

"I don't know how you can say that, son. Y'all got those kids to take care of."

"I know but I can't stand to see us hurting them with all of our bullshit. Excuse my language, Mama."

"There's nothing I can say except I hope you two work it out."

"It'll work itself out one way or another."

"Did you see the news earlier?" she asked, changing the subject. "They're offering a reward for information on who killed that woman."

"I saw it. I know that detective is coming for me."

"Don't even let it bother you. I'm you're alibi, son."

"I know. It's late. Go on to bed, I'll talk to you soon. Love you."

"You're my heart, Ernest."

The phone rings again and this time it's Megan.

"Hello," he said, bracing himself for news that might be a hard punch to the gut.

"How are you?" Megan asked, being coy.

"It's late, what do you want?" Ernest said, losing patience with her.

"I guess you probably know about the reward the family is putting up. I wanted to let you know that I'm on your side."

"Lady, the police have never been on my side," he said.

"You've got to trust somebody," she said.

"Not in my world," Ernest said, hanging up.

Twenty-Five

While he was in the shop working, Ernest was the picture of contentment. He was the man who'd had a vision and ushered it into fruition. With his diverse staff of professionals his business continued to prosper. His new customers were now considered regulars. He was the envy of his competitors at Cummins Station just a few blocks away. Nowhere in that picture could you see his nerves on edge because of the ticking time bomb threatening to go off at any moment. Twenty-five thousand dollars was a big enough incentive or enticement for anybody to point a finger. The question was who it would be. Anybody who had ever walked into King Cut knew Ernest Shaw was a suspect in the case. At these prices would those loyalties hold or be disregarded. Sure snitches get stitches but sometimes they get paid.

It was about 5:00, an hour before they would stop taking anymore walk-ins and lock the door. Ernest had kept the TV turned off and the music playing nonstop. He didn't want to field any discussions about Eva's murder and the reward.

His plan had worked all day until one of their regulars came in and said, "They say it's going to snow tonight and I can already feel the frost in the air."

"Uh-uh," Carla said, turning on the TV, "I need to see the news before y'all get me snowed in up here. I've got to drive all the way to Murfreesboro."

"Don't worry about it, you're welcome to come and stay with me," Leon said, teasing her.

Carla laughed as she changed the channel until she found the local news. It was imperfect timing with the news beginning with the announcement about the $25 thousand reward.

"Oh shucks," Jayne said, "They're getting serious about catching whoever killed your friend, Ernest. If I knew anything I would definitely call."

"I would call in a heartbeat," Carla said, "That could be a down payment on a house. Leon, you could get a new car."

Leon didn't answer. He pretended his focus was on his customer.

"What about you, Ernest," Jayne asked, "Are you sure you don't know anything we could tell the cops to get that money?"

"I don't know what to tell you," Ernest said, walking back to his office.

***

A couple of hours later when the shop was closed and everybody else was gone, Leon came back to the office to check on Ernest.

"I'm gone, man," he said, sticking his head in the office. "I've that stop to make."

Leon had been going by King Cut once a week to check on the place and pick up booth rents and utility bills.

"Let me ride with you tonight, man," Ernest said, getting up and grabbing his jacket. "It's been too long since I've been over there." He wanted a chance to kick back and have a drink with his old crew.

"Trail me in your car, that way we don't have to come back by this way."

"That's cool with me," Ernest said, grabbing his keys.

Ernest knew the way to King Cut with his eyes closed but it felt good to let somebody else take the lead for a minute. He relaxed against the heated leather of the car seat and fixed his eyes on Leon's license plate as he drove along on the side streets. It was barely a twenty minute ride. That's when Ernest realized that geographically he hadn't gone that far from where he started.

When he followed Leon's old Buick into the parking lot it all looked the same, not one thing was different. For a minute he almost wished he hadn't made the move and then none of the madness in his life would have happened.

He walked into the barbershop still behind Leon to the familiar sound of the bell above the door jingling.

"What's up, E," Jeff said, raising his eyes off his iPad where he was scrolling through music for his next track. "Surprised to see you back on the block."

"What can I say, I missed seeing your black ass," Ernest said, giving him the brother handshake and shoulder bump. "Andrea gone home already?"

"She was rushing home to see some Tyler Perry show she's hooked on," Jeff laughed.

"You got what I need?" Leon asked, keeping it all business while he waited in front of Jeff's station.

"I got you," Jeff said, tossing him a zipped pouch with the words SunTrust on it.

"Now what you got to drink in here," Leon said, sitting

down at his old work station and kicking his shoes off.

"Ain't nothing changed," Jeff said as he pulled out a bottle of Hennessey. He poured them all a couple of shots in clear plastic cups. He drained his cup in two gulps. "You know they got a billboard up about a reward for ol' girl over there off the interstate on Charlotte Pike."

"I haven't seen it," Ernest said, nursing his drink.

"It ain't nothing but that black Columbo wannabe trying to get somebody to roll over on you, E," Leon said, holding his cup out for another shot.

"That's a joke," Ernest chuckled, "The white chick is trying to get me to roll with her."

"All these white chicks want that dick, man," Jeff laughed, "I would do her, E. Fuck her and I bet she'll get the nutty professor off your back. The only thing she really wants to know is what you did to blow that other chicks mind."

"You got that right, Jeff," Leon said, laughing until he almost choked.

"Ain't no way, man," Ernest said, "I'm done with the insanity. All I want is some peace and a goodnight's sleep."

***

"You look like you hit the Mega Millions," Megan said, sitting at her desk cracking and eating pistachio nuts.

"We got a hit," Rodney exclaimed, wearing a toothy grin that spread from ear to ear.

"What are you talking about?"

"The reward did exactly what we wanted it to do. We got a witness who saw Ernest Shaw going out of a lower level door at the Renaissance Hotel around 12:30 that night."

"What witness, and how did she finger, Shaw?" Megan asked doubtfully.

"She was walking with some friends from the Katt Williams concert to the Public Library parking garage where their car was located. She saw this guy she knew who used to cut her son's hair at King Cut come rushing out of the hotel. She said she didn't think anything of it until she heard the report on Crime Stoppers about the murder."

"And you think that will hold up in court?" Megan smirked.

"It's circumstantial but at least it was enough to get a warrant for his arrest."

"It's your call," Megan said, subdued.

"Why are you looking so down in the mouth?" Rodney asked lightheartedly, "I know you hate to lose that $20, but damn."

"Cut the gloating and let's go," she said, grabbing her puffed vest.

As soon as they stepped foot out the door a strong wind whipped Rodney's trench coat up in the air. He squeezed the lapels around his neck to hold out the cold.

"I don't know how you stay warm in that thing," he told Megan, shivering. "It doesn't even have any sleeves on it."

"What is it with you? You sound like my grandmother. You might need to start taking a multivitamin for your old ass."

"I sense a little attitude this morning, partner. That must mean you didn't get your chance with loverboy."

"Shut up, Rodney. You are too full of yourself."

"Not at all, and just to show you how benevolent I'm feeling I want you to drive. Run all the lights you want. I'm ready to bring Ernest Shaw's arrogant ass in."

Megan felt sorry for Ernest. She had truly hoped that he hadn't done it. She thought he was a real interesting guy and wanted to get to know him better. She had reached out to him but he hadn't responded. Honestly she wished he had even though she knew that you never mix work with pleasure.

The morning rush hour had subsided and the traffic up Broadway flowed like a smooth river. For once Megan didn't have to change lanes or run through any lights. She made a left at 12th Avenue and after one block she could see the television crews and press waiting.

"No you didn't," she said, glancing over at her partner.

"Oh yes I did. We busted our asses to get this collar and they busted our balls the whole time. So today we're about to get all the shine."

"You know you're rotten, don't you."

"Yeah, but I'm not by myself am I," he said, smiling at her.

Megan pulled the car over in a no-parking zone across the street. Rodney was out of the car as soon as it stopped. She took her gun out of her holster as she hurried to back him up. She didn't think it was necessary but it was proper procedure. Rodney wanted the drama of busting through the door but a customer was coming out when they got there and held the door for him.

Ernest had seen the car when it pulled up. He had been expecting them from the first time he saw the TV bulletin about the reward. He took off his smock and was standing at the receptionist desk waiting. Nobody else in the shop noticed.

Rodney snatched Ernest's arms behind him.

"I'll be damned," Leon said with his scissors in mid-air.

"Ernest Shaw, you are under arrest for the murder of Eva Hamilton," Rodney growled as he handcuffed him. "You have the right to remain silent. If you do say anything, it can be used against you in a court of law."

"What the hell is going on?" Jayne said, shocked and confused by the whole scene.

Megan put away her gun. Hearing all the commotion, Erik and Halina had rushed to the front. Carla held her hand tightly over her mouth. Cameras converged at the door and reporters held microphones in their stretched out arms.

Wilson kept talking as he soaked up the attention. "You have the right to a lawyer during questioning. If you cannot afford a lawyer, one will be appointed for you if you wish."

Ernest's expression remained blank even when a cold gust of wind smacked him in the face as Rodney pulled him out onto the sidewalk. Megan took the lead through the reporters back to the car. Rodney slowed up where the cameras could get a close-up of Ernest as they took him into custody. He wanted to humiliate him, bring him back to the low-life thug that he was.

Cramped in the backseat of their cruiser with his arms behind his back, Ernest had a flashback to the night almost twenty years ago when he was in the same position in the back of a squad car. That day he had sworn to himself that he would never be in that position again.

***

Leon was on the phone with Vince before they had Ernest in the car. Next he called Rochelle and then Miss Sheila. After that he did what he knew Ernest would want him to do.

"I know we're all disturbed about what just happened. I'm sure this situation will be resolved and Ernest will be back. In the meantime we need to do what he has us here to do and that is to take care of business."

Carla answered a phone call; Erik went back to the massage room, Halina went back to her area, and Jayne went back to her client's cut.

Twenty-Six

Through the arraignment and the bail hearing Ernest continued to do what he had a right to do, he stayed silent. He answered no questions and made no statements. The lawyer Vince had hired for him gave his plea of 'not guilty.' After convincing the judge that his client was not a flight risk, Ernest was released on a $1 million bond. He had spent three days in jail.

The first call he made after Vince picked him up from the Criminal Justice Center was to his mama.

"Mama, I'm out. Vince got my bail."

"I need to see you, son."

"Not tonight, mama. Give me a few days."

"All right, child, as soon as you can though."

"Bye, Mama, I love you."

"You're my heart, Ernest."

Next he called Rochelle and talked with his kids. He should have gone over there but he didn't want to see anybody. He was ashamed of everything that had happened and for publicly embarrassing his family.

"Thanks for being there, man," he told Vince when they got back to his house.

"You're my brother, E, I got your back."

"I'll be out of here in a few days after I get a place for my mama."

"You know you can stay here for as long as you need to."

"Yeah I know but I don't want to put you out."

"You're family, man. Anyway I'm about to grub, your mama asked me to pick up some food from Mary's for you."

"Go ahead, I'm beat. After I take a hot shower I'm hitting the sheets."

***

The hot water pulsating against his back felt like heaven to Ernest. He hadn't bathed in four days. After he washed his hair and scrubbed the filth of the jail off his skin he watched the dirty suds circle and go down the drain. It would be so simple if the rest of the dirt in his life could follow it. He stepped out of the shower into the steam filled bathroom and wrapped a towel around his waist. When he opened the door to the guest bedroom Rochelle was sitting on the bed with his things packed.

"I want you to come home, Ernest," she said sincerely.

Ernest dropped his head and leaned against the dresser. "I'm exhausted, Chelle."

"I didn't come over here to argue. I'm worried, the kids are worried, and we want you home."

"We haven't resolved any of our problems. I'm not ready. It's not fair to the kids for me to keep going in and out of the house."

"I'm sorry for my part in everything," she said remorsefully. "I know that I was jealous and insecure. I was wrong for punishing you when you were straight. I want us to start over."

"Nothing has changed, baby. We're still the same people."

"I know that I need to change," she said, "I need you to be patient with me."

Ernest shook his head. "I'm not blaming you for what I did and you didn't make me do any of the things I did."

"We'll be fine, babe, if you come home. We owe it to the kids."

"I finally realized that us staying together for the kids probably hurt them more than it helped them."

"That's not true. They're hurting more now."

"I can't come back there and then have to leave again," Ernest said, staring at the ceiling. "If they convict me on this shit I'm going to do some serious time. It's better that they get used to me not being around."

"You're my world, Ernest. Don't you know that?"

"I don't want your life revolving around me, Chelle. It makes me feel like I'm trapped in a cage like a dog. You only want to let me out to go to work and then chain me back up. I can't live like that."

Rochelle didn't know any other way to persuade him so she started unbuttoning her blouse.

"Haven't you missed me?"

"I can't," he told her firmly.

"You ain't shit," she said, storming out the room.

She didn't even have to say that. He already felt it.

***

Rodney was strutting around the station like a peacock. He probably measured an inch or two taller from all the congratulations and commendations that swelled his head as well as his chest. He was standing at the coffee machine beside a fresh box of donuts gloating and shooting the breeze with a fellow detective when one of the sergeants called his name.

"Hey, Wilson," he yelled from across the room, "There's somebody here to see you."

"Sure thing," Rodney answered, thinking it was another reporter wanting to do an interview. "I'll be in the office in a minute."

Rodney refilled his cup and wrapped one of the bear claws in a napkin to munch on while he talked with his visitor. He was somewhat startled to find a small middle-aged Arab or Armenian looking guy sitting in the chair beside his desk when he walked in. Meyers was at her desk quietly going through some files on her computer.

"Hello, I'm Dt. Wilson. You wanted to speak with me?" he said, addressing his guest.

"Yes, detective, my name is Avetis Darbinyan. I own the Marathon Gas Station on 8th Avenue North across from Farmer's Market."

"Yes, Mr. Darbinyan, what can I do for you?"

"I saw the arrest of that guy on the news for the murder of that woman at the Renaissance Hotel."

"Uh-huh," Wilson said, biting in to his bear claw."

"You've got the wrong guy."

Megan ears perked up at those words. She closed the file she was reading and began to listen intently. This was more than worth the price of movie tickets that she had to pay Rodney when he arrested Ernest.

"What are you talking about?" Rodney asked him, completely confused.

"Like I said I own the drive-in market on 8th Avenue North. There was a car parked out front the night that woman was killed. I thought the car was suspicious, like maybe they wanted to rob me or something. I started to call 911 but I thought I'd check it out myself first. It was a guy who looked like he was drunk and had passed out. He wasn't hurting anything so I let him sleep it off. He's the guy you're charging with that murder. You can check my surveillance camera and the date. He was there practically all night."

Wilson couldn't swallow the sticky dough mixture caught in the back of his throat. He felt like he couldn't breathe. His stomach retched and he gagged into the napkin that held the other half of his sweet snack. This couldn't be happening to him. How could this meek specimen of a man come in there and ruin his victory lap.

"Do you have a copy of the tape, sir?" Megan asked, coming over to the man.

"Yes, ma'am, I brought it with me," Avetis said, handing her a jump drive.

Megan put it in Rodney's computer and opened the file. It showed Ernest pulling into the gas station and parking. He never got out of his car. The date and the time 9:45 flashed in the bottom right hand corner. Megan went forward on the time. He pulled his car out of the parking lot just after 3:00.

"It looks like your witness lied," Megan told Rodney. "There's no way she saw him at the hotel at the time she said."

Rodney still hadn't spoken. He'd figured the girl was lying and just wanted to get her hands on the money but that hadn't mattered to him. It was up to the jury who they wanted to give the benefit of doubt. Now it had blown up in his face.

"This doesn't make any sense," Rodney said finally.

"I just didn't want to see that guy go to jail if he didn't do it," Avetis said.

"That's being a good citizen," Megan said, patting him on the shoulder, "Thanks so much for coming in."

Mr. Darbinyan got up, shook Megan's hand, and walked out of the office.

"So are you going to tell the Lieutenant or am I?" Megan asked him with a satisfied look.

"Why don't you go ahead, you seemed to be pleased with the revelation."

"It's nothing personal, partner," she said, taking the jump drive out of his computer. "Isn't that what you said?"

*****

Ernest hadn't been back to work since the day he was arrested. It had been a week of him lying around the house watching talk shows and reality TV in the day, football and classic boxing matches in the evenings. He had already made up his mind to stop hiding out and go to work the next morning when he got the call from his lawyer that the charges had been dropped. He could barely sleep that night he was so excited.

Driving down Franklin Road, he was about to call his mama when his phone rang. She had been calling him all week and for the first times in his life, he hadn't answered. He answered without hesitation thinking it was her.

"Hello," he said happily.

"It's Megan," the voice said.

He was about to hang up and then he changed his mind. "What do you want, detective?"

"I wanted to let you know that you don't have anything to worry about. You have an airtight alibi. The man who runs the drive-in market on 8th Avenue had you on camera passed out during the time of the murder."

"I'm sure that rained on your partner's parade," he said.

"It thunder stormed," she said with a chuckle, "My question is why did you lie?"

"Isn't it obvious, I didn't know where I was," Ernest said, hanging up.

Ernest stopped the car, got out, and stared at the sidewalk.

He needed a minute to compose himself and process what Megan had told him. Up until that moment he wasn't sure if he had murdered Eva or not. Now knowing he hadn't killed her freed him from the mental prison he had been locked in for months. He was elated, overjoyed. When he lifted his head up the first thing he saw was McDougal's Liquor Store. That wasn't an option. He looked around and saw a sign that said, ZolliKoffee. He crossed the street and bought a large latte and a dozen muffins to go.

Ernest balanced the coffee and muffins in one hand while he turned the lock on the door of In Earnest with the other. His heart continued to beat fast from the exhilaration of the day. Coming through the entrance it was the only time he had walked in there without wondering how long it would last. He sat the muffins down on the counter of the receptionist area and went back to his office. He turned on the light and then his computer. He found a small stack of mail and then a long string of emails. He turned on the jazz music that normally flowed through the intercom and went back out to brew fresh coffee for the crew when they arrived.

With a fresh smock on, he sat down at his station with his latte and one of the still slightly warm blueberry muffins. He bit into it and it was the best thing he had tasted in a long time. It was indeed a blissful moment as he gazed out the front window.

A couple of minutes later he saw Leon park and come across the street.

"Good to see you, man," Ernest said as soon as he walked in the door.

"I guess you heard what happened," Leon said, sounding despondent.

"Yeah my lawyer called me last night," Ernest said, thrown off by Leon's reaction.

Leon bit his bottom lip and shook his head. "I guess bad news still travels fast."

"Are you for real? That's the best news I've had in a long time."

"That's cold, E, they could have been killed. They're family."

"What in the hell are you talking about?" Ernest said, disconcerted.

Then Leon realized he didn't know.

"It was King Cut," he told him, "The shop was robbed last night."

Ernest sat his coffee down. "Dammit, what happened, did anybody get hurt?"

"Jeff and Andrea were having a card party after hours and then two guys came in with guns blasting. Three people got shot, one of them was Jeff."

"Oh no, man," Ernest exclaimed in disbelief, "Is he all right?"

"Yeah, he's good. It went in his left shoulder and came out his back. He's at Skyline."

"What about Andrea?"

"She's shaken up but she wasn't hurt."

Ernest got up and practically snatched off his smock. "I'm going over there."

"Settle down, man, it's all taped off. You can't get in there."

"I can't believe it," Ernest said, shocked.

"You were right, E. It was time to go."

Ernest put his smock back on and took several big gulps of his coffee. He was still trying to regain his celebratory mood when Carla came in.

"It's about time, boss man," Carla said with a smile when she saw Ernest. "I was starting to get worried about you."

"There's nothing to worry about," he said, smiling back

at her. "I made you some coffee and there are muffins for everybody."

"Just what I needed," Erik said, walking in and grabbing a muffin. "I didn't eat any breakfast trying to be here on time."

Halina and Jayne walked in next.

"I'm glad you're back," Halina said. "We missed you."

"Thank you," Ernest said.

"Are you back for good or is this just until a trial or something?" Jayne asked, twisting her fingers in the air. "I'm working my hands to the bone covering for you. Halina probably can't even fix this."

Ernest laughed. "I'm here for the duration. There won't be a trial, at least not for me."

That's when Detectives Wilson and Meyers walked in.

"We'd like to speak with you in private," Megan requested, cutting Rodney off from making a public scene.

Ernest led the way back to his office. He closed the door behind them after they walked in. He leaned back on his desk while Megan stayed near the door. Rodney came over and stood in front of him.

"I know you think this is over but I'm going to nail you," he said, breathing down on Ernest. "I don't care what that tape says."

"Don't waste your time, detective. Your case has gone cold," Ernest told him.

"You're lucky. If we were someplace else you wouldn't be spouting off," Rodney said with spit flying from his teeth and lips.

"Unsportsmanlike conduct," Ernest said.

"This isn't a game, Shaw. You will go to jail."

"Not because you want me too," Ernest retorted.

Rodney sneered at him. "I can't stand your kind. You're nothing more than a pimp."

Ernest stretched out his arms. "Why do I have to be that, brother?"

"You manipulate women with your dick and use them to get what you want."

"At least I have one."

Rodney balled up his fist in anger. "You're just another small time hustler who found a way to take advantage of somebody's weakness."

"That's bullshit. You don't know anything about me," Ernest said, standing his ground. I'm something you will never be. I'm doing my own thing while you're out here shuffling for the man."

"Just because I don't like killers doesn't mean I'm working for the man. I'm out here to make the wrongs of people like you right again."

"If that's what you tell yourself to help you sleep at night, then more power to you."

"I'm not going to rest until you're back in that cell where you belong," Rodney said, pointing a finger in his face.

"I'm tired of this. If you have anything on me, arrest me, if not, stop harassing me. This is my business. If you come around here again I'll sue the whole Nashville Police Department."

"Let's go," Megan yelled to Rodney from the door.

He stared down at Ernest with contempt, wishing he could punch him just once in his smartass mouth. It would have made it so much easier to walk away. Instead he felt like a gambler who had laid it all on one bet and then threw snake eyes. There was no reason to stay but it was so hard to leave empty-handed.

Megan tugged at the sleeve of his trench coat. "Come on partner," she said, feeling the same sense of loss but for a completely different reason.

Ernest smiled to himself feeling like the champion of a hard fought match as he watched Megan pull Rodney out of the door.

***

Ernest and Sheila were sitting over dinner at her new three-bedroom townhouse across from the Kroger on Franklin Road. Buttons stood on her hind legs with her front paws in Sheila's lap eagerly waiting for an intermittent morsel from the table.

"It's been so long since I could relax and enjoy a decent meal," Ernest said, slicing the potato beside his baked chicken.

"I'm so relieved that all that ugly mess is behind you, son."

"More than that, Mama, I feel a lot better with you living here. It was worrisome with you staying at the duplex. Once people found out I had the new place I kept thinking they might break in on you thinking you had money in there."

"It didn't bother me none. I've known everybody around there since you was a baby. Anyway if it makes you happy for me to be here then I'm glad."

"Plus the kids can come by whenever they want."

"You know I don't mind you staying here with me, Ernest, but have you given any thought to when you might go back home?"

Ernest frowned. "I don't know. My head is cluttered with so many questions. I think I'm getting paranoid or something. When I'm around the people closest to me, I'm not comfortable. I feel like I can't trust them, like they're hiding things from me."

"Stop thinking like that, child. You can trust your wife and your friends."

"I didn't kill Eva, Mama."

"I know that, son. I killed her," Sheila said matter-of-factly. Ernest froze for a moment. Then he shook his head to dislodge the words from his brain. Sheila looked at him waiting for the reality to sink in.

"You did what?" he asked, shaken and horrified at what she told him.

"I did it. I killed her," Sheila told him calmly. "I went in like I was the housekeeper and I cleaned up the situation."

"You couldn't have, Mama. You went to dialysis that day. I know it makes you sick. There's no way you could have done it."

"I was sick, sick as a dog, but I was sicker about what she was doing to you. I knew I had to pull myself together because my family was in trouble."

To Ernest the whole thing was incredulous.

"How did you know where she was?"

"Rochelle told me that she kept calling you. So I sent a text to Eva from your old phone. I'd taken it from the house a while back 'cause Rochelle kept going through it and it was driving her crazy. I pretended I was you and texted her that you wanted to see her. She answered back and said that she was at the Renaissance Hotel and wanted you to come there. She gave me the room number and said she would leave a room key under the vase on the table by the elevator."

"Who took you downtown?" he asked, continuing to question her in disbelief.

"I caught the bus down there. I followed someone inside through the door where the employees come in. I hung up my coat and put on a uniform I got off of a rack. Then I caught the employee elevator up to her floor. When I first came in the room she thought I was the maid. She asked me to go turn down her bed and draw her a hot bath. So I did. She came into the bedroom and started undressing so I went back out into the sitting area. Halfway to the door, I heard the sound of water splashing when she got into the Jacuzzi. I stopped. I just stood there for a while, I don't know how long. I didn't know what I was going to do. I stepped to the door to leave, opened it, and then she called out your name. She said for you to come in and massage her neck and shoulders. I went back into the bathroom, walked over to tub, pulled her head back, and then I slit her throat with your old straight razor."

"Why, Mama," Ernest cried out from the agony of hearing her story. "You didn't have to do that. I could have handled it."

"She was going to ruin you, baby. She was rotten fruit. She was going to spoil everything you've worked for. I couldn't let her hurt what's mine."

Tears began to roll down his face. "I'm so sorry."

"What are you crying for, child?"

"I can't believe I put you in that position. It hurts my heart, Mama."

"Boy, I'm your mama. I'm here for you, you're not here for me. You're here for your children. I couldn't let you lose your family. Ain't nothing worth that."

"All of it was my fault," he said with his face buried in his hands.

"It's over now," she said, rubbing him on the back. "You've got to let it go."

"I don't know what to say."

"There's nothing to say. Besides, I don't want to talk about it anymore."

"I love you, Mama," he said after a while.

"You're my heart, Ernest.

Epilogue

Ernest scanned the room to see which machine his mama was connected to. She was near the end as usual. He grabbed a chair on his way to sit next to her.

"Sit on down, son," Sheila said, smiling, "I'm so glad to see you."

"Good to see you too, Mama."

"I haven't seen you in over a week. How are things going?"

"Business at the shop is great. I think it's about that time for me to expand. I've already started looking for another spot. Rochelle is doing real good in her accounting classes at Nashville Tech. She thinks she might want to help me manage it."

"What about King Cut?"

"Jeff hired two new barbers. It's his place now. Andrea left. She said it wasn't the same anymore. She does her regulars at her house and hosts her card parties there too."

"I guess she's happy," Sheila giggled. "She doesn't have to get too far from her kitchen or the TV."

Ernest laughed too. "That's my girl though."

"So what's Vince doing with himself lately?"

"Believe it or not, he's getting married."

"You're right, I can't believe that. I never thought that boy would settle down."

"He didn't either," Ernest chuckled.

"By the way, they tell me I'm moving higher on the list for a kidney."

"That's great news. I can't wait until you can get off this machine," he said, watching it pump and churn.

"Well, enough about me, son, how are you doing?"

"Everything is fine, Mama, no worries."

"That's good, baby, Now tell me what your friend has been up to."

The End